KEEPER OF THE MOON

HARLEY JANE KOZAK

HARLEQUIN® NOCTURNE™

Recycling programs
for this product may
not exist in your area.

ISBN-13: 978-0-373-88565-7

KEEPER OF THE MOON

Copyright © 2013 by Harley Jane Kozak

www.Harlequin.com

Printed in U.S.A.

Dear Reader,

Back in 2006, I found myself singing backup in the Killer Thriller Band, and there I met for the first time my fellow Killerettes, Heather Graham and Alexandra Sokoloff. Our friendship has been forged in the fire of nonfunctioning sound systems, stuck elevators and demonic wigs. In fact, it was almost predictable that we'd end up writing a series about L.A. vampires, werewolves, shapeshifters and elves—and the women who love them.

In Hollywood, my current hometown, it's not unusual to create "art by committee" but what *is* unusual is working with people you love and having this much fun. I've already forgotten which of us came up with this castle or that character; I just feel lucky getting to tell a part of the story.

Although this is my fifth novel, it's my first romance, and I would not have attempted it without the encouragement of the talented and generous Heather and Alex. I am exceedingly grateful that they invited me to hop on board the Keepers' series. Happy reading!

Harley Jane Kozak

To Katharine Harto Coen,
Who knows all about true love . . .

Chapter 1

Magic hour.

It's the first or last hour of sunlight, when the day is opening or closing up shop, an event so commonplace that only certain breeds of humans notice it—movie people, for instance, who treasure the footage shot in those fleeting moments for the way it can render an aging star young, a dull actor luminous and a plain landscape…enchanted.

Sailor Ann Gryffald loved magic hour, especially sunset, loved to end her seven-mile run on a downhill slope as the sky turned red and the canyon faded to black. The name itself was a kind of incantation to her, like all movie terms. She'd been around film sets most of her life and couldn't remember a time when she hadn't known the meaning of "magic hour" and "second meal" and "martini shot."

But Sailor wasn't only an actress, so she knew that magic hour had other meanings lying just under the surface, the way L.A. itself could hide under a veil of smog. The moments separating the worlds of day and night were when portals opened, shapes shifted with little effort, and even the most unimaginative human might stumble upon signs of the Otherworld.

Sailor was part of that Otherworld. She was a Keeper, a human born with a distinctive birthmark, and the mandate to guard and protect a particular species. In her case, the birthmark was a tree and the species were the Elven. These were not the tiny elves of popular culture in green jackets and felt hats, but tall, intensely physical creatures whose element was earth, whose beauty was legendary, whose powers included healing, telepathy and teleportation. The Elven loved Hollywood, and Hollywood reciprocated, rewarding and occasionally worshipping their charisma and physical beauty. Of course, most humans had no knowledge of Others, had no belief in, and thus no perception of, the extraordinary qualities and abilities their neighbors possessed. It was Sailor's job to preserve that. A Keeper's first obligation was to keep secret the very existence of the species, the Elven and vampires, the were-creatures, shifters, leprechauns and ogres whose natures the "real" world could not accept.

Sailor was new to the actual job, had taken it over from her father only months earlier, and found it something of a yawn. But with her birthmark came a fraction of the Elven powers and their beauty, so all in all, not a bad gig. She also had a strong sixth sense that told her things, like…

There was something in the air right now.

Sailor slowed her pace. She was a mile into her run, heading west on Mulholland at a good clip, shoes pounding the dusty road. It wasn't darkness she felt; the sun wouldn't set for another hour or more, and the moon was already out. It was a heaviness, making her want to look behind her, making the hair on the back of her neck—

"Hey!" a man yelled.

She turned and spotted him at the end of a driveway, waving his arms as if she were a taxi.

"Hey, what?" she called back, squinting. Did she know him? Were they friends?

"You're breaking the law," the man yelled. "Your dog's off-leash." He was dressed in a suit, standing alongside a Porsche in front of a small mansion.

Figures that he'd drive a Porsche, she thought.

"He's not a problem," she called back.

"He's a problem if he pisses in my yard."

The man's yard was as dressed up as he was, a flawless green lawn accessorized with white rosebushes, more suited to Beverly Hills than the canyons.

"He's not going to piss in your yard." Sailor jogged in place and snapped her fingers. Jonquil, a huge, fierce-faced mutt with the temperament of a rabbit, loped over to her. "We're thirty feet from your yard."

"There are leash laws," the man retorted. "You're not supposed to let your dog urinate at will."

She laughed. "What are you, the pee police? There are jackrabbits, deer, coyotes, all urinating at will, rattlesnakes, bobcats, possums—"

The man gave her the finger and moved into the house.

Sailor lowered her voice. "Go ahead and pee, Jonquil." But the big mutt stared at her and inexplicably began to whine.

A rush of wind hit Sailor, so cold she thought, *There must be some mistake. I must be dreaming,* followed by a flutelike sound blowing in her ear, a flapping of a wing next to her cheek, striking her face. She swatted at it wildly, but something sharp sliced right down the middle of her chest, ripping through her shirt. *Man, that's going to hurt in a minute,* she thought.

Jonquil was both whining and barking now, nearly crying, *if dogs could cry*, Sailor thought, as her legs faltered, refusing to hold her up.

And then she was falling, with the fading sunlight hitting her full in the face, falling onto the gravel and pavement of Mulholland Drive.

Damn, she thought. *I'm checking out.*

Darkness.

Alessande saw the woman go down. She'd been out gathering fenweddin for a medicinal tea, as fenweddin was best plucked in late afternoon, in full bloom. Alessande was on the hillside, blending in so well that she was effectively invisible both to the woman, whose mind was elsewhere, and the man from the mansion, who wouldn't notice her unless she walked naked onto his lawn. The dog had looked her way, wanting to play, but Alessande was on a schedule, so she sent him on his way with an abrupt thought command.

But then the air changed, and Alessande turned her attention to it, letting the argument of the humans fade into the background. She took two steps backward, touched a bay laurel tree and contracted her energy until she was dense as the tree's trunk, connected to it and virtually invisible, protected from a malevolence she could feel but not identify. Then she watched the malevolence materialize. It began as a blinding bit of light that arranged itself into a creature with wings, moving so violently that she could barely see the talon tearing open the woman's chest.

And then it vanished. As abruptly as it had come, it was gone.

Alessande exhaled, disconnecting from the tree. She moved quickly to the woman, pushing aside the dog that was licking his human's face, apparently trying to revive her.

The wound wasn't deep, and it was nowhere near the carotid artery, which was good. But the woman was unconscious, and that *wasn't* good. Alessande lifted her carefully. She was tall for a human female, but not heavy, so after picking up a set of keys fallen on the road and sending reassurance to the dog, Alessande moved swiftly. It was rush hour and only a matter of time before a car came along, which would mean curiosity and offers of help. She needed neither, at least not the sort of help a mortal could provide.

She moved down the hillside, directly into the brush, the dog following closely. The woman's bare legs were getting badly scratched, but it was faster than taking the road to her cabin, and made it less likely that they would be spotted by a passing car. Alessande was dressed in earth tones and blended into the canyon, and while the woman wore hot-pink shorts and a white tank top, now stained with blood, the angle of their descent would hide them from Mulholland. Within minutes they'd reached her screen door, which she kicked open.

When Alessande laid the woman on the sofa and took another look at the long gash, she was relieved to find the blood already clotting. On a hunch she lifted one of the woman's eyelids and then the other, and let out a long, slow breath.

The whites of the eyes were perfect, bright and healthy. But the irises were deep scarlet.

Declan Wainwright pulled on a pair of black jeans and a Grateful Dead T-shirt, getting ready for the workday, which in his case began at night. The part he enjoyed, at any rate. He had to deal with banking and office hours like anyone else, but he handed off as much as he could to his frighteningly talented assistant Harriet, without whom, he liked to say, he would be mad and penniless.

Not that Harriet listened to him. "Blarney," she called it when he talked like that, knowing full well he came from England, not Ireland. Outside of calling him Mr. Wainwright, Harriet was one of the few people who showed Declan no deference, which was one reason he loved her. Another was that she terrified people seeking access to him. She had the face of a horse, and the voice of a drill sergeant. In fact Harriet Brockleman would be the perfect human, in Declan's eyes, were it not for the fact that she turned off her own phone at nine-thirty each night, went to bed and was unavailable to him.

"Mr. Wainwright," she called through the beach house intercom system, "are you at home to Vernon Winter?"

"No. Take a message." Declan exchanged his diving watch for a vintage Rolex, and looked out the French doors to the ocean. The tide was coming in. He wasn't going to interrupt a perfect sunset by listening to the dour predictions of his stockbroker.

The waves beckoned, and he moved out onto the deck.

The house on Point Dume was four stories tall. The master bedroom occupied the top floor, guest rooms took up the third, then the main living area, and at the bottom, built into the cliff, the maid's quarters and his office. The upper deck, where he stood now, made him feel he was in the crow's nest of a ship, out at sea. It was one reason he could stay in L.A., putting down roots, when part of him longed to just set sail and keep going.

The moon was full. It had already risen, its tenure overlapping with the setting sun, and he could feel its energy. His gaze moved to a spot on the beach marked by death. More than a week had passed since the woman's body was found, and each day it weighed on him more. The woman had once been his lover. Their affair had been as brief as it was passionate, but long after both had moved on to other lovers, the bond had lingered.

Elven women did that to him.

And now she was dead, tossed carelessly onto the beach by an unknown killer, and the rage he felt wouldn't let him sleep, or work, or play.

Enough was enough. Time to act.

He moved to the edge of the deck, closed his eyes and breathed in the salty air. He let thoughts slip away, his own energy moving into his astral body, the energy field surrounding him. He waited. After a moment there was a gentle shattering of the boundaries that held him in place as a man, a mortal.

And then he was floating.

He spoke not in words but in thoughts, addressing the woman so recently dead. "Charlotte, I will avenge you. Use me."

Charlotte did not appear. But a tornado of currents circled him, the wind picking up, telling him it was no small thing to choose this path, that he was altering his destiny by involving himself in the mystery of her death. He stayed resolute and unmoving until he felt the spirit world acquiesce and the wind die down.

Declan let out a long breath. He'd done it. He'd shifted the course of his immediate future. He couldn't know what that future would bring, only that he would now encounter people and events that would pull him into the orbit of a murderer.

A sound broke into his reverie, pulling him back into his body, onto his deck. It was a high-pitched squeal he couldn't identify. A child?

Crying.

He looked below, to the beach, to the right, to the left. Nothing.

And there it was again.

He closed his eyes to pinpoint the location of the cries. They seemed to come from under the house. His mental focus shifted to the sand four stories below. He couldn't see it, but he could feel it. Warmth. Life. Terror.

He took the outside staircase two steps at a time, thinking of the *panga*, a Mexican fishing boat, that had washed ashore a month before from Tijuana, carrying undocumented immigrants, dehydrated, half-drowned. What if it was happening again right now? What if one of them was just a—

Baby. The sound was recurring, a cry interrupted by the waves crashing on the shore. It must have found its way to the storage space where he kept the kayak and the beach furniture, in the area formed by the stilts and the rocks. He hit the sand and was instantly ankle-deep in surf. He clambered barefoot under the deck and then worked his way upward to the dry area, barely able to see in the underbelly of the house, where it was already night.

And there it was, clinging to a plank.

A cat.

He could just make it out in the last moments of sunlight filtering through the slats. An unhappy cat, gray, frightened, mewling.

"So you're the baby." He felt its terror and in response, slowed his own breath. "Come on, then."

But the cat was panicked, hissing, and as he moved closer it stood upright on its hind legs in a freakish posture, displaying its own underbelly. Female, clearly. Her neck seemed stuck to the wall. Declan inched closer and pulled his cell phone from his pocket, used the flashlight app and saw that her collar was caught on a protruding nail. The cat was so freaked out that she was in danger of strangling herself. He put away the cell and crooned to her, using a hypnotic voice. "Come on, girl, let's get you somewhere safe. Warm and dry…nice bowl of milk…tasty piece of fish…" He pulled his T-shirt over his head and draped it around his hands as a shield from her claws, then grasped her and held on, letting her struggle as he worked on unhooking the collar. But for that he needed his hands, so cradling her against one shoulder, he endured her scratches until he'd released it, at which point she wriggled out of both his grasp and her collar. In a spark of movement she took off under the house and into the darkness.

Leaving Declan behind, wet, bloody, shirtless and swearing, and holding her collar.

Minutes later he was back inside the house, dripping on the bleached wood floors. He set his cell on the kitchen counter, its screen showing a voice mail message from Alessande Salisbrooke. He would call her later.

"Look at this," he said to Harriet, who'd brought him a towel. He handed her the collar, which had the Gucci logo on the leather and two green gems hanging from the metal ring like charms on a bracelet. "I believe those are real."

"Emeralds? Leave it to you, Mr. Wainwright, to rescue a cat and end up with a fortune. Does it have a name?"

"The cat? Her name is Tamarind."

"Yes, here it is on the tag. With a phone number. Shall I call it?"

"You needn't bother," Declan said, already stripping off his wet jeans. "There won't be anyone home."

Alessande had the door opened before Declan could reach for the doorbell. She ushered him inside and took a long look out at the horizon, as if scanning it for information. "Thanks for coming," she said.

"My pleasure."

"Took you long enough." She closed the door.

He laughed and put an arm around her. "Took me no time at all, you ingrate. I came as soon as I listened to your message. What's up?"

"I found a woman up on Mulholland, unconscious. I need help with her."

"You have a dozen family members within shouting distance."

"They're Elven. I don't want any Elven near her."

"Why not?"

By way of answer, Alessande led him into the living room, where a girl—a woman, actually—lay on the sofa. She was covered by a blanket, so he could only see a long arm and the top of her head. A large yellow dog lay beside her. The dog raised his head at their entrance, but Alessande made a hand gesture and he relaxed, tail thumping on the stone floor.

"Is she sleeping," Declan said in a low voice, "or unconscious?"

"She goes in and out. It's like she's drugged. Go check out her eyes."

"Her eyes?"

"Lift her eyelid."

He approached the woman. She had red-blond hair that spilled down the side of the sofa like a waterfall. His pulse quickened even before he came around and saw her face. It was heart-shaped, stunning in repose, with long eyelashes pointing the way to high cheekbones. A face he'd seen when it was awake and animated. Her extreme vulnerability now touched something in him. "I know her," he told Alessande.

"Who is she?"

"In a minute." He didn't want to say the name aloud, knowing sleeping people will sometimes hear themselves called and pull themselves into consciousness. With a finger he brushed back a lock of her hair, gently, and with a growing suspicion of what he would find, he lifted an eyelid. He stared.

After a moment he turned to Alessande. "How exposed were you to her?"

"Enough. I carried her down the hillside. I'd begun to treat her wound when I thought to check her eyes."

"Get any blood on you?"

"On my jacket. Nothing on my skin, as far as I could see."

"You were lucky."

"Do you think I'm all right?"

"I think if you weren't, you'd already be dead."

The woman grew restless, and her eyelids fluttered. Declan, acting on impulse, said quickly, "I don't want her seeing me just yet. I'm going to shift."

He closed his eyes and slowed his breathing, focusing on his astral body. Then he let in another image, the first person who came to mind—Vernon, his stockbroker. He would do. Vernon was shorter, somewhat heavier and fifteen years older than Declan, with a lot less hair. Declan watched the details coalesce and let the image take him, turning himself around so that he was now inhabiting Vernon's body, looking at the world from his perspective.

He opened Vernon's tired eyes and looked into the eerie eyes of the beauty who, until a minute ago, had been sleeping.

As images slid into focus, Sailor waited for something to look familiar, but in front of her was a man she didn't know, in a house she didn't recognize. A cabin, really, but a sophisticated one. She could see past the man to a woman, and beyond the woman to a kitchen, state-of-the-art, very modern, with a Wolf range. In a bay window hung an ornament, a carving in wood that she knew well, because her great-aunt Olga had an etched glass version of the same image: a tree with roots so long they circled up to meet its branches. Sailor's eyesight was remarkably good, which was strange. Then again, at this point everything was strange.

Her head hurt and her chest burned. She was lying on a sofa covered with a soft blue blanket. The blanket was stained with blood.

"How are you feeling?" the man asked.

"I don't have a clue," she said. "What happened to me?"

The woman came closer. Elven. Typically beautiful. She was at least six feet tall, both athletic and voluptuous in the particular way that distinguished Elven women from human, except when the humans were surgically enhanced. She had white-blond hair and green eyes so pale they looked haunted. "You were attacked," she said. She held a bottle of rubbing alcohol and sterile gauze.

Jonquil stood, sensing a party taking place, his huge tail wagging exuberantly.

"Sit," the woman said, and the dog sat so eagerly that Sailor wondered if the stranger were a dog trainer. The woman said, "Do you remember it at all? It was half an hour ago."

Sailor thought about it. "There was a bird, or—wings, at least. It sort of sliced me open." She looked down at herself and moved back the blanket to see that her sternum was bleeding, her chest exposed. She pulled at her torn tank top and jogging bra, trying to cover herself.

"Let's have a look," the man said.

"Are you a doctor?" Sailor asked.

"Why else would I want to look at your naked breasts?" he asked, which made her laugh, but that turned into a cough, which hurt.

"Come," he said. "Let's see how bad it is." He wasn't re- motely attractive, she thought, and he was old, at least as old as her own father, but there was something about his hands and the way he moved that—well, it was ridiculous, but she found him appealing.

He, however, was focused on her wound. He frowned, so she said, to distract him, "It's not deep, is it? And it burns a bit, but I have a high tolerance for pain. I can't imagine why I passed out."

The man glanced at the Elven woman, then said to Sailor, "You're not in the habit of passing out?"

"Are you kidding? I'm as healthy as a horse. A healthy horse, that is. Well, obviously. It's a ridiculous saying, isn't it? Because it's not as if there are no sick horses in the world. They can't possibly all be dying accidental deaths."

"Are you always this talkative?" he asked.

"No."

He glanced at the Elven woman again. She handed him the gauze and rubbing alcohol.

"What? What is it?" Sailor asked. "Why do you keep looking at each other?"

The woman said, "Whatever it was that attacked you—"

"Other," Sailor said.

"What?"

"It was Other, whatever attacked me."

The woman moved closer. "What are you?"

"What *am* I? I'm a Gryffald. Sailor Ann Gryffald, to be exact."

"Are you kin to Rafe Gryffald?"

"He's my father."

The woman frowned. "You're the Keeper's daughter?"

Sailor winced. "Keeper" wasn't the sort of word you said in mixed company, and the man applying rubbing alcohol to a gauze pad appeared to be mortal. The first rule of Keeperdom was nondisclosure. "The question is," Sailor said, nodding toward the man, "what's he?"

He looked up and gave her a smile. "Don't worry. I'm a friend. You can speak freely."

Sailor looked to the woman for confirmation. She nodded.

"Okay, then," Sailor said, and then, as the alcohol touched her wound, "Ouch. My father is the former Keeper. He's now serving on the International Keeper Council at The Hague."

"So your uncles are—"

"Piers and Owen. Keepers of the vampires and shapeshifters, but also currently serving on the International Council."

"And you've inherited the family proclivity toward—"

"Otherworld management? Yes. I am the current Keeper of the Elven."

"Bloody hell," the woman said. "The grown-ups have left the building."

Sailor shrugged. In her three months on the job, she'd gotten several negative reactions to her youth and inexperience. The truth was, while she looked like a teen, she was twenty-eight. The three Gryffald brothers, Sailor's father and two uncles, were well-respected in the Otherworld, but respect isn't always passed on to one's heirs, and while Sailor had been born with the mark of the Keeper, she'd assumed she had decades to prepare for the role. Fate had decided otherwise. When her father had summoned her home from New York, she'd come. There was no question of refusing—Keeping was the family business—but L.A. wasn't rolling out the welcome mat.

"Yes," Sailor said. "I'm no happier about it than you are, but anyhow, nice to meet you. Except I haven't met you."

"Alessande Salisbrooke," the woman said.

"And I'm Vernon Winter," the man said.

"Okay, nice to meet you. So what's my diagnosis here, doc?"

"I'm not a doctor."

"I thought you said you were."

"No, I'm a stockbroker."

"Why are you examining my chest? No, never mind. Stupid question."

He smiled and once more she found herself drawn to him. *Was* he mortal? She was no longer sure. "I'm doing it because she can't," he said, nodding at Alessande. "She shouldn't be touching you, because the Elven are highly susceptible to what you've got, which is a disease. You're both lucky to be alive."

"Lucky to be alive?" Sailor said. "Because of a scratch on my chest? It was weird, the attack, but hardly life-threatening. And I have no diseases. What are you talking about?"

"I'm putting on the kettle," Alessande said, moving into the kitchen as she talked. "You've heard about the film stars who've died these past weeks from what the media calls the Celebrity Virus?"

"Charlotte Messenger and Gina Santoro?" Sailor said. "Of course. And last week an acting student from the California Institute of the Arts, who wasn't exactly a celebrity, and a junior agent at GAA, also not a celebrity, but quite beautiful. Oh. And a sitcom star."

"Did you know any of them?" Alessande was making kitchen noises, opening cupboards.

"Personally? No. I've followed the story online."

"What else do you know about it?"

"Nothing," Sailor said.

"Good God." Vernon Winter taped gauze on her wound. "Don't you Keepers talk to each other?"

"You mean like send around an email blast? No. What's it got to do with us?"

"You realize the dead women were Elven?"

Sailor snorted. It was an insult, suggesting that a Keeper couldn't recognize Elven, or, for that matter, vampire, pixie or were. Shapeshifters, by their nature, were trickier and took longer for her to figure out, but except for them, Sailor found it hard to believe her fellow humans were unaware of Others living among them. It was like being unable to distinguish cats from dogs. She said, "I could spot Elven characteristics since I was a toddler. Gina Santoro and Charlotte Messenger? Flamboyantly Elven. The sitcom star? Not. I don't know about the two. I only saw Facebook photos." Elven charisma was hard to discern in a still photograph.

"What tribe?" he asked, challenging her.

Who *was* this guy? "Gina was Rath," she said. "Obviously. Charlotte looked multiracial. Déithe, of course. Maybe Cyffarwydd, as well. Hard to say, with all her plastic surgery. And I'm not just talking ears." Softening ear tips was a practice as common as ear-piercing for Elven children. "Why, is this a test?"

"Everything's a test for a Keeper as new as you," Vernon said. "And looking like a high school cheerleader isn't going to help your cause."

Was that a compliment? Was he *flirting?* "I don't have a cause. And I don't have to make my case, because I was born a Keeper. It's not a job I'm auditioning for or even one I particularly want, but I'm a Gryffald, so I'll be good at it. And I don't know what your interest is in this as a stockbroker, but if you're used to judging people by their faces—"

"It's not your *face* I was judging."

He *was* flirting. How crazy was this? Sailor was about to respond, but Vernon's face wavered, suddenly becoming younger. Darker. Handsome. Light shimmered around it.

She blinked several times. Okay, the attack had somehow affected her eyesight. That was scary.

Then he went back to being plain again. Homely. Non-shimmering. Her vision was fine. That was a relief.

"Back to the issue at hand," Alessande said, coming back into the room. She carried a plate of gingersnaps, and Sailor could hear the teakettle on the burner in the kitchen. "The so-called Celebrity Virus is what my tribe is calling the Scarlet Pathogen. It's only affecting the Elven. Except that now here you are, an Elven Keeper, exhibiting one of its key symptoms. Whatever attacked you? It infected you. You're not bleeding much, thank God. With the others, there were rumors of excessive bleeding."

"But—" Sailor's mind was reeling. How could she have a disease? An hour earlier she'd been on a seven-mile run. "Wait, wait, wait. None of this is true. First, that sitcom girl wasn't Elven. She was completely mortal. And not very talented, I'm sorry to say, because I don't like to speak ill of the dead. And second—"

"The sitcom girl didn't have the disease," Alessande replied. "She overdosed on meth. One of our people took the 9-1-1 call and leaked misinformation to the press."

"Why?"

"To draw attention away from the Elven. Standard procedure. Mortals see patterns, even where they can't understand them. The human girl disrupts the pattern."

Sailor glanced at Vernon. Despite Alessande's assurances, it unnerved her to speak of mortals this way in front of one. "But—okay, you said I have the symptom, but then you said I'm not bleeding abnormally. So what symptom are you talking about?"

The teakettle whistled. Alessande gave a nod to Vernon, then went to the kitchen. He crossed to the front entryway and lifted a mirror off the wall.

Sailor watched him walk toward her with the mirror and grew fearful, her hands reaching up to her face, her mind racing with images of what had been done to it when she was unconscious. She didn't consider herself excessively vain, but she was an actress, after all, and fairly pretty, and so...

The man handed her the mirror. She looked at herself...

...and gulped. Her eyes were no longer green, but a deep shade of scarlet.

Don't freak, she told herself. *Keep it together. Could be worse*. She took a deep breath, then turned her gaze resolutely to Vernon. "Okay, what does it mean?"

He looked directly at her, and because she had a fair amount of the Elven telepathic abilities, she could read his thought: *Good. You didn't panic*. "We don't know what it means," he said. "Yet. We'll find out."

"You don't know? So I could be going blind, or—"

"How's your eyesight now?"

"Fine. Great."

He nodded. "I wouldn't worry, then."

"They're not *your* eyes," she pointed out. "So, wait." She spotted the other woman reentering the room. "Alessande, you can catch it from me?"

"We don't know," the Elven woman replied. "But so far, so good."

"So what's the cure?"

Alessande brought in a tray of tea. "We've yet to find out. It's not like we can send out a press release and confer with the CDC."

True enough, Sailor thought. When times were good, the Others lived easily under the radar among humans, blending in with little effort. It was during crises that the mandate for secrecy created problems.

Alessande handed Sailor an earthenware mug, steaming-hot and filled with roots and leaves. "Sip. Don't burn yourself, but keep on sipping."

"What is it?"

"*Siúlacht.* You picked the right hillside to tumble down," Alessande said. "Not too many of us can make a good batch of *siúlacht*. I'm one of them."

The scent arising from the mug evoked a memory, but the memory refused to coalesce. Sailor took a sip and shuddered. The bitterness was intense, but so was the effect. Her senses sharpened, her sinuses cleared and she felt energy return to her.

"It's a delicate situation," Alessande said. "On one hand, we need to study the disease, find out whether other cities have experienced it, but on the other hand, we need to downplay it. So far, only the Elven community knows, along with some high-ranking vamps and shifters. And werewolves—Antony Brandt, the coroner, and others with inside jobs, who can control the flow of information."

"But not the Elven Keepers?" Sailor asked. "That doesn't make sense."

Alessande and Vernon looked at one another.

"Well, shit," Sailor said, intercepting the look. "So the other Keepers *do* know. Everyone knows but me."

"Probably the Antelope Valley Keepers don't know," Alessande said reassuringly. "And San Pedro. That guy's clueless. Bakersfield, too."

"The San Pedro Keeper died last month," Vernon said.

"Great," Sailor said. "So except for my colleagues out in the sticks, and the dead ones, I'm the only one the Council doesn't bother to inform? I'm the Canyon Keeper, for God's sake."

"If you'd had the information," Vernon said, "what would you have done with it?"

"That's hardly the point, is it?" Sailor asked.

"It may be exactly the point. If you're so new at this that you plan to share news that's confidential—"

"Hey, give me some credit, would you? They either don't trust me, or they consider me too inconsequential to bother with. Whichever, it's insulting. And for that matter, what are *you* doing with all this insider information?"

He hesitated, and Alessande said, "He's my friend. I trust him with my life. Keep drinking. You've had a trauma and a racing heartbeat won't improve things."

"I'm fine, I'm calm, I meditated this morning." Sailor took a last gulp and set the mug on the coffee table. It was strong stuff, whatever it was—she'd already forgotten the name. The Elven were good at that sort of thing, the healers of the Otherworld. She pushed herself up off the sofa. "Alessande," she said, "thanks for rescuing me. But it's my job to protect your species, not vice versa, and if I'm contagious, I'm not doing you any favors being here. Not to mention that I have work to do, and I can't do it lying on your sofa."

Alessande nodded. She reached for a sheath attached to her belt and pulled out a dagger with a four-inch blade. "Someone or something out there means you harm," she said, placing it on the table. "Can you use a dagger?"

"Yes." Sailor picked it up admiringly. It was beautifully etched, and she shared the Elven preference for blades over bullets. "I'll get it back to you."

"Go straight home and stay there," Alessande said. "Don't go out again tonight."

Sailor started for the door, but Vernon stepped in front of her, barring her way. She felt an energy between them that excited her. When she stepped around him, he grabbed her. His touch was electrifying, but she couldn't understand why, and that alarmed her. There *was* something Other about him, but she couldn't identify it.

"Take your hand off my arm," she said.

His grip tightened. "Don't be stupid, girl."

Sailor almost laughed at his effrontery. "Dude," she said. "Who're you calling girl? Not to mention who are you calling stupid? I'm the one holding a knife."

He smiled fleetingly, and the shimmery thing happened again, changing his face. A shock went through Sailor as she stared at him, the surge of sexual energy intensifying. Then the moment passed and he was the homely stockbroker once more. Had she just imagined the change? Or was something truly affecting her vision?

Vernon let go of her arm. "I'm serious. You should be examined by a doctor, one who understands Others. Your Council needs to study this disease."

"Come, Jonquil," she said, and snapped her fingers at the dog, who hopped up from the stone floor and ambled after her. She walked around Vernon, opened the door and then turned back to him.

"The Council," she said, "can kiss my ass."

Chapter 2

When the woman was gone, Declan returned to his own form. Being Vernon Winter had been a constricting experience and a mildly painful one. Among other things, the man had arthritis and fallen arches. But it had been worth it.

"Not a bad job of shifting, for a Keeper," Alessande told him, gathering up the tea things. "I saw you lose the shape only three or four times."

"I counted six," he said. "It's a miracle she didn't notice."

"She's young. The young are not observant."

"We're all young to you, Alessande." Declan knew her to be nearly a hundred, although she looked thirty in human years. The Elven didn't begin to show their age until well into their second century. "But it may have been the Scarlet Pathogen. Her eyes looked bloody scary." More scary than he'd let on to Sailor. She'd been stoic about it, which showed some character, but of course, she hadn't been looking into her own eyes for the past half hour. And he hadn't *stopped* looking at them. They were mesmerizing, whatever their color, and he wondered why he'd never noticed that before in their acquaintance. "What's the disease doing to her on the inside, that's what I'd like to know."

"That's what we'd all like to know."

Declan followed Alessande into the kitchen. "We shouldn't have let her walk out of here."

She looked at him. "What should we have done, kidnap her? She's fit, she's armed and she'll be home in minutes— the Gryffald estate is a mile down the road. The *síúlacht* she drank will give her speed and strength enough to take on anything. It will last an hour, two at the most."

"And then?"

"It will wear off and she'll drop. She'll sleep the sleep of the dead for a good twelve hours or more, but she'll be in her own home and safe enough. I've been to her house, years ago at a dinner party her father gave. There were layers upon layers of protective spells cast." Alessande handed him a mug of coffee, although he hadn't asked for any.

"Hope they've kept it up. Spells fade." He sipped his coffee. "We should've gotten a blood sample from her, have Krabill take a look at it."

"The *síúlacht* will mask the effects of the pathogen. Better to wait until it's worn off."

"Wait twelve hours? I don't have that much patience."

Alessande shrugged. "The *síúlacht* will be out of her system long before that. Krabill works nights, doesn't she?"

"You're suggesting I rouse the girl from her dead sleep to take her to Krabill's office?"

"You've roused me from a dead sleep once or twice, if memory serves."

He smiled briefly. "She won't like it as much as you did."

"Can Krabill develop an antidote, do you think?"

Declan turned his attention to the twilight sky. "Maybe,

but that's not the point. Those four women didn't just catch this disease. It's my guess they were deliberately infected."

"Why do you say that? Because this one was attacked?"

"And because Charlotte was found on the beach at Point Dume."

"Where did you hear that?"

"I watched the coroner take her body away."

Alessande's eyes grew wide. "My God, what was she doing there?" Most Elven had a fear of water that was both logical—being near it physically weakened them—and deeply emotional. "She'd never have gone there voluntarily."

Declan shook his head. "Charlotte wouldn't go near a swimming pool, let alone an ocean. Someone forced her there," he said, "or dumped her there. She was murdered, whatever story they're giving out. The more we learn about this pathogen, the more we'll know about the killer who used it. And I want that killer."

"As murder weapons go, it's not very effective," she said. "It didn't kill Sailor. Besides, that winged creature didn't need a pathogen. If it wanted her dead, those talons alone could've opened an artery, and even I couldn't have saved her."

"All right, I don't pretend to have any of the answers now. But I'll get them, I promise you."

She looked at him speculatively. "Why did you not want her to see you? Why did you shift?"

Declan met her look. "Sailor Gryffald and I don't get along. I wanted to see what she's like when she's not on the defensive."

"And why don't you get along?"

He thought back to a recent encounter at his nightclub. "I expect I may have offended her at some point."

"I expect you did."

Declan laughed. "What does that mean?"

"You're a great friend to your friends and a cold bastard to those beneath your notice."

"That's not true."

"It certainly is."

"Well, she's never been beneath my notice. She's a Gryffald." The Gryffald family had been players in the Los Angeles Councils long before "player" was part of the cultural lexicon. Of course, the current Gryffalds were all young, three neophytes in a city where experience was power. Sailor's cousins had proved more capable than he'd expected... but this one?

"She has the pedigree," Alessande said, reading his thoughts in the disconcerting way the Elven had. "Give her a chance."

"She's an actress, for God's sake. Hardly training for a crisis like this." He turned away from her and looked out the kitchen window, watching the color drain out of the sky.

Alessande moved next to him. "Well, we all have an uphill battle, haven't we? The girl was attacked by something Other, and that is bad news for our world. Once it becomes known, I fear for what my species may do to yours, Declan, and to the vampires, as well. None of you Keepers will have it easy if it comes to war."

"I won't let it come to war, Alessande."

"You may not be able to stop it."

"Watch me." He drained the coffee in his cup and set it down. "Fate put that girl in your path. And you put her in mine. Now I'm calling Kimberly Krabill, and we're going to find out what this bloody pathogen is and how it works, and how the killer acquired it."

"If Sailor doesn't like you, how do you propose getting her to your Dr. Krabill?"

"Charm." He smiled. "If she's coming down from *siúlacht,* she'll be too weak to resist."

Alessande looked into his eyes. "Tread carefully. I saw a portent tonight. When she was unconscious." She hesitated, then said, "For love of that woman, someone will die. And love may bring death to *her,* as well."

"My heart isn't in danger."

She laughed softly. "You don't know yourself at all, do you? But be warned, Declan. I don't think Sailor Gryffald is long for this world."

The sky was dark now, night fully arrived. Declan breathed in the canyon air, watched the lights of distant houses go on one by one. Like fireflies, he thought, and then tried to remember when he'd last seen a firefly. They weren't native to California any more than he was.

It had been instructive, meeting Sailor as a stranger, unencumbered by the undercurrent of hostility that characterized their encounters. More than instructive. With no chip on her shoulder, he found her exceedingly attractive. He wondered if Alessande had been right, that he was a cold bastard. Maybe. The truth was, he found actors to be self-absorbed and vain, with few exceptions. It was hardly their fault. The business was so harsh that survival required a high opinion of one's own talent and specialness. Sailor was showing more substance than he'd expected, but she was hardly ready to assume the position of Canyon Keeper. His plan was to get her to Krabill and let the doctor oversee her recovery while her colleagues—himself, for starters—took charge of the crisis. Good luck for the investigation to be able to observe the disease. Sailor Gryffald was more valuable in a hospital bed than on her feet.

And more vulnerable.

He shook off Alessande's last words. *Portents aren't facts*, he reminded himself. *They're like dreams, open to*

*interpretation, symbolic. We've had enough dead. I have no
intention of letting Sailor Gryffald join their ranks.*

Declan slowed his heart by an effort of will, and then
lowered his eyelids on a long exhale, sent a command to
the region deep in his solar plexus, watched the molecules
rearrange themselves.

He turned himself into a hawk and flew home.

Sailor knew she was moving as fast as she was because
of the strangely named brew that Alessande had given
her. A long-forgotten memory suddenly emerged from the
depths of her mind: she'd been a child, sick with bronchi-
tis, and her mother had given her the same brew, bade her
drink it despite the bitterness. It had been like a miracle
then, and it was the same now. She could feel it continue
to sharpen her senses and heat her blood, and wondered if
there would be a backlash when it wore off, some kind of
potion hangover. Her theory, backed up by personal research
in her college days, was that the better the high, the worse
the morning after. She couldn't remember the aftereffects
when she'd been seven, only that one moment she'd been
ill and the next playing tag with her cousins.

However much the potion helped the symptoms, it was
unlikely, Sailor guessed, to actually cure this poison or
virus—no, what had they called it? A pathogen. The pathogen must be resistant to the usual Elven healing powers.
Otherwise Charlotte and Gina and the others would have
healed themselves. Might the pathogen have some magical component? She assumed that the medical community,
the one comprised of Others, was searching for the cure.
She would worry about that later. The first thing to do was
get home.

Should she teleport? No, because Jonquil would be left
to find his own way alone. Besides which, teleporting took

a physical toll on her. She had a surge of energy now, but who knew how long it would last? Better to conserve it.

She had been teleporting since the age of two and a half, according to her mother, which so unnerved the poor woman that she'd called her husband home from work to make Sailor stop disappearing from her bedroom and reappearing in the playroom when she was supposed to be napping. Because Sailor wasn't truly Elven, her powers would never be as strong as theirs, and she needed constant practice to move herself more than a mile at a time. Still, she was very good at it, for a Keeper. Not that she'd always used it responsibly. Keepers, too, had to survive the teenage years, and Sailor's had been rocky.

She continued jogging, her focus on Jonquil's tail ahead of her, the full moon above, her grip on the dagger Alessande had given her. If the thing, the Other, whatever it was, returned, it would not catch her unaware. She didn't run with an iPod, because it interfered with situational awareness, and now, especially, she needed access to all six senses. She would recognize the warning signs this time: the whoosh of wind, the drop in temperature, the quieting of the cicadas. This time she would be ready. She had always been good with a knife.

Don't be stupid, girl. That man's words reverberated in her head. Stupid? She was in her element out here. Running was her passion, and these roads were as familiar to her as her home. No one was going to scare her off her own turf.

Her thoughts returned to the man. He wasn't in the least attractive, and yet there was something about him that she found...magnetic. Perhaps it was his confidence. There was nothing sexier. Or maybe her strange wanton reaction was due to the moon, just risen, perfectly full. It was in Scorpio, the most carnal sign of the zodiac, and yesterday had been Beltane, the ancient Celtic celebration of fertility. A trifecta of sexual energy.

Even so, that man…who was he and why was he privy to Elven inside information? He knew more about the current crisis than she did, and he was nothing. He was merely mortal.

Or was he?

She stopped in her tracks and Jonquil stopped, too, curious. Of course. It was so obvious, she was embarrassed to have been almost oblivious to it. The attack must have thrown her off her game, affecting her powers of observation. Sailor had seen the shimmering effect enough, witnessed her cousin Barrie practice her own shifting skills. How could she not have recognized it? "Vernon" was merely a costume, a convenient face and body to house a man—or woman— who was a shapeshifter. Or, like Barrie, a Keeper of shifters. Although that was less likely. She doubted a Keeper could sustain a shift for half an hour, especially a shift into human form. Humans, Barrie said, were tough.

So Alessande hadn't been altogether straight with her, and some shifter out there was also playing her. Some shifter with powerful sexual energy. And, of course, the entire Elven Council—excluding the dead guy in San Pedro and the idiots in the Antelope Valley. And she mustn't forget the winged Other that had attacked her. There were a lot of people withholding information. She would need a flowchart to keep them straight.

But she knew whom to find first. As soon as she changed clothes and did something to disguise her eyes.

She reached Laurel Canyon and took the lead, hugging the shoulder to avoid the traffic, knowing Jonquil would do the same. They were running downhill now, practically at a sprint, and within two minutes Lookout Mountain was

in sight and they were taking a right onto the private road
that led to the House of the Rising Sun, high on the hill.
Her home.

The House of the Rising Sun was actually a compound
with three houses, built early in the twentieth century by
Ivan Schwartz, a magician who went by the stage name of
Merlin. Sailor had grown up in the main house, which her
mother had always called the Castle House. Sailor's cousin
Barrie lived in Gwydion's Cave, the residence Merlin had
built for their grandfather. And Rhiannon, the third cousin,
occupied Pandora's Box, the original guesthouse. Merlin,
who had long since passed from this world to the next,
nevertheless preferred to stay on at the House of the Rising Sun—as a ghost.

A Tiffany lamp burned in the main hall, giving Castle
House a ghostly glow. Had she left it on? Maybe. She did
tend to be careless....

She followed Jonquil to the kitchen and filled his water
bowl, watched him lap it up, then refilled it. The kitchen
was old, with beat-up soft wood floors and knotty pine
paneling installed in the 1950s, which was decades before
she was born, but she knew the history of the estate going
back to the 1920s. The house was old even when it was new,
Mediterranean Gothic in style, with as many antiques as its
owner could fill it with. Sailor loved all of Rising Sun, but
especially Castle House, and especially the kitchen. She'd
grown up in the oversize room, baked cookies with her
mother, done homework at the old pine table, warmed herself near the wood-burning fireplace, napped on the ratty
sofa covered with homemade quilts. She thought of Alessande's kitchen, with its polish and new appliances. If there
was an opposite to state-of-the-art, this was it.

She looked out the window over the sink and saw a light

on in Pandora's Box. Apparently Rhiannon was home. Out the back door she saw Gwydion's Cave illuminated, as well, which meant Barrie was there, probably writing. The three houses were connected by tunnels, one of the estate's many splendid oddities, but as adults, the cousins mostly stayed aboveground. For the moment Sailor had Castle House to herself, and could shower and map out what she would say to her cousins before—

A door slammed open. A gust of wind came through the kitchen. Already spooked by the lamp, Sailor reached for the dagger she'd set down.

"Sailor! You home yet?" a voice called, and a door slammed shut. "Where are you?"

"Kitchen," she called back, and looked around for a dish towel to throw over her bloody shirt, but too late, because her cousin Rhiannon was walking through the archway, accompanied by Wizard, a dog so large he made Jonquil look dainty. Sailor clutched the shirt close and reminded herself not to make eye contact with her gorgeous relative.

"You've been out all this time?" Rhiannon reached down to pet Jonquil, who greeted her and Wizard with enthusiasm bordering on hysteria, as though he hadn't seen them both a few hours earlier. Rhiannon glanced at Sailor. "Are you slaughtering something for dinner?"

Sailor looked down at the dagger in her hand and set it on the butcher block in front of her. "Oh, I— This is just—"

"Very slasher movie, that thing." Rhiannon frowned at it. "Listen, Dad called. Mine, not yours. Apparently the rumor that we missed paying one lousy electric bill—or, okay, two bills—"

"Three."

"Three lousy electric bills, fine. So somehow he heard that they turned off the power because—and you'll love this—the alarm system is wired to his computer, and he happened to check in and was able to see that the system was down, so he called the company, who ratted us out, and—" She stopped, taking in her cousin again. "What have you got all over yourself? Paint?"

There it was. Could she talk about the attack without divulging everything else? Probably not. "It's nothing. Go on."

"That's it." Rhiannon picked up an apple from the fruit bowl on the counter and peeled off the sticker. "My dad and his gadgetry. You'd think he could relax the surveillance, knowing that I'm engaged to a cop, but no." She rubbed the apple on her sweater, apparently an alternative to washing it, and took a loud, crunching bite. She peered at Sailor as she chewed. "You're a mess."

"You're looking a bit 'circus refugee' yourself," Sailor replied, with a sideways glance. Rhiannon's lanky body was draped in plaid flannel pants, a tie-dye T-shirt and an argyle sweater, everything in colors so at odds with her flame-colored hair that Sailor felt nauseous.

"Cleaning closets," Rhiannon explained. "Carving out space for Brodie. Trying on stuff before I hand it off to the Goodwill, in case I still like it. It's insane how tiny the closets are in Pandora's Box. How come nobody in the 1920s believed in storage space? It's like junk wasn't invented until 1985. Never mind me. Look at you. Your shirt's filthy. What did you do, fall down the hillside?"

"Yeah, something like that. Listen, Rhi, I just need to take a shower and—"

"It's like you got run over. And the dagger—is it antique? Let me see that."

Sailor, in proffering the dagger hilt-first, let go of her own shirt.

"Sailor!" Rhiannon shrieked. "What in God's name happened to you? Look at your chest."

"What?" another voice called. "What did I miss?" And into the kitchen sauntered Barrie, the third cousin.

Barrie was petite by Gryffald standards, but the toughest of the cousins in many ways. When she saw Sailor's state, however, she turned tender. "You poor thing. What did you do to yourself?"

"It's not a big deal," Sailor said. "Just a jogging…incident. Accident. Happens all the time on the trails. I'm clumsy."

Rhiannon took Sailor's hands in her own and turned them over. "Really? So you trip and fall, but you don't skin your knees or scrape your palms, you fall directly on your sternum?"

"She probably ran into a tree," Barrie said.

"With arms outstretched," Rhiannon said.

"Very common among runners," Barrie added. "It's why they don't route marathons through forests."

The two women looked at Sailor expectantly, and for the first time got a good look at her face.

"Holy hell!" Rhiannon screamed. "What's with your eyes?"

"Good God," Barrie said. "Are those…colored contact lenses?"

"No. But if you have a spare pair, Barrie, I need to borrow them."

"If you want to borrow anything," Barrie said, "start explaining."

Sailor sank into the sofa as a wave of weakness rolled over her. "I need coffee."

"I'll make coffee, you talk," Rhiannon said, walking across the kitchen.

Barrie plopped down on the sofa alongside Sailor. "This isn't some extreme ploy to get the night off work, is it?"

"Damn. Work." Sailor sat up on the sofa. "What time is it?"

"Eight-twenty."

"Okay. I'll make this fast. Something happened tonight, which—"

"Is it to do with us?" Rhiannon asked.

"Tangentially, yes. It has to do with the family business."

"Oh." This time the two spoke in unison.

The cousins were all Keepers. Born in the same year, one red-haired child to each of the Gryffald brothers, the girls came into the world with the birthmarks of their fathers. Barrie's destiny was to oversee the shapeshifters, Rhiannon's the vampires. The girls had shared childhood memories, holidays and vacations, then gone separate ways as adults. Now they were back together and living in the family compound rent-free, if not expense-free. Their Otherworld work didn't come with a paycheck, and all three of them had real-world professions—for Sailor, acting. Which meant, at the moment, waitressing.

"The thing is," Sailor said, "I'm not sure I should talk about it."

"Screw that," Barrie said.

"Okay, but what if I tell you what I know and you feel you're honor-bound, as a Keeper, to discuss it with—"

"Who?" Rhiannon asked from across the kitchen.

"Whom," Barrie said. She was a journalist, and she believed in precision.

Sailor shook her head. "Shifters. Vamps. Your fellow Keepers." She looked at Rhiannon. "Your fiancé. Especially him. You tell Brodie, he's going to want to talk to me, and he's got to stay away from me. Because he's Elven."

Rhiannon frowned. "What's that got to do with—"

"You know what I hate?" Sailor continued. "Someone swears you to silence and tells you something, and then it turns out they themselves were sworn to silence, which means they're expecting more of you than they expect of themselves."

"You hate that?" Barrie asked. "Because I don't have a problem with it. Everyone does it."

"But isn't it much better," Sailor persisted, "if someone were to ask you later, to be able to say, 'Golly, I didn't know anything about it'?"

Barrie nodded. "Yes, if I were the sort of person who's ever said 'golly.'"

"I'm going with Barrie on this one," Rhiannon said. "Screw that. We're family."

Sailor took a long look at her cousin Rhiannon in her strange clothes and another look at her cousin Barrie, and the two of them looked back at her with Gryffald eyes.

After a deep breath, she told them the story of her evening.

Declan Wainwright stood outside the gates of the House of the Rising Sun. He'd parked off Lookout Mountain and hiked the few hundred yards to this spot, where he could see into the main house—Sailor's house—one of several on the compound and the only one showing movement. He counted three people and assumed they were the Gryffald cousins. He was waiting for Sailor to be alone, to pass out from fatigue, as Alessande had predicted, so that he could make his way into her bedroom and extract some blood. He'd worked his way through college as an EMT, so that would be easy. If she was deeply asleep, she wouldn't even wake. He would return in the morning to get her to Kimberly's lab, recruiting her cousins to help, if necessary. But for now, he needed her blood.

And, to be honest, he needed to see that she was safe.

He wasn't used to waiting. Harriet excelled at expediting

things for him, a perk of money and power. He'd spent the past hour texting with her, rearranging his calendar, rescheduling meetings planned for the next morning and setting up two for tonight. One was with Kimberly Krabill, the physician, and the other was business. He glanced at his watch.

He would have to break in. If there was as much magic here at the House of the Rising Sun as Alessande had indicated, he couldn't do it by shifting. He'd once become a sparrow and encountered an enchanted force field so strong that he'd lost his shift energy, felt his wings fail and fallen twenty feet to the ground. Better to take his chances as a normal burglar. The grounds had a dilapidated aura, suggesting that nonmagical security was minimal. Declan liked trespassing anyway; it made him feel like a kid again.

At the age of ten he'd told his foster parents that he would rather eat what came out of a garbage can than what came out of their frying pan, which had resulted in a hard kick to his gut. "Compared to what that drugged whore of a mother fed you," his foster father had bellowed, "this is the dining hall of the *Q.E. Two*."

Declan had waited until nightfall, climbed down the fire escape and made his way to Southampton's docks, which he knew well enough, his mother having numbered a few sailors among her client base. When he'd found the *Queen Elizabeth II* in her berth, his curiosity grew.

He'd turned himself into a swallow and flown aboard.

The ship had delighted him. He'd reverted to human form and stayed aboard and in his body all the way to New York. For him, it was second nature to steal food, sleep in small places and keep out of the way of grown people. He could do it all without resorting to his abilities, most of which he didn't understand, a few of which scared him. His mother, in one of her lucid moments, had told him that there were others like him, maybe not in Southampton, but in big cities and also in America, quite a lot of them. Keepers, she'd called them. With birthmarks like his.

She'd been right. America was filled with them. Keepers and shapeshifters and Others of all sorts, creatures that looked human but had other qualities and talents, magical, fascinating, at times frightening to a ten-year-old…

Few things frightened him now.

The lights in the house went out. A door opened, and he could hear two people saying goodnight to one another. That would be Rhiannon and Barrie, he thought. They all lived on the compound, so it was likely they'd left Sailor in the main house and were heading to their own. Their voices trailed off, along with the sound of footsteps on a stone path. When it was quiet, he scaled the wall easily and made his way to the main house.

Entering the house—a small castle, really—required only the removal of a window screen and crawling through. He used his cell phone flashlight to look through a stack of mail on the kitchen table, confirming that it was Sailor's house. Then the dog appeared—Jonquil, she'd called him—greeting him like an old friend. Apparently he and "Vernon Winter" smelled the same.

"Where is she?" he whispered, scratching Jonquil's soft ears. "Upstairs? Asleep?"

Jonquil, as if he understood, bounded up the winding staircase. Declan followed, his footsteps disturbingly loud on the creaking stairs. He searched each room, and while he found Sailor's bloodstained jogging clothes on the floor of the master bedroom, he did not find her.

Where the hell was she?

Chapter 3

Sailor made it to the Hollywood Bowl, resplendent under the full moon, in seventeen minutes. Parking was a nightmare, of course, but she would be leaving long before the rest of the crowd, so she blocked someone's Acura and left her Jeep, moving fast before parking security could bust her.

She was determined to see Charles Highsmith, the head of the Elven Keeper Council.

Learning Highsmith's whereabouts had been simple: a call to his office pretending to be a veterinary assistant concerned about one of his polo ponies had yielded the information that he was at the Hollywood Bowl, had been there since six at an open-air pre-concert "business picnic" and was unreachable. Of course, one person's "unreachable" was another's piece of cake, Sailor decided. The Hollywood Bowl wasn't the Staples Center; because the criminal element was less addicted to the Los Angeles Philharmonic than to the Lakers, security was lax. She was prepared to use her limited powers of Elvenry and her considerable powers of lying to make her way in, but the usher guarding the entrance was listening to the concert, and she slipped by easily.

She walked carefully. The house was dark, with all the lights focused on the orchestra, but the full moon illuminated the way and made her aware of the occasional Elven. How contagious was she? She hadn't infected Alessande, so surely an accidental touch wouldn't do it, but how to be sure?

She made her way to the Garden Boxes, where her father had season tickets, hoping that Highsmith was there, too, and once again her luck held. Highsmith was on the aisle, wineglass in hand.

Under normal circumstances she would have been embarrassed to spoil anyone's concert experience, but now she touched Highsmith on the shoulder and met his affronted look calmly. The full moon would highlight her scarlet eyes, which she hadn't yet hidden behind her cousin's contacts. She needed no mirror to tell her how frightening she must appear. It was written all over his patrician face.

"Remember me?" she said. "I'm Sailor Gryffald."

They walked to the exit in the near dark, accompanied by the notes of Mahler's *Symphony No. 5*. Highsmith led the way. He was an inch or so taller than she was, with an athletic body and a commanding presence that was almost military, even when he was wearing khakis and a polo shirt. His muscular back registered displeasure, which Sailor chalked up to a control freak facing a situation not of his making. She found the man intimidating and—okay, this was weird—attractive. Was that some *siúlacht* side effect?

In the parking lot he led her to the VIP section and

clicked a remote at a black Rolls-Royce Ghost. He let her in the passenger side and turned on the lights. "Look at me."

He studied her eyes in a clinical manner. She in turn registered a man in his fifties with a hard, handsome face and close-cropped, steel-gray hair. For a split second he looked at her, rather than her eyes, but before she could see his thoughts he switched off the interior light and opened his car door.

"Don't you want to know how it happened?" she asked, but he was out of the car and opening her door before she knew what he was doing.

"Let's take a walk."

"Why? Is your car bugged?" she asked, but she climbed out.

He didn't answer until they were several yards away. "Cars are vulnerable. That much electronic circuitry makes it difficult to cloak with protective spells. Tell me what happened, please."

She recited the facts once more, striding through the parking lot. The night had grown cold, but she knew she was running a temperature and welcomed the chilly breeze. Highsmith listened without comment, asking for only a few points of clarification. When she'd finished, he said, "How did you find me here?"

She ignored that, not wanting to get his assistant fired. "The question is, why didn't I know about the Scarlet Pathogen until I became infected with it?"

"We're giving no official response while events are still unfolding."

"Events are unfolding right into my bloodstream," she said. "And anyway, who's 'we'? I'm part of the Council. Shouldn't I be one of the official responders?"

"No. The executive committee takes care of that."

"Are you serious?"

"It's protocol."

"And who's the executive committee? You?"

"Keep your voice down."

Sailor looked around. A chauffeur stood outside a limousine talking on a cell phone twenty yards away, the lone human in sight. She lowered her voice, but not her intensity. "I was attacked. Deliberately infected, which means that maybe those dead Elven women were deliberately infected, too. Maybe they didn't just pick up the disease on location, which is what the news reports suggest. I expect you would know. I expect you have contacts in the law enforcement community. Because you're the head of the Council."

He looked at her speculatively. Then he nodded. "Yes. The police are investigating the deaths, and if they haven't yet been ruled homicides, they will be any day now."

"Who are their suspects?"

"If my sources shared that kind of confidential information with me, do you really think I would share it with you?"

"If it would help us find a killer, yes. Don't you think I have a right to know?"

"I think you're a novice in a job you neither understand nor appreciate, despite your pedigree. Being the victim of an attack doesn't change that."

"But it's motivating me," she said. "And I'm a fast learner."

"Congratulations."

His sarcasm was like a slap in the face, and Sailor felt her temper rise. "My assailant was a winged creature, a bird or a bat. That's either a shifter or a vampire, and once word of that gets out—and that's my call, isn't it?—all hell will break loose. So you and your executive committee and your protocol and your old boys' network can shut me out, Charles, but you'll be doing so at your own—"

"Young woman." His voice stopped her cold as he turned

and looked at her face-to-face. "You've been through a disturbing experience. I'll make allowances for that. But don't
think for a moment that you are my equal simply because
you bear your father's name. I'm the Council's President
and you are its youngest member, and you haven't earned
the right to address me by my given name, let alone speak
to me in that manner."

She was now seriously pissed, but he held up his hand.
"If you intend to make an enemy of me so early in your career, you're not just rude, you're ignorant."

Sailor closed her mouth, anger and embarrassment fighting it out inside her.

"Word of this must not get out," he continued, "or you
will cause a great deal of damage. Keep your mouth shut.
You should stay out of sight, as well. Your eyes will attract
attention."

"Shouldn't you be worried I'll transmit the disease to
the Elven?"

His eyes narrowed. "Naturally," he said, and looked at
his watch. "I'll call for a Council meeting within twenty-
four hours, and you'll hear from me in the next twelve.
Until then, stay home. I'll send my own physician to your
house tomorrow to examine you. Where are you parked?"

"I don't need an escort, thank you."

"Then I'll return to the concert, where my absence will
have been noted. You'll have been recognized, as well.
That's how rumors begin. It was an unfortunate move on
your part, coming here. That's why it's imperative you go
home now. I'll have to do some damage control."

"I'm sure you're quite capable of it. Sir," she added, with as
much sarcasm as she could fit into one syllable. She walked
away before he could respond, pleased to have the last word.

Go home? Ha. She had things to do, and going home
was far down on the list.

* * *

Declan knocked on the door of the first of the two guest-houses he came to, interrupting what he imagined to be the early stages of foreplay between Rhiannon Gryffald, the Canyon vampire Keeper, and Brodie McKay, her Elven lover. He was on good terms with both, so he spent a minute in friendly conversation before saying to Rhiannon, "Where's your cousin?"

"Which one?" she asked, innocence written all over her lovely face.

"Sailor."

"Oh." She smiled. "Work, I expect. She waits tables at the House of Illusion. The late shift."

She went to work? In her condition? Declan hid his reaction and asked, "Did you see her tonight?"

Rhiannon hesitated for a fraction of a second. "We don't run into each other as much as you'd think."

Declan saw Brodie raise an eyebrow, which told Declan a several things: Rhiannon knew about the attack on Sailor, but she wasn't about to tell *him,* because she hadn't even told her fiancé. And her fiancé, who happened to be a cop, would no doubt ask her why she'd just lied to a friend and fellow Keeper as soon as Declan was out the door.

And if Rhiannon was able to keep secrets from an Elven who would be looking her right in the eye, she was very talented indeed. Telepathy through eye contact was an Elven specialty, right up there with a strong sexual appetite. Declan wondered how his friends would reconcile the two tonight.

"Thanks," he said. "Have a nice evening."

The House of Illusion sat atop a hill on Hollywood Boulevard, east of Laurel Canyon. It was fully illuminated in all its medieval glory, turrets and battlements beckoning tourists and natives, skeptics and believers, devotees and the merely curious.

Declan had a soft spot in his heart for the place, having first seen it as an eighteen-year-old on his first night in L.A. He'd since outgrown its brooding kitschiness, but the tapestries, silvery mirrors and brocade sofas gave him a feeling of history, of Olde England, even—were he sentimental—of homesickness. Many of the furnishings had come from the British Isles, from castles fallen on hard times. The stained glass and stone fireplaces retained bits of history and, in some cases, magic.

The bar was an ornately carved mahogany affair, and Dennis, the gnome tending it, dressed for the period in a striped shirt and high-waisted trousers with suspenders. Declan would never require a uniform for his own wait-staff, and the guy had his sympathy.

Declan took a seat at a barstool, ordered a club soda and said, "Do you know a waitress named Sailor Gryffald?"

Dennis said, "Sailor? Sure. She's due in—" He glanced at the clock behind the bar. "Seven minutes ago."

Sailor had made the trip up the long winding drive to the House of Illusion more times than she could count. As a child she'd come with her parents, eyes wide, heart pounding, both terrified and mesmerized by the gargoyles, the heavy wooden doors, the moat that snaked around the castle. These days she didn't drive over the ornate drawbridge that was the public entrance but around the back to employee parking.

Her waitress training had required her to memorize the history of the place, some of which overlapped with her family history. Ivan Schwartz, its founder, was the magician who went by the stage name of Merlin and was now their family ghost-in-residence. His star was rising in the

1920s, when he built not only the House of Illusion, but the House of the Rising Sun estate, his personal kingdom. He was a social creature, keeping friends in residence, foremost among them Rhys Gryffald, Sailor's grandfather, for whom he'd designed Gwydion's Cave. But whereas Rising Sun was welcoming even in its current state of semi-decay, the House of Illusion was modeled after the haunted Carisbrooke Castle on the Isle of Wight. It was meant to evoke chills, and it generally succeeded.

Tonight, though, her chills were from another source. Whatever Alessande had given her was fast leaving her system, taking with it energy, heat and mental clarity. The temperature had dropped twenty degrees since sunset, and Sailor couldn't stop shivering, although the wound on her chest was now hot to the touch. She'd covered it with a gauze pad and buttoned her black velvet waitress dress up to her throat to hide it. It hurt, but pain she could handle. This weakness was another story.

Tough it out, she told herself, as she tied on her apron and reported to her manager, Kristoff, to be assigned a station. He was staring at his table chart and barely acknowledged her. "You're late. You've got station two, but Lauren's busy with a bachelorette party, so take the four-top for her and the deuce next to it." Then he looked up. "What on earth?" he said, and she instantly looked away. "What's going on with your eyes?"

"Yes, sorry, Kristoff, had trouble with my contacts tonight."

He frowned. "Are your pupils completely dilated? Are you on something?"

"No, just colored lenses. My cousin talked me into them."

"Black? Black contact lenses?"

They weren't black, they were green, but in combination with the scarlet of her irises they resulted in a shade of mud. She'd borrowed them from Barrie, and while Barrie's prescription was mild, it was enough to make Sailor nauseous.

"Dark brown, actually. Yes, okay, not my best look."

"It's a terrible look. Customers will think you're a drug addict."

She wanted to tell him she didn't much care, as long as they tipped her, but flippancy didn't go over well with Kristoff. "Sorry," she said. "You really don't want me working blind. I'd be walking into walls."

He shook his head. "We're wasting time. Get to work."

She breathed deeply, trying to adjust to the noise, pace and stress of the restaurant, an atmosphere she ordinarily found bracing. Tonight, though, it felt like an assault. She looked at her watch. Twenty minutes until the second dinner seating, which preceded the midnight magic show. A half hour from now she would either be working at a fever pitch or falling hopelessly behind, and the latter could cost her her job. Kristoff wasn't her biggest fan.

There were no other Elven on staff, thank God. And if any came in as customers and Kristoff seated them at her station, she would just have to get Lauren to switch tables with her. Lauren was her friend, but a mortal, so Sailor would have to come up with some plausible excuse.

But first she had to stay awake.

She was taking the drink order at the deuce when she overheard a snippet of conversation behind her. "...only thirty-three. Her whole career ahead of her. I heard it was food poisoning," a man said, to which his companion replied, "I heard it was a parasite picked up on location. Both of them were working overseas."

She knew they were talking about the dead actresses, but when she cast her eyes around the candlelit room, she couldn't figure out which table she'd been listening to. The vampires at table six? Ivan Schwartz had been, among other things, a ventriloquist, so he'd played with acoustics when building the House of Illusion, with results that were sometimes magical and sometimes maddening.

The dead Elven. Her heart hurt to think of them, had hurt all week, because she was tied to them in ways she didn't even understand. But now her conscience hurt, too. She should have been more proactive. Even believing their deaths were from natural causes, as had been reported, she should have asked questions. Now that she knew they were dead precisely because they were Elven—Gina and Charlotte, and the other two, the acting student and the talent agent—she was appalled at her earlier inattention. How irresponsible could she be? For the first time she was glad that her dad was on the other side of the world, because she couldn't bear to see his disappointment.

"Hey, sister. Y'okay?" It was Julio, her favorite busboy, clearing plates from the table next to her.

"I've been better."

"You look bad, baby."

"I feel worse."

"You need something?"

"About fourteen hours of sleep."

"You change your mind, want something else, you let me know."

"I don't do drugs, Julio."

He looked affronted. "Hey, I'm a full-service dealer. Herbs, homeopathic, healthy stuff. Legal, even. Chinese medicine. Not just party powders and pharmaceuticals." He looked over her shoulder. "At the bar. *El turista.* I think he wants you."

Sailor turned. A customer, swiveling on his barstool, was snapping his fingers, signaling her. *El turista* was what Julio called any customer he considered too ignorant to be local and this one confirmed the designation by drawling, "Waitress, hand me one of the menus you got there."

"Customer," she said, "I'd be happy to." She strolled toward him, holding out a laminated menu. "But is that how you get your wife's attention, by snapping your fingers? Because here in L.A. that's how we summon our dogs. And I'm not your golden retriever."

Before she could reach the customer, Kristoff stepped in front of her, taking the menu. He handed it to *el turista*, then steered Sailor toward the kitchen. "I don't know if you're sick or hung over or what your problem is," he hissed, "but talking to a customer like that? I'd fire you right now if we weren't overbooked tonight, with two waiters calling in sick. You're on very thin ice. Are we clear?"

"Yeah."

"Good. You'd better give me a five-star performance the rest of your shift. I see three tables in your section needing attention. And I believe your appetizers are up."

He marched off, leaving her to retrieve two burning-hot plates laden with crab cakes. He was filling up her section all at once, and she wasn't going to be able to handle it, not in her condition. But she couldn't handle being fired either. Jobs were scarce, and it had taken footwork, luck and family connections to score this one. She wasn't letting it go without a fight.

"Julio," she said, before heading back out onto the floor. "There's this tea made of twigs and things, and—"

"Chinese?"

"No. It's some Gaelic word, starts with an *s*. Tastes awful. I know it's a long shot, but—"

"Siúlacht."

Her eyes widened. "That's it."

"Yeah, I have some. Not the tea. Capsules. My supplier, he gets them from some Druid lady in the Valley. Hang tight, *mija*, I'll get them."

* * *

Other than being clearly exhausted, Sailor looked good, Declan thought, watching her from the far end of the bar. She looked better than good, in fact, communicating with Dennis in waitress/bartender shorthand, garnishing the drinks on her tray with speed and precision. She was dressed as someone's idea of a French maid, a sleeveless dress in black velvet, with a ridiculously short skirt. Someone's idea of sexy.

Okay, she was his idea of sexy, too. Especially her long legs, in black stockings with a seam down the back, stockings that showed a bit of thigh at the top. Her wild hair was pinned up, with one errant lock in her eyes, but she didn't have a free hand to deal with it, so she kept tossing her head, which didn't solve the problem but gave her the look of a spirited filly. He wondered what she would do if he walked over and pinned it back for her. By his calculations she had to be close to the breaking point, and he searched for an opportunity to step in and…what? Stop her from keeling over, perhaps, when the *siúlacht* abruptly left her system. What he would like to do was pick her up and carry her into one of the back rooms and lay her down on a Queen Anne sofa.

From there his thoughts turned to darker, more erotic images.

Julio found Sailor while she stood at the bar, waiting for a drink order, eyes closed, asleep on her feet, like a horse.

He slipped the *siúlacht* into her pocket.

She opened her eyes with a start, pulled one of the pills from her pocket and sniffed it, then nodded. The pills were rough to the touch, and she imagined grass and twigs compressed hundreds of times, hardened into a caplet. "They smell just like the tea," she said.

He nodded. "The same, I promise. I gave you two. You take one now, you save one."

"I owe you."

Julio shrugged. "You take care of me, *mija,* so I take care of you."

She felt as if she was going to go into a coma waiting for Dennis to fill her drink order and knew she was fast reaching the point where she wouldn't care about her job, her customers or the state of the world so long as she could close her eyes. She looked at the glass of ice water on her tray, took a quick glance around the bar and then, satisfied that no one was looking at her, popped a pill in her mouth and swallowed. She knocked back the water, placed the glass on the bus tray, then replaced it with a fresh one from the bar.

Dennis came back with two white wines. "You okay, Sailor?"

"Give me ten minutes. I'll be fine."

It was *siúlacht,* all right. The aftertaste was unmistakable, and with it came the same memory of her mother giving it to her when she was a child. But now she wasn't feeling the effect—

And then it kicked in, like a hockey puck to the stomach. Within seconds she was wide-awake, ears buzzing. She could focus and move, and ten minutes later she was not only on top of her station, she was helping Lauren with hers. It was when she was ordering three Irish coffees for the bachelorette party that she saw, at the far end of the bar, Declan Wainwright.

Her heart skipped a beat. And then another.

Damnit.

Declan had been watching her for half an hour, waiting for the moment to step in and get her out of there without creating a scene. He'd done a glamour on himself, nothing taxing, not full-on invisibility, just enough so that she wasn't aware it was him at the bar, seeing him only as some random customer.

And then she'd popped a pill.

He'd seen the surreptitious glance around, her eyes disguised with colored contact lenses—where on earth had she gotten those?—that told him the pill was something other than aspirin.

He was sure that no one else saw, but at that point he was locked onto her and could practically hear her thoughts: *I hope this works.* As an Elven Keeper, she had the Elven transparency, both sending and receiving thoughts telepathically. He wondered if she was gifted in all aspects of Elvenry, including their version of witchcraft.

Damn the girl. She was tainting her own blood, clouding the best clue they had to whomever was killing the species she was supposed to be protecting. And she'd done it right before his eyes. He was angry enough that his glamour fell away before he realized it, leaving him openly staring at her.

And now she was staring back.

Sailor literally stopped breathing.

If there was a man living who was more erotically appealing than Declan Wainwright, more her type, better able to take her breath away, she didn't want to meet him. One was enough for this lifetime. When she was around him she wasn't herself, and self-consciousness, painful for anyone, was particularly bad for an actress. It killed creative energy. Her attraction to him rendered her graceless, inarticulate and gauche—and that made her defensive.

Breathe, she told herself.

And why was he here? It was one thing to encounter him after hours at his own nightclub, where a drink or two could ease her awkwardness. Here she was at a disadvantage, dressed in an absurd French maid uniform—with sensible shoes—perpetually in danger of being yelled at by Kristoff. How embarrassing.

Her cousins considered Declan a friend, especially Rhiannon, but Sailor had gotten off on the wrong foot with him years earlier, and then again a few months ago, and now every encounter seemed to make it worse. She'd pegged him as someone with a bias against actors/waiters, against any artist who wasn't—yet—A-list. Which pissed her off.

What pissed her off even more was how susceptible she was to his charms, like nearly every woman in L.A., which made her a cliché. She had no defense against his rakish appeal, his jet-black hair and sky-blue eyes bordered by laugh lines, the early warning signs of middle age. He was close to forty, Sailor knew, a decade older than she was, but he didn't look it. His body, surfer-lean, was always in jeans and a T-shirt. And he had a timeless aura of…cool. As the owner of the Snake Pit on Sunset, he was a staple of the late-night club scene, as well as being a producer, entrepreneur and unerring judge of talent in the indie music world. A star maker.

And he had all the confidence that came with that. He was used to women coming on to him, and she wasn't going to join that club. He was never going to know how she felt about him, not if she had anything to say about it.

What was he was doing at the House of Illusion? It wasn't to see her, that was for sure. She wasn't in his social sphere. But he was staring at her now, so she could hardly ignore him. They were acquaintances. It would be too weird. Damn.

She served her Irish coffees, asked Lauren to keep an eye on her station, then wiped her hands on her apron, brushed her hair from her eye, and—heart pounding—walked over to him.

"Mr. Wainwright?" The formality was tongue-in-cheek, acknowledging the prickliness of their relationship.

Declan swiveled on his barstool to face her. "Miss Gryffald," he said drily. The way he pronounced her name betrayed his Celtic origins. The guy had an accent that would make a tax code sound seductive.

"I wanted to ask you—" Damn. She was shaking. "I'm wondering if there's anything you could tell me about Gina Santoro or Charlotte Messenger."

"Why?"

"Excuse me?"

"Why would I?" he asked.

"Why would you know anything about them? Or why would you tell me?"

"Yes."

Did some people enjoy toying with other people? she wondered. Some endorphin rush? "You would know about them," she said, "because they were both part of the club scene and you *are* the club scene, and there's not much that goes on between 2:00 a.m. and sunrise that you don't know or can't find out. And you would tell me because you're a shapeshifter Keeper and you were friends with my uncle Owen, and because I'm an Elven Keeper and it couldn't hurt you to have an ally on my Council—a new one, I mean. And not to be ageist, but…a young one. One who's not going to be collecting Social Security anytime soon." She was talking too fast and with too much energy and saw Dennis glance her way.

"I already have a number of allies," Declan Wainwright said, his voice low. "And if you think trading on your family name will earn anyone's respect, you're not much like your uncle Owen. Or your father."

Sailor was now breathing heavily, her face burning along with the wound in her chest. "You know what?" she said.

"Maybe you think that because I'm just a waitress-slash-actress I shouldn't be talking to you except to take your order—"

"You shouldn't be talking at all, in a room that—"

"—and that your money means you can afford to make enemies. I can see how you might think that. And yet it would be so easy to win someone's gratitude and loyalty, someone who might have information that could be useful to you, but I'm sure you have your reasons for being an arrogant b—" She stopped, aghast. Had she just almost called him an arrogant bastard?

He swiveled his barstool until he was facing her dead on. Smiling. His trademark grin, something she'd seen but never provoked. "Go on, pet. Don't start editing yourself now."

"Oh, my God. My mouth. I'm sorry. Look, I've got—"

"A temper?" He was still smiling. "I'd say so."

"I was going to say 'customers.' But yes, a temper, too." She turned to go.

"Wait." He reached out and caught her wrist.

She turned back and stared, electricity surging through her at the touch. His hand was strong, but his hold was gentle. She could easily have pulled free, but she didn't. Her heart was beating fast.

With his free hand Declan made the "Check, please" gesture to Dennis, and when Dennis made the "It's on the house" gesture back to him, Declan stood, and pulled her closer. He was taller than she by a few inches, and she was forced to look up at him.

He leaned in, and she couldn't imagine what he was doing—for one crazy moment she thought he was going to kiss her neck—but it was only to whisper in her ear.

"What did you take just now?"

"What do you mean?" She was practically vibrating with the nearness of him.

"The pill."

"Oh." She shook her head. "Just—it's called *siúlacht*. It's nothing, it's—"

"I know what it is. Bloody hell." He let go of her, and stepped back, turning to shield his thoughts from her. "All right. Come to the Snake Pit after your shift. This—" he gestured at the bar "—is no place to discuss business."

She gulped. *Shit.* She'd talked about Keepers, shifters, Elven in a room constructed for eavesdropping. It had been a huge lapse in judgment.

He put a twenty on the bar for Dennis. "And do me a favor?" he added. "No more pills tonight. Not even vitamins."

"Okay, but—"

"You think no one's looking?" Declan raised an eyebrow. "Look around you. Mirrors and magic. Everything you do, love, someone can see."

Declan watched her walk away, surprised at his own flare of temper, which had made him more sharp-spoken than he'd intended. But her talking openly about Keeper matters in a place like this and on top of that downing a second dose of *siúlacht*… What bad luck. The *siúlacht* would mask the effects of the Scarlet Pathogen all over again. That set them back two or three hours, hours that could have been spent tracking a killer by other means. Maddening. What a waste of time.

But it was more than that. If he were to be honest with himself—and he worked hard to be honest with himself, to not turn into the arrogant bastard she thought he was—he had to admit that the one he was mad at wasn't Sailor but himself. Because she stirred up something in him—she

had just enough Elven in her to be his type, with her overt
sensuality, her long golden limbs and red-gold hair—and
the last thing he needed now was a romantic entanglement.
Sailor's path had crossed his because of this crisis, and it
was the crisis that mattered. Finding the killer. Not her.

Alessande's warning came to mind. The Elven passion
for portents and premonitions irritated him because he
didn't like being told what not to do, even by supernatural
sources. This time the warnings were unnecessary, redun-
dant, telling him what he already knew: Keep this strictly
business.

And it was hardly her fault that she'd messed up his evening's agenda, because she had no idea she was part of it.
Taking *siúlacht* wasn't a bad call on her part; it was a perfectly reasonable response to her condition, taking more of
what Alessande had given her hours earlier. *Not everyone's
an addict, mate,* he told himself. And even if she were, it
wasn't his business.

How had she lasted this long, though? He and Alessande
had underestimated her stamina. But she would show up at
his club, he had no doubt. She wanted something from him.

Would she be safe, though, driving the streets of Hollywood after midnight? Safe from what had attacked her
this afternoon? Whether her assailant was a vampire or a
shifter, neither was likely to enter her car while she was
driving. And once she reached the Snake Pit she would be
on his turf, and anyone trying to mess with her there did
so at their peril. *Let them try,* he thought, and instinctively
flexed his muscles.

Damn. He was going to have to watch himself. Feeling
this protective toward her was a bad sign.

He signaled Dennis, who came over, wiping a shot glass
with a bar towel. "Do me a favor?" Declan asked, pulling
out a business card.

"Sure."

Declan nodded toward Sailor, visible in the next room. "Sailor Gryffald. I don't think she's well. Call me at this number, would you, if she shows any signs of weakness? Maybe see her to her car?"

"I'll do better than that," Dennis said. "I'll follow her, see she makes it to the door of the Snake Pit." He smiled at Declan's look. "Acoustics, friend. I can hear everything at this bar."

Sailor watched Declan leave with mixed feelings. On the one hand, she'd been both unprofessional and immature, and she desperately wished she could rewind the conversation. On the other hand, no matter how gracelessly, she'd achieved her goal: he had agreed to talk to her about the murders, and Declan Wainwright was a major resource. The challenge now would be to extract from him everything he knew, not just the stuff he would tell anyone. And to get him to share his connections, which were vast.

Okay, the real challenge would be to retain some self-possession in his presence and not act like a kid with a crush.

Fortunately Sailor loved a challenge.

The only thing she couldn't figure out was why Declan Wainwright cared that she'd ingested some homeopathic twigs and leaves.

And how she was going to survive hanging in the city's hottest after-hours club dressed in her waitress uniform.

Chapter 4

Declan's assistant, Harriet, had set up a business meeting for midnight, texting him Reggie Maxx's confirmation before calling it a day, leaving her boss to his nighttime assistant, Carolyn. Declan stood now in a corner of the Snake Pit's main room, surveying his club in full swing. The place ran well in his absence, a fact he knew because he was in the habit of shifting and showing up to observe operations. It took him a full minute to spot Reggie, because he was looking for a man on his own and Reggie had brought a date. They were on the dance floor, the date a well-built blonde with a short skirt and a serious shimmy, Reggie a tall, sandy-haired man towering over his fellow dancers.

"Hey, Declan," Reggie said, coming over to shake hands. He was breathing heavily, flushed from the exercise. The Elven Keeper was in his early thirties, just shy of handsome, but with a freckle-faced charm and impressive physique.

"Hope you don't mind—this is my associate, Kandy. We wanted to, uh, see the band."

"Not at all. Thanks for agreeing to meet on such short notice," Declan said.

Kandy shook his hand with enthusiasm. "Are you kidding? I told Reggie he had to. You're like a celebrity, you don't need notice. And I'm Kandy with a *k*, so I'm easy to remember." She wore six-inch stilettos studded with metal, which also made her easy to remember, Declan thought. "I made Reggie bring me along, because I've never been to the Snake Pit and I've lived in L.A. like three whole years."

"Then I won't interrupt your night for long."

Kandy giggled. "This *is* our night. I love your accent, by the way. You're Australian or one of those, right?"

"English and Irish, love," Declan said.

"Ooh, Black Irish. That's where you get that smoky look and those baby blue eyes, right?"

Reggie turned to her. "Kandy, Declan and I need to talk business, so why don't you take a little tour of the place? Just don't get in trouble."

Declan hailed his bartender and told him to keep Kandy supplied with whatever she wanted, then led Reggie toward a staircase leading to the underground level.

Reggie gave a sheepish laugh. "She's…a great assistant, actually. Paralegal. Draws up real estate contracts like you wouldn't believe. Anyhow, she wanted to come and she's… persuasive."

Declan could well believe it. As an Elven Keeper, Reggie would have a strong measure of his species' sexual appetite, and their magnetism. There were mortals who found the Elven irresistible without, of course, knowing what they were dealing with, and Kandy was their prototype. "No surprise," Declan said. "She's pretty, you're a guy, it's a full moon."

"Yeah, true." Reggie said. "Anyhow, I'm very curious as to what you wanted to see me about."

Declan led Reggie into his office, a futuristic-looking space in gunmetal gray. He closed the door. "I need information."

"Name it."

"The Scarlet Pathogen deaths. Anything you can tell me about them?"

Reggie looked around, as though someone might be hiding under the concrete desk. "Why are you asking me?"

Declan gestured toward a leather sofa, inviting Reggie to sit. "You're one of the few Elven Keepers it's not a chore to have drinks with. What are you drinking, by the way?"

"Scotch, straight. Thanks. But what I meant was—I'm not a cop."

Declan moved to a bar across the room. "No, but you're the Coastal Keeper, and Charlotte Messenger's body was found on the beach. Your jurisdiction."

Reggie grimaced. "Well, there's that."

"And you know the cops are involved, that this is more than a health department matter, a communicable disease." Declan handed him a glass of scotch and sat on a leather chair opposite the sofa.

Reggie took the highball glass. "Yeah, that's true." He took a sip of scotch, avoiding eye contact. He didn't want his thoughts read.

Typical, Declan thought.

He hadn't encountered the Elven or their Keepers until his late teens, when he'd headed west from New York City. The dry heat made Southern California a favorite Elven habitat, and their incandescent looks made them naturals in the film industry. Outwardly social, they thrived on the admiration of lesser mortals, not to mention casual sex, but Declan knew that at heart the Elven were as clannish as

Gypsies, distrusting outsiders. Reggie was now exhibiting that Elven reticence. "I don't expect something for nothing," Declan said. "Excuse my directness, but we're both businessmen. I'd like you to handle a real estate transaction I'm planning."

Reggie blinked. "Don't you have a Realtor?"

"For my Hollywood properties. This involves Malibu. I want to buy Dark Lagoon."

"Dark Lagoon's not for sale."

"That's about to change," Declan said.

"Interesting." Reggie sat forward, all ears now. "But why Dark Lagoon? It's not even attractive. Have you walked around there?"

"Frequently. I'm obsessed with wetlands. The lagoon is a stopover for migrating birds along the Pacific Flyway."

Reggie laughed shortly. "Sorry, not into birds. Too... flighty."

Declan smiled. "Ever seen a golden eagle drag a goat off a cliff?"

Reggie eyed him speculatively. "You can't do anything with the place, you know."

"That's the point. I want to save it from being developed. Save the coastal commission from having to spend their own money to buy it and protect it. I'll pay a fair price, even a generous one, then donate it to them."

"Happy to help, then," Reggie said. "I'll take a look at the property tomorrow. There's a house just south of there that I rent out to film companies, and I'm meeting a location scout at noon."

"That can't be pleasant for you, hanging out on the beach." Even Elven Keepers, Declan knew, disliked water. It wasn't necessarily the full-blown phobia it was for the Elven themselves, but for some, it came close.

"In this economy, I'll put up with some unpleasantness."

Reggie took a long sip of his drink, then said, "So what do you want to know about the celebrity deaths?"

"The night Charlotte's body was found. Because it was your district, I assume someone notified you?"

"You'd think." Reggie put down his glass and lowered his voice. "Elven Keepers operate a little differently. You shifters have some autonomy. We go through a chain of command, an executive committee."

"With Charles Highsmith leading that committee?"

Reggie glanced at Declan. "Off the record, right?"

"Completely."

"Yeah, Highsmith controls things. I mean, theoretically we could overturn his decisions, but it's like herding cats to get a consensus on anything, especially if Highsmith's against it. Anyhow, it was Highsmith who got the call from the sheriff's department when they found Charlotte."

"Who's the contact in the sheriff's department?"

"Guy named Riley. Werewolf."

"But no one contacted you? Malibu's your district."

"Highsmith called me the next day to tell me it was under control," Reggie said. "Meaning the flow of information was contained, the right cops were assigned to the case, the right medical examiner doing the autopsy."

"But Elven women keep dying," Declan said. "Doesn't Highsmith consider that worth controlling?"

"As a matter of fact," Reggie said, "he's called a closed meeting for tomorrow. I got an encoded email ten minutes ago, telling me and the other Elven Keepers to stand by. Time and place to be announced."

"Now what prompted that, I wonder?"

Reggie shrugged. "You understand, what gets said in closed meetings I can't share with you, Declan, much as I'd like to. Closed meetings are a big deal. We haven't had one since winter solstice."

Over five months ago. "Was Rafe Gryffald at that one?"

Reggie nodded. "I think Rafe Gryffald was the only thing holding Highsmith in check the last ten years."

Declan paused, then said, "Met his daughter yet? Sailor?"

"No. I've seen her around, but we haven't met. Why?"

"She may be there tomorrow, but she'll be in over her head and could use a friend."

"Happy to help. Can I ask what's your interest in this?"

"I have friends among the Elven," Declan said. "Also, the other species are about to get involved, so we'll need interspecies cooperation, which has to start with the Keepers."

"I'm all for that. But to be honest, you should be talking to Highsmith, not wasting your time on the second string, which would be me." Reggie gave Declan a wry smile. "Not that I'm not flattered. All I can tell you—and it's not much—is that the cops are convinced these deaths are homicides, and they'll be making that announcement anytime now."

Declan nodded. The moment they'd found Charlotte on the beach, he'd known in his gut that her death was a murder. But now, it seemed, the whole world knew it, and that hardened his resolve.

Reggie was watching him closely, reading his thoughts to some degree. "And you have a personal stake in this, don't you?" he asked. "Didn't you used to date Charlotte Messenger?"

"Yes."

"Bad luck, her being found so close to your house."

"Bad luck her being dead at all," Declan said. "But worse luck for her killer."

"Why is that?"

Declan smiled grimly. "Because I am going to send him to hell."

* * *

The bouncer must have been given her name, Sailor thought, because he waved her through with no questions. *Elven,* she thought, and gave him wide berth, then entered the darkly atmospheric club.

She'd been a regular at the Snake Pit since turning legal. Back then it had been the heady thrill of drinking alongside celebrities. But some months ago she'd been part of a movie deal made right there at an A-list table, a role she'd been euphoric about playing—until the deal fell apart. The whole incident had left a bad taste in her mouth, and since then she'd avoided the chaotic main room, sticking instead to the quieter venue next door where Rhiannon could often be found singing and playing her beloved Fender. In the main room the music—and crowd—was rougher-edged.

Sailor made her way toward the stage through throngs of people, some dressed to the nines, some with the grunginess of migrant farmworkers. She took care to steer clear of any Elven. She was still in her waitress uniform, black polyester velvet, but theatrical, and with enough spandex to cling to her like an ace bandage. She'd traded her comfortable shoes for a pair of heels she kept in the trunk of her car, but she still longed for a shower and some real clothes. Her arms were bare and the concrete room cold, with a blue mist coming up from the floor, but she welcomed the sensation. She suspected she was running a fever.

Unless it was the thought of seeing Declan at any moment that was raising her temperature.

The band was tuning up, an unwashed quartet wearing chain mail, but Declan wasn't anywhere nearby, so she climbed a spiral steel staircase to a cavernous green room furnished with cubist sofas, where one couple openly snorted cocaine and a trio of uncertain gender engaged in some act of sex. No Declan there, either.

But she noticed something. Her vision was sharper than usual, colors more vibrant and people more attractive. It had happened at work, too, now that she thought about it. Not all night, not consistently, but in waves. Similar to what she'd experienced when she'd awakened in Alessande's house. Once she'd taken the *siúlacht* she couldn't recall it happening anymore. Until now. So maybe it was a symptom that the *siúlacht* suppressed, and maybe now the *siúlacht* was wearing off.

She descended to the basement, a different scene altogether, with its own bar and two poker games in progress. She asked a cocktail waitress where she might find Declan Wainwright, and the woman nodded toward a corner.

Sailor saw the back of his head, his black tousled hair, and then her heart did a fluttery thing and her bravado started to slip. Not good. She needed confidence if she hoped to be taken seriously. Unless she could get her game on, this wouldn't work.

A restroom was to her right, and Sailor slipped in. It was stark and dark, illuminated by floating votive candles, on the assumption that no one wanted to see herself clearly at this hour of the night. Sailor leaned in to stare at her flickering reflection, giving herself the equivalent of a half-time locker-room talk. *"I know that in Hollywood terms Declan Wainwright is a rock star and you're at the bottom of the food chain. But in Otherworld terms, you're both Keepers. And that's why—"*

Three women entered the bathroom, two heading for the stalls, one stationing herself at the adjoining sink. Sailor glanced at her: nightclub-chic, exotic clothes. Great. Here *she* was in her cheap uniform with her crazy eyes, talking to herself.

"Be careful, sister," the woman said.

Sailor looked at her, startled. The woman was applying

lipstick, her face close to the mirror. She paused, pressed her lips together to blot them, then said, "The one who can fly through the air, he is not to be trusted. Nor can you trust your own kind."

"Excuse me?" Sailor said.

The woman shrugged, still looking at herself in the mirror. "I'm a messenger. I hear words, I repeat them. Does the message mean something to you?"

An image of the winged creature flashed through Sailor's mind. "Yes, I think so. But who are you?"

"I just said. A channeler, okay? I hear messages. Usually from the dead. Not always. Runs in the family. Kind of a drag. Anyhow…" With a last look at herself, she turned to go.

"Wait," Sailor said. "Can you tell me more?"

The woman sighed, then looked up and to the left, as if listening. "'Location, location, location,'" she said. "Mean anything to you?"

"No. Anything else?" Sailor asked.

"No, that's pretty much it."

"You can't elaborate on this message?"

"Nope."

"Well, can you tell me who's sending it?"

The woman looked up and to the left again. "Okay, this is kinda weird, but did you ever see the movie *Ginger Girl*? That's who she looks like. *Ginger Girl*."

"Gina Santoro."

"That's the actress? Yeah, okay. Her. But is she even dead?"

"Yes," Sailor said, "she's dead."

The messenger left the ladies' room, and Sailor turned back to the mirror. Gina Santoro, a star so out of her league they would never have socialized in life, had taken the trouble to seek her out in death. *To hell with Declan Wainwright and his club and his wealth and his status,* Sailor told herself. *I've got a job to do, and he's going to help me.*

She straightened her collar, made sure her bandage was in place and went out to face him.

Declan was on his laptop but looked up at her approach. "Is this a good time?" she asked.

He held up an index finger and continued to focus on his computer screen, watching what looked to Sailor like the sizzle reel of a very young jazz band. The song ended, and he shut the computer with a snap. He turned to face Sailor, flipping his chair around so that he was straddling it.

"So you made it. Good," he said, and gave her his full attention. "What have you got?" he said with a beckoning motion.

She studied him. He was friendlier than he'd been two hours earlier. Not so scary. Okay, he was a little scary. Mostly because he had the most astonishing face. High cheekbones. Piercing eyes. Blue. Cool blue in a hot face. Good grief, he was handsome. "What have *you* got?" she asked.

"Information on Gina Santoro and Charlotte Messenger. That's why you're here, right?"

"Yes," she said, giving herself a mental shake. "But how exclusive is your information? Because mine is quite exclusive, and I'm not trading it for something I can see on *Entertainment Tonight.*"

"I can do better than that. But let's start with you."

"Why?"

"Because *you* approached *me.*"

"Oh. Yes, of course." She felt as if she were burning up. "By the way, is it hot in here? Do you have the heat on?"

He was looking at her intently. Barrie's annoying contact lenses made his blue eyes loom large. Very nice eyes they were, too. "The heat?" he asked. "It's summer, and this is a nightclub. Hot, sweaty bodies and so forth. So, no. Are you feeling all right?"

"Yes, never mind. Here's the story. I was attacked." She told him, in a few words, what had happened. Surprisingly, he expressed no surprise. And maybe she was getting better at telling the story, because he asked no questions except "Who else have you told?"

"Charles Highsmith."

That *did* surprise him. His eyebrows shot up. "In person?"

"No, I texted him," she said, deadpan. No good Keeper communicated Other business by phone, and certainly not by email or text.

"Cheeky." Declan smiled. "So you've been busy. And how did Charles Highsmith respond?"

"He told me to go home, get some sleep and keep my mouth shut."

"I see you follow orders well," he said drily.

"Yes, it's a talent of mine. So now Highsmith's called a Council meeting for tomorrow. A closed one, not the usual social gathering they invite everyone and their dog to. So he's taking this seriously. Okay, that's quite a bit that I've told you. So, your turn. What do the cops know?"

"You've got a cop in the family," he said. "Brodie McKay. Why don't you ask him?"

"Because for one thing, Brodie's not the kind to blab about police business. Possibly my cousin Rhiannon could get it out of him, because she's sleeping with him, but I'm not. For another thing, he's Elven, so it would take him about four minutes in my company to psychically download everything that's in my head and in return give me only what he thinks I should know. Not that he's not a great guy," she added. "But he thinks of me as a little sister."

I won't have that problem, he was thinking. She read the thought in his eyes and nearly gasped. What did he mean by that?

Aloud, he said, "You've told no one else?"

She flashed on her cousins but decided to dodge the question. "Secrets carry energy. Stories told too often lose their energy. You can tell a shopworn one when you hear it, can't you?"

"I can."

"So," she repeated, "your turn. What do the cops know?"

"DNA tests showed that Gina Santoro and Charlotte Messenger shared a sexual partner."

"Wow. Who's *your* informant?" she asked.

"A shifter at LAPD," Declan said.

"Name?"

He smiled. "Let's leave that out for now."

So he would share news but not a news source, Sailor thought. Interesting. "What about the other two victims?"

"They're testing them," he said, "but the results haven't come back."

"Okay, so this guy Gina and Charlotte hooked up with—it *was* a guy?"

"Yes."

"Was the sex consensual?"

"Don't know," he said. "The crime scenes were apparently messy, but whether it was rape or highly energetic foreplay, they're not saying."

Energetic foreplay? Did he have to be talking like this? With his accent? Coming out of his mouth, the word *foreplay* actually constituted foreplay. "Crime scenes?" she asked. "That implies homicide. The deaths haven't yet been ruled homicides."

"True."

"But they will be shortly."

"Right again."

"Oh. You know that already." She was a bit disappointed that she hadn't reached a conclusion ahead of him. "Anything else they can tell from the DNA besides gender?" Sailor asked. "Race?"

He nodded. "Caucasian. And something else—the man was Other."

Just like my own assailant, she thought. "Really? DNA shows that?"

"Not at your average crime lab. Obviously. But Antony Brandt sent a sample to a lab in Denver, run by a vampire. The vamps love genetic studies."

"So what kind of Other was he?" she asked.

"That could take weeks to determine. Right now they can't even say if he's species or Keeper."

"What do you mean 'Keeper'?" Sailor asked. "Being a Keeper shows up in DNA?"

"Yes."

"Wait. You're saying my blood—and yours, for that matter—is different from normal humans?"

Declan raised an eyebrow. "Does that surprise you?"

"Hell, yeah."

"Why? You and I have abilities the average human would consider magical. It's a fraction of what our species can do, but even so—"

"Are you kidding?" Sailor felt her voice rising and brought it back down. "Charlotte, Gina, Brodie, any Elven you can name could be in Nome, Alaska, in four seconds. Without breaking a sweat. I've trained like an athlete my whole life and I can teleport only a mile or two. If I don't work on it every day, I can't get across the street. You can't even compare the two."

"Calm down, love," he said. "Why is this so upsetting to you?"

That shut her up. He'd called her *love*. For the second time that night. It was just a figure of speech to him, some Brit thing, but for a moment she couldn't find her voice. She looked away from him to see if the visual thing was still happening, where everything and everyone looked intense and attractive. But the rest of the room looked normal.

Which meant her reaction to him had nothing to do with the Scarlet Pathogen.

"It's true that you and I have to work at our abilities," he said, his face softening. "But a human could work her whole life and still not teleport off a barstool. It's not in her. But it's in *you,* Sailor. In your blood. Why does that bother you?"

"I don't know exactly. It's the whole Keeper thing. I'm used to thinking of it as this little idiosyncrasy, like having perfect pitch or a photographic memory or some kind of athletic ability. Not something that defines me."

He was looking at her with great interest, she realized. Even…kindness. "Take out those contact lenses," he said.

"Why?"

"I want to see your eyes."

Sailor felt another wave of heat go through her. She felt suddenly shy, reluctant to let him see the alarming color of her irises or what they might reveal. Without the contact lenses, she would be strangely vulnerable. And at close range, under this kind of scrutiny, could she mask her thoughts?

"Afraid?" he asked.

The magic word. "No," she said, "I'm not." She took out one lens but wasn't sure where to put it. Declan moved to the bar, going behind it to fill a shot glass with water. She followed him, staying on the customer side. "Drop it in," he said, then gave her a second glass for the other one. "Sorry I haven't got any saline solution for you." The bartender looked their way but left them alone. Declan leaned across the bar, getting into Sailor's space, into her face. She held her ground, feeling reckless. Feeling excited at being this close to him. Eight inches closer and they could kiss.

Could he tell how much she would like that?

His hand came up, and he touched her cheekbone gently. She nearly jumped at the heat of his fingertips. "Your eyes," he said. "The color isn't scarlet, it's paler than that. And it's not constant, it fades and intensifies."

"I feel it," she whispered. "It's going on inside me, as well. I can feel what you're describing."

"I want you to see my doctor tonight. She's a shifter, and I trust her. I need to know what's traveling through your bloodstream. I need to understand this pathogen."

And just like that, the spell was broken. The thought of being examined by a physician, with Declan Wainwright watching, was not appealing in the least. Talk about vulnerable. Paper gown, harsh overhead lights, unflattering angles. Not at all erotic.

"Yeah, let's hold off on that one," she said, blinking and straightening away from him. "I've got things to do. I'll be happy to see your doctor tomorrow, though."

"Sorry, Sailor." Declan moved to let himself out from behind the bar. "Tomorrow you can see Highsmith's doctor. Tonight you're seeing mine. C'mon. I'll drive."

"Wow. You're a little bossy, aren't you?"

"Yeah. Character flaw."

She moved to the table to collect her purse. "Not that I don't enjoy the attention, as the only live victim of a rare disease—but no doctor tonight. I'm tired, I'm badly dressed, and I have to go home and walk my dog. Do you have pets?"

"No."

"Well, then, you wouldn't—" To her annoyance, she found herself wobbly on her feet. Immediately Declan was at her side, his strong hands grasping her shoulders, and she had to admit, there were worse places to be than in the hands of Declan "Dreamy Eyes" Wainwright. But then one of his hands found the back of her neck. She had just the briefest moment of panic as he squeezed a bit tighter than was comfortable, and she could think of only one reason someone would do that.

And then she felt herself falling a long way down.

Chapter 5

It wasn't the first time someone had passed out in the Snake Pit. People had even died there. So there was a protocol for it, and when Declan saw Benjamin, his bartender, heading for the register, he knew it was to press a button on the security panel and alert his bouncer, a muscular hulk capable of hauling away passed-out sumo wrestlers. But his bouncer was Elven. Too susceptible to the Scarlet Pathogen to risk touching Sailor.

And to his surprise, Declan realized he didn't want anyone else's hands on Sailor Gryffald.

"It's okay," he called to Benjamin. "I've got this."

He'd held on to her as she went limp and grasped her by the rib cage. Then he readjusted his grip and picked her up. She was long-limbed and tall, not easy to haul around, but he was happy to do it. Holding her in his arms felt natural. One thigh beneath its black silk stocking showed red scratches from having been dragged down the hillside that afternoon. Her arm, too, had scrapes. And there was the bandage on her chest that he himself had put there hours ago. He felt a rush of some emotion he couldn't put a name to.

And one he could: regret. He hadn't planned to render her unconscious. But the opportunity had arisen, and he'd taken it, his need to get her to a doctor overriding civility.

His bouncer was at his post at the door. When he saw his boss, he made a move to help, but Declan told him sharply to step back. "She's not feeling well," he said. It wouldn't take the large Elven long to figure out what was going on. Everyone was talking about the Scarlet Pathogen, and he knew Sailor Gryffald was a Keeper. He would start to connect the dots. There would be no keeping any of this secret for long.

One of his busboys—a leprechaun—was in the alley, emptying bottles into the Dumpster. Declan had him help get Sailor into his Lamborghini Aventador. She was stirring now, making moaning sounds, and he only hoped she wasn't going to throw up when she regained consciousness. His feelings for her were complicated, but the way he felt about the car's upholstery was not.

Kimberly Krabill's office on Beverly was only minutes away, and by the time they arrived, Sailor's eyes were open. "Where are we?" she mumbled, letting him help her out of the car.

"Someplace nice," he assured her.

Krabill buzzed them into the building and met them as they got off the elevator. She was blonde, cheerful and, like most shifters, of indeterminate age. She wore jeans and a sweatshirt, which made her look nothing like a physician, and she told Sailor to call her Kimberly and then worked a little glamour, altering her own voice and her facial features until they both resembled Sailor's. She was not quite shift-

ing, merely inspiring trust by suggesting a woman who Declan assumed to be Sailor's mother. It worked. Sailor went
willingly into the inner room and onto the exam table, her
focus on Kimberly. He was noticing how strongly Elven
Sailor was, how many of the species' characteristics she
had. Most Elven had little use for hospitals or doctors, being
such gifted healers themselves. But Kimberly was no ordinary doctor, as Sailor would soon figure out, if she hadn't
already.

"All right, sweetie," Kimberly said, peering at her eyes.
"Let's see what's going on here. Sailor's a pretty name.
I've always wanted to meet you. I know your uncle Owen.
Good man."

"Yes," Sailor agreed. "But it's been suggested that I not
try to cash in on the relationship."

Declan smiled. She was recovering her wits quickly
enough.

Kimberly took Sailor's vital signs, pronounced her temperature normal and her blood pressure good, then put a
stethoscope to her chest. She listened for a bit, and then
took out a pocket flashlight and shone it into her eyes. "So
interesting," she said.

"Yes," Sailor said. "Interesting."

Kimberly guided her gently onto her back and turned
to Declan. "Step outside, would you? I'm going to examine her wounds."

He took a seat in the small waiting room, listening to
their conversation and the click of a camera as Kimberly
photographed the talon marks on Sailor's chest.

A minute later Kimberly came out of the exam room.
"I've changed the dressing. Just need to make a quick phone
call," she said, and headed down the hallway and into her
office.

Sailor appeared in the doorway and fixed him with a

look. "Do you always get your way by knocking people unconscious?"

He looked up at her from the room's one comfortable chair. "I've been downgraded to Wainwright?"

"You've been downgraded to worse than that," she snapped, pacing the tiny room. "I'm censoring myself. That was a despicable thing to do."

"You're right. And I'm sorry. Look at me," he said, and when she ignored him, he stood and put a hand on her bare shoulder. She turned quickly and for a moment he thought she would slap him, but instead she shot him a fierce look. Once again something surged through him. Sexual heat. He ignored it. Her eyes were far less scarlet than they'd been earlier. He could see specks of green—her own eye color, if he remembered correctly. "You don't seem any the worse for it."

"I vacillate between enraged and asleep," she said. "Okay, what did you use to knock me out? Magic?"

"Jujitsu."

Her expression changed. "Can you teach it to me? That particular move?"

"Yes."

"Can you teach me the defense against it?"

"The best defense," he replied, "is to not let your opponent get close enough to use it on you."

"Great. Back up, would you?"

Declan laughed. He thought he saw the corner of her mouth twitch in response, but at that moment Kimberly came back into the room.

"Okay," she said, "I've just talked to Antony Brandt, whom I woke out of a sound sleep. I can't believe people are actually in bed at—" she looked at her watch "—one-eighteen in the morning." She glanced at Sailor. "Tony Brandt is a senior pathologist at the coroner's—"

"I know Tony," Sailor said.

"Brandt?" Declan asked. "You're bringing in Brandt? How many are we going to involve before it makes the morning paper?"

"Don't get snippy," Kimberly said. "I couldn't do this work without interspecies cooperation. Tony Brandt and I routinely consult with one another. There are too many physiological differences among the species for any one doctor to have that kind of expertise. It's more like being a vet than a physician, and if you can find someone better at it than me, feel free."

Declan said, "We need you. We love you. Go on. What did Brandt say?"

"Tony did the autopsies on Santoro and Messenger, and has another scheduled for tomorrow morning. Female, age twenty."

"The acting student from Cal Arts," Sailor said. "I don't know her name."

"Yes." Kimberly opened a cupboard and took out surgical supplies. "Tony said to get him a blood sample and he'll get it to his lab guy. And we're to keep her here under observation."

"Her meaning me," Sailor said.

"Yes."

"Well, pardon me, but I'm not being kept anywhere. I'm going home. You're welcome to a blood sample, though."

Kimberly stared at her. "Your eyes. The color isn't constant. The scarlet pigmentation has receded."

"Yes," Sailor replied. "It comes and goes."

"Can you feel it happening?" Kimberly brought out her tiny flashlight again.

"My eyes don't feel at all different," Sailor said, "but at times my vision gets hyperclear. And I get a really excited feeling. Kind of trippy. And I get very talkative. And surges of energy."

"That," Declan said, "could be the *siúlacht*."

Kimberly frowned at Sailor. "You took *siúlacht?*"

"You say it like I'm an addict," Sailor said. "I was given it this afternoon and didn't like it at all. Nasty stuff. Twigs and leaves and God knows what. Cricket testicles."

"She was found by Alessande Salisbrooke," Declan told Kimberly, "who gave her a dose of it."

"I drank only half a cup," Sailor said, "but I'll say this, the effect was fantastic. Invigorating. I felt like I could run a marathon."

"*Siúlacht*'s been around forever," Kimberly said, going to a cupboard and pulling out a tray of surgical supplies. "The Elven have traditionally used it to help them recover after teleporting. But only in emergency situations, because when it wears off, you're *really* wiped out. It's also extremely difficult to make. What time was that?"

"Early evening," Sailor said.

"Its effects would be long gone by now. Enters and leaves the body quickly. Did you take anything besides *siúlacht?*"

Sailor said, "No, that's it."

"That's not quite it," Declan said. "What about the pill you took two hours ago?"

"That was *siúlacht*, too. Here, I have another." She pulled it out of her pocket and handed it to Kimberly.

"My God," Kimberly said. "I've never seen it in pill form, or even heard of it." She sniffed it. "Certainly smells like *siúlacht,* though."

"Can I have it back?" Sailor asked.

"No, you can't," Declan said.

"I'm asking her, not you," Sailor said, sitting up. "What are you, the *siúlacht* police?"

Kimberly put a restraining hand on Declan's arm.

"Would you please behave yourself?" She turned to Sailor. "Nobody's judging you."

"He is," Sailor said. "Your Keeper there."

"I am," he said.

"Declan, shut up," Kimberly said. "*Siúlacht* is neither illegal nor addictive, and it's about as immoral as green tea. But, Sailor, right now I need to understand the symptomology, sort out what the pathogen's doing to you as opposed to what the *siúlacht*'s doing."

"I can tell you right now what the *siúlacht* did," Sailor said. "Saved me from falling face-first into the salad bar. And I'll tell you what the Scarlet Pathogen does. It makes colors brighter and faces clearer, and people and landscapes and wallpaper and billboards beautiful and intense. Like putting on your 3-D glasses in a 3-D movie. But with an emotional component, too. And then it fades, and everything goes back to normal and I get sleepy."

"Interesting," Kimberly said.

"Yes, except all the symptoms stopped when the *siúlacht* kicked in. But I'm getting sleepy now, so I'm guessing the *siúlacht* is fading and the trippy 3-D episodes will be returning."

"Let's see how much they increase as the *siúlacht* leaves your system."

"I'll take notes and report back to you," Sailor promised. "But I'm not staying here 'under observation,' because I have a lot to do tomorrow and I'll be getting an early start."

Declan started to protest, but Kimberly patted him on the arm, saying, "Save it. I don't keep people against their will." She set about preparing a syringe and a set of test tubes. "But I'll tell you this, Sailor, you've been infected with a potentially life-threatening disease. You're a Keeper, so you share some genetic coding with the Elven, for whom this is apparently a death sentence. You're the first non-

Elven case of the disease we know of. That makes you important." She tied piece of rubber tubing around Sailor's bicep. "Until we understand the symptoms, avoid driving. Also, avoid being alone, and not only because of the disease. Because you were attacked, we'll assume you have enemies." She pushed the needle into Sailor's vein. "I want to see you tomorrow. As the *síúlacht* leaves your system, I want to know what's going on with your blood."

Sailor didn't seem to have a problem with needles, Declan noticed. She smiled at the doctor. "Kimberly, you are a very beautiful woman, do you realize that?"

Kimberly blinked. "Uh, thank you."

"You're welcome. Are you romantically involved with Declan?"

Both Declan and Kimberly said, "No."

"Okay, just wondering. Because the two of you are individually really quite attractive, so I have to figure it's at least occurred to you to hook up. And you, Kimberly, have particularly lovely ears. Do you like my ears, by the way? My mom had them altered when I was three, because they were extremely Elven. Can you even tell? Can I open a window?"

Kimberly raised an eyebrow. "Let's finish up here first." She removed the first test tube and started on a second. "You're sweating. That was sudden. I think you're running a fever."

"Look at her eyes," Declan said. "Twice as red as they were five minutes ago." The scarlet of her irises had intensified, coinciding with her rise in temperature and change in mood.

Kimberly finished taking blood, pulled off her latex gloves and stuck a thermometer in Sailor's mouth. "Is that another symptom of these episodes, the sudden rise in temperature?"

Sailor said, "Mmm-hmm," and Declan thought back to Alessande's house and Sailor's very friendly, very chatty reaction to Vernon Winter.

The thermometer beeped, and Kimberly removed it. "One hundred one point two. Fastest onset of fever I ever saw. Just sit tight till it drops. Also, keep in mind that pathogens work in mysterious ways. There may be symptoms that haven't begun to manifest. Impossible to predict what's incubating and may show up in the next few days or even weeks. So pay attention to—"

"Okay, it's over," Sailor said.

"What is?"

"My temperature. It's dropped. The vision thing is gone, too."

Kimberly popped the thermometer back into Sailor's mouth and pulled out her flashlight, but Declan could see that it was just as Sailor had reported. The scarlet had faded to an unearthly pink.

"Kimberly," Declan said, "who will you be consulting with on her condition?"

"I'll talk to anyone who can help me treat her. Strictly Others, of course." She removed the thermometer.

"You saw the talon marks on her chest," Declan said. "And you know what that implies about who or what attacked her. It's not just a medical condition we've got here, it's a political one, as well. Just keep that in mind."

"Politics isn't my concern," Kimberly said.

"Well, it's mine," Sailor said, buttoning her dress up to the neck once again. "Like him, I'm a Keeper. I may be the only known carrier of a pathogen *and* the target of some criminal-minded Other, but I'm also responsible for a large number of Elven in this city. That's my priority. So thank you for your help, and I'll be back when I can."

"She'll be back within twenty-four hours," Declan said.

"Hold on," Kimberly said. "I want another blood sample before you go, to see if the change you just experienced shows up chemically."

Sailor sat through the process again, but hopped off the table the moment the needle was out of her arm. "Last thing," she said to Kimberly. "I assume you honor the usual doctor-patient confidentiality stuff and will communicate with no one but me about your findings?"

"You and my fellow scientists. Unless you want family or friends to be given information," Kimberly said. "Would you like to designate someone?"

Sailor glanced at Declan. "I'll let you know," she said, and walked out of the office.

It was a sensual experience, sitting in the passenger seat of Declan's Lamborghini, all black leather except for the steering wheel, which was suede. He called it the "Aventador." The outside resembled a spaceship and the dashboard was lit up like a cockpit, and with the engine rumbling under her she half expected to become airborne. He was careless of speed limits, and that suited her. It was impossible to tear through the streets of Hollywood in a car this powerful without feeling joy. She was aware of his body inches to the left of her, the tensile strength of his hands and forearms, the black T-shirt, the silky black hair. Despite everything that had happened to her that day, nothing could top this, riding in the car with Declan Wainwright, a man she'd been mad for since she'd been an underage teen sneaking into the Snake Pit, completely beneath his notice.

He was noticing her now. She could feel it.

"Nice car," she said.

"Thank you."

"Lousy gas mileage?"

"Bloody awful."

She looked at him, and he glanced at her. She looked away. Then she glanced at him again, because of course she couldn't let him see she was too shy to maintain eye contact. And then *he* glanced at *her* again, and this time he smiled. She smiled, too, and then glanced away yet again. Okay, this was torture. She *was* too shy to maintain eye contact. She had the craziest feelings going on. She wanted to climb onto his lap, face-to-face, heedless of traffic safety and romantic discretion.

Toughen up, she told herself. "So, Wainwright," she said, adopting a breezy tone, "by my calculations you owe me. I've given you my story, and I've seen your doctor—not that I had a choice—so everything I know, you now know."

"And?"

"And in return I want access to all your sources, networks of information, friends on the Councils."

He laughed. "Greedy little beggar."

"Too much?"

He looked at her in the dark, and she couldn't read his expression.

"It's not for me," she said. "It's not like I'm asking for an acting job. I want to know who's killing the Elven."

"We want the same thing," he said, braking as they came to a red light at Crescent Heights. He turned and faced her. "So you're proposing a partnership."

"Am I?"

"Aren't you?"

The thought of being partners with Declan, spending time with him, was so heady that Sailor could hardly imagine it. She took a deep breath. "Okay, I am."

"Why me? I'd think you'd go to your cousin Barrie with all this. She's a shifter Keeper, too."

Wow. He had no idea how she felt about him. It was both a relief and a disappointment. "You're higher up the food chain," she said. "Barrie would understand that. I need friends in high places on other Councils, because I don't have any of my own. That I know of. I haven't been to any meetings yet. Closed ones, I mean. The open meetings don't really count, they're just social events."

"Then how were you sworn in?" His right arm stretched across the back of her seat, behind her headrest.

"We have a labyrinth in our backyard. We use it for rituals. Darius Simonides did the honors, standing in for my dad." She was aware of his arm, so close. She imagined she could feel the body heat emanating from it. Of course, he was just stretching, she told herself. Working out the kinks in his muscles. The biceps and triceps. It didn't mean anything. He wasn't coming on to her. Sometimes an arm is just an arm. In need of a stretch.

"Bit irregular, isn't it? Vampire swearing in an Elven Keeper?"

"Darius is my godfather," she said. "And yes, he's a bit irregular." She sat perfectly still, not wanting to touch his arm and then have him politely pull it away, confirming that it was just a stretch, nothing more. "Back to you," she said. "You really haven't shared any real information with me yet, besides some measly DNA details. And I'd like some." She closed her eyes, pretending this was a normal thing, riding in this car, with this man, his arm around her. Almost around her. Okay, around her seat.

"Ah, but you've nothing left to negotiate with, love," he said. "You've given it all away."

"Oh no, I haven't, 'love.' Not by a long shot. But I'd sure like to."

"Seriously?" he asked.

Her eyes popped open. She felt a slow burn crawling up her neck, suffusing her face. "Did I just say that out loud?" she asked. "Oh, my God, no. Please tell me I didn't say that out loud."

"Afraid so." Declan turned back to the road, a smile on his face. With his left hand he turned the wheel hard and pulled over to the right, onto the residential road that ran alongside Laurel Canyon. He came to a stop.

"This is a nightmare," Sailor said, heart racing. "It happens when I get really sleepy. It's not even the Scarlet Pathogen, it's me, I've done it since I was a kid. I think I'm having a thought, and the next thing I know, it's a conversation, I've said it out loud, and—"

He put the car in Park with his left hand, which couldn't have been that easy to do, she thought, and then his right hand, the one next to her face, snaked around her neck. She didn't resist; she just went along with it as the warm palm on the nape of her neck, on her hair, pulled her toward him.

He stared into her eyes, and then his gaze dropped to her mouth and he pulled her in closer. And then his lips found hers.

She responded without hesitation. His mouth was warm. His face was scratchy. Everything about him felt familiar, his scent, the sound of his breath. She felt she could kiss him forever, never move from this spot. It was a kiss filled with curiosity and wonder, slow and sweet, unexpected and…something she had dreamed about since the first time she'd laid eyes on him.

But this was better than a dream.

A motorcycle zoomed by them, speeding up Laurel Canyon. The spell was broken.

Declan pulled back and looked at her. It wasn't easy to return his look, because she had trouble masking her thoughts at this range. Of course, at this range so would he. Her curiosity overcame her reticence, and she raised her eyes to his.

All she saw was desire. And pleasure. "You're quite

something," he said softly. Then he turned away, shifted gears and pulled back onto the road. "Okay, I was wrong," he said.

"About what?" She cleared her throat. "I...can't even remember what we were discussing."

"Our business deal," he said.

"Oh. Of course."

"I probably shouldn't have done that," he said. "Kissed you."

"Why not?"

"Because we were in the middle of negotiations. At least *I* was." He looked at her and grinned. "That's an intriguing habit you have, talking in your sleep while still awake."

"I'm not sleepy now. That woke me right up."

"Don't get too lucid. I'll have you home in minutes. And you need rest."

"I think we better close the deal first."

Declan smiled. "What's your offer?"

"Okay." Sailor switched gears—reluctantly. "What you need, you and Kimberly Krabill, is me. You want access to my symptoms, my blood samples—how, by the way, does that find us the killer?"

"It's just one angle, but it's a good one. He has a signature, and it's distinctive. It's the Scarlet Pathogen. Figuring out his motive could also lead me to him. Figuring out how he got access to his victims, that's another angle to work. And I plan to. But the strange way he's killing women, that to me is the obvious place to start. Also, it fell into my lap, and I pay attention to synchronicity. Understanding the pathogen could tell us how he got hold of it."

Okay, Sailor thought. *Declan's interest in me is primarily scientific. Good thing to know.* "But if I'm lounging around on some exam table being studied, I don't get to be out there doing my job."

"Yes," he said, looking at her, "but being studied may lead to the development of the antidote. Don't you care about being cured?"

"Yes. Although so far I'm not finding the symptoms all that—" she yawned "—debilitating. I just don't feel sick. A sudden rise in temperature, the world going Technicolor for a minute or two, people looking attractive—I can live with it. My eyes are probably scary, but as long as I don't have any auditions…"

"Sailor," he said, "have you asked yourself the obvious? Do you have any enemies?"

"I've been thinking about that. And no. I mean, Kristoff, my manager at work, he doesn't like me much, but he's hardly going to assault me for putting too much foam on the cappuccinos."

"Glad to hear it."

"Let me ask you the obvious," she said. "Why are you so intent on finding this killer? The Elven are mine to worry about, not yours. And it's not as if you're a cop."

He didn't answer for a long time, so long that she thought he hadn't heard the question. "I made a vow to someone," he said finally. "It was a long time ago, but I'm still bound by it. I don't break promises."

"Okay." It wasn't okay, really. She wanted to know much more but didn't want to risk a rebuff. The energy between them had changed. Declan had turned serious, and she had no idea how to connect with him again. "So, then," she said. "Partners?"

He glanced at her. "I've got a few conditions."

"Go ahead."

"You have to tell me the truth. I've got nothing against lying, it's a good tactical device. Just don't do it with me."

"Have I lied to you?"

"You said you've told no one but Highsmith about your attack. That was a lie. You told your cousins."

"Well, of course. Family. That hardly counts. Any other conditions?" she asked.

"No drugs. If you're an addict—"

"One *siúlacht* pill hardly constitutes—"

"—don't be high around me."

"Declan, I'm not an addict. Life is trippy enough. I don't even smoke pot." Not since college, anyhow.

"All right."

What was his issue with drugs? Sailor wondered. And where was the guy who'd been kissing her five minutes earlier? She wanted *him* back again. "And these conditions, I assume they're reciprocal," she said.

"Reciprocal?"

"Because I don't care about your recreational habits. But, Declan, don't lie to *me,* either."

He looked at her for so long that she was afraid they would crash into the mountainside, and just as she was reaching the point of panic, he looked back at the road and shifted gears, roaring up the canyon.

"Done," he said.

Sailor was practically dozing when Declan reached the House of the Rising Sun, even though it was mere minutes later. But by the time he parked and reached her side of the car, she was popping open the distinctive scissor door as if she'd been born in a Lamborghini.

"Partners," she said, refusing his offer of a hand out, "open their own car doors."

He smiled. "Okay, tough girl." But he caught up to her just as she tripped on the flagstone path leading to the heavy door of the castle she called home. And he held on to her arm in spite of her "I'm okay." Her bare skin was cool to the touch, not inflamed with the feverish heat of a pathogen episode.

He'd loved kissing her. He hadn't meant to do it, he shouldn't have done it—and he wanted to do it again. Things were getting more complicated than he'd bargained for.

Sailor fumbled in her pocket and pulled out her phone, then frowned. "Where's my purse?"

"My bad. Back at the Snake Pit most likely."

"My house keys are in it, along with my driver's license, maxed-out credit cards and tonight's tips."

She must be really distracted, Declan decided, not to have noticed this earlier. He took out his cell and made a call to Carolyn, his nighttime assistant. "Your purse will be waiting for you behind the bar, main floor," he told Sailor, hanging up. "So how do we get into your house?"

She led him around to the back, crawled through the doggie door, then unlocked the dead bolt and let him in.

"Burglar's paradise, this is," he said.

"Only skinny burglars," she pointed out.

"And no alarm system?"

"We haven't paid the bill," she replied. "And it's a drag to keep turning it off and on anyway, so we stopped bothering with it."

"Brilliant strategy," he said. "So you're completely unprotected?"

"No, I have a vicious watchdog." She looked around. "Jonquil! Jonquil? Where are you? Here, Jonquil!" She moved through the ancient house, turning on lights as she went, leading Declan to the kitchen. Jonquil was lying beside the kitchen stove, in his doggie bed. He looked up, made thumping noises with his tail on the floor, shuddered, yawned and then fell back to sleep.

"Airtight security," Declan said. "And what about magic?"

She yawned. "My dad and uncles used to do lots of spells and enchantments. Me, not so much. Anyhow, I think I can take it from here. Unless you intend to follow me to my bedroom, see that I make it into bed?"

There was nothing suggestive in the suggestion; she was so tired she was in danger of falling asleep in front of him. "I do," Declan said. "I don't like you staying here alone."

"I'm not alone. My cousins are in their respective houses fifty yards away, connected by tunnels to this one. And Alessande Salisbrooke gave me a dagger. I'll sleep with it under my pillow. There's nothing to worry about."

He steered her toward the staircase. "Still, I'm going to walk you up."

She yawned again. "Okay."

Her bedroom was a huge wallpapered affair complete with fireplace and large bay windows whose locks wouldn't deter a ten-year-old. He checked the closets and adjoining bath, and then, finding nothing, made her show him the dagger she intended to sleep with. He said good-night and told her to lock the bedroom door after him. She gave him a wave and had her French maid outfit unzipped and was pulling it over her head as he walked out. Was she too tired to be self-conscious, or was she unaware of how seductive she was?

Declan walked around the old house, this time memorizing the floor plan on all three stories, doing what protective magic he knew, got reacquainted with the half-comatose dog and then went back to check the door of Sailor's room. It was unlocked.

Careless girl.

He opened it and went inside.

She was fast asleep in the old four-poster bed, one bare arm stretched out along the white duvet, her long hair scattered about the pillow. Her breathing was slow and steady, her face untroubled.

Something stirred in him. *I shouldn't be here,* he thought. *She's not my concern.*

But he settled into an armchair in a corner of the room and watched her sleep until the moonlight turned into daylight and the world felt safe from dark magic.

Then he walked downstairs and outside, and drove down the mountainside.

Chapter 6

The first thing Sailor did upon waking was think about Declan Wainwright. Specifically, about kissing him.

The second thing she did was check the bathroom mirror. Her eyes were still scarlet, a fine color for underripe plums but disturbing in a human face. Other than that, she was okay. Her wound looked uninfected, and she decided to leave the bandage off. She was sore, no doubt from being hauled around, but it was no big deal, and she'd slept nearly four hours, enough to restore her to functionality. But she'd left Barrie's colored contacts at the Snake Pit, so she would have to wear sunglasses until she could get them back from—

Declan. She caught her breath. So many things had happened in the past twelve hours, and so much needed to be done in the next twelve, before her next waitress shift, but all she could think about was him.

Had she really spent much of last night driving around

L.A. with him? And kissing him? She looked again in the mirror and watched herself blush, as if he were there watching.

She studied her naked body. Would he find her pretty? Stupid question. Straight guys of all species tended to like unclothed girls. And how would he look in the nude? Wonderful. Some things you could just tell, even hidden under jeans and a T-shirt.

Where would his birthmark be?

She turned profile to look at her own, a perfect oak tree on her left hipbone. Strange to think that everyone in the Council meeting today would have that same oak tree somewhere on their bodies. That they all shared DNA.

That disturbed her. To know the blood coursing through her veins distinguished her from other humans, from her own mother— Was this who she was? Was this her identity, as indisputably her as the family she was born into?

No. In a week or two this crisis would be behind her, and her mind would be on headshots and auditions and hunting for an agent. But for the moment she was a Keeper, and that was what had awakened her after four hours of sleep.

That—and Declan. And what would he be to her once this crisis was over? What was he even now? What had that kiss meant last night?

He was attracted to her at least. Amazing. She'd always felt like a presumptuous teenager around him from the first time she'd seen him in his club, when she had in fact *been* a presumptuous teenager, underage and easily intimidated. But years had passed since then, years in which she'd moved to New York, gone to college, grown. She'd returned to Los Angeles a different person in so many ways—except one. When she'd walked into the Snake Pit eight years had fallen away and she'd once again been a gawky teen, this time with a chip on her shoulder.

But last night had changed all that.

And maybe her value to him really was about the pathogen coursing through her, but this was a chance to do more, to prove herself as a Keeper, his equal. Time to get to work.

She threw on jeans and a sweatshirt, and spent an hour on her laptop doing internet research on the four dead women, then went downstairs, pausing on the landing to touch Great-Aunt Olga's glass window ornament. It was the tree symbol. The tree trunk itself was actually a man and woman, limbs intertwined, naked. She and her cousins had found that nakedness hilarious when they were little. "It's the symbol of the Ancients," Aunt Olga would tell them reprovingly.

Now their nakedness looked beautiful to her.

In the kitchen she fed Jonquil, plugged in her cell phone and checked her answering machine. Charles Highsmith's assistant had called confirming, in code, the time and place of the meeting that afternoon. Sailor had to pause to find her decoding notes, hiding under a stack of bills, before listening to her last message. This one was from Darius Simonides's assistant, asking her to return his call.

Sailor grabbed the phone.

Darius Simonides was arguably the most powerful talent agent in Hollywood, head of the biggest agency—and a vampire. He was also Sailor's godfather.

She cleared her throat several times and mentally rehearsed what she would say, hating her desperation to please this man. When the assistant answered, she said, "This is Sailor Ann Gryffald, returning—" before being interrupted.

"Mr. Simonides would like to see you in the office this morning at eleven-twenty."

"I'll be there," Sailor told her.

Global Artists' Alliance, or GAA, as it was known, occupied a good chunk of Wilshire Boulevard in the heart of

Beverly Hills. It was a light salmon-colored slab of concrete that put Sailor in mind of an upscale penitentiary,
and she wondered if the agents' assistants saw it like that,
the young MBAs and MFAs so underpaid and overworked
they were nearly indentured servants. For those aspiring to
be represented by GAA, however—and Sailor was of their
number—the pale peach prison was Shangri-la.

Keeping her sunglasses on, she gave her name to an
astonishingly attractive receptionist at the front desk and
was directed to the third floor, where another headphoned
beauty directed her to a hard couch. On a coffee table were
trade publications. Both *Variety* and *The Hollywood Re-
porter* had headlines referring to the dead celebrities, but
she read the articles as an insider—a Keeper. She caught
a few errors that she assumed had been fed to the trades
by the publicity machine that operated in the world of the
Others. Did the Elven have their own PR firm? Why hadn't
her father filled her in on this?

The fact was, Rafe Gryffald hadn't expected to be ap-
pointed to the International Council. He'd figured on working in L.A. for years, letting his daughter live her life, see
the world, pursue her artistic aspirations. Which, up until
yesterday—

"Ms. Gryffald?" a woman said. "This way, please."

Sailor followed her down the hall. The woman wore a
silver wrap dress that hugged her perfect, fat-free body and
indicated an intriguing absence of underwear. Her gray
heels were very high, making her ability to walk an art in
itself. She showed Sailor to an anteroom and asked if she
wanted coffee, water or Diet Coke. Apparently no actor
in the history of GAA had requested regular Coke. Sailor
wanted to compliment her on being so sexy, but she had a
dim idea that this might not be taken well and it might be

best to say nothing, even though she felt really chatty all of a sudden. And hot. Damn. *Here we go again.*

The assistant moved off, and a man approached, elegant and grave, introducing himself as Joshua LeRonde—a higher class of assistant, as he was allowed a name—and told her that Darius would see her, if she would please follow him.

And on they went, to the inner sanctum.

The office was like a hotel suite, tasteful and spacious, with a wraparound view of both Century City and downtown. The view was obscured at the moment, windows shrouded with translucent curtains, protecting Darius from the piercing sunlight he found so unpleasant.

He wore a white shirt and pressed black pants with a snakeskin belt, and a Ulysse Nardin watch. Sailor had never seen him in anything he couldn't wear to officiate at a wedding or a funeral, and she'd known him her whole life. He was taller than she was, with dark hair with a touch of gray, beautifully cut, very pale skin and extraordinary hands, with long, graceful fingers. He looked fifty, but of course he was far older.

"Here you are," he said, coming from behind the desk to kiss her on both cheeks in the European way.

"Godfather."

He smiled. "Godchild." He peered at her, still within kissing distance, which made her as wary as if his fangs were extended, and then he removed her sunglasses with the gentleness of an optician. It was an intimate gesture. She felt a stirring inside. How could she be finding Darius so appealing? Handsome, aristocratic, yes, but good grief, he had at least a hundred and fifty years on her. Plus he was her godfather.

"Ah." His hazel eyes stared into her own. "What have we here?"

"I had a—an incident. Yesterday. An encounter." She gestured to her chest, but she was wearing a dress that buttoned nearly to her neck, and she wasn't about to unbutton it. It was very bad form to do that with a vampire, unless you were inviting him to feed.

"Really? Have a seat and tell me." He tucked her sunglasses into the pocket of her dress, another gesture she found intimate and almost erotic. He then moved behind his desk as though ascending a throne, which in a previous century had probably been the case.

She told him of the attack, of being found by Alessande. She left out the part about the shapeshifter posing as Vernon the stockbroker, because that would make her look slow.

"But no lasting effects, other than your remarkable eyes?"

She reported the sharp vision that occurred every few hours, the visual beauty of everyone she encountered. "It happened just now, in fact," she said. "And then there's sleepiness. If Alessande hadn't given me *siúlacht,* I wouldn't have made it off her sofa."

He raised an eyebrow. "Would that explain your passing out some hours later at the Snake Pit?"

"Okay, that wasn't actually—how did you hear about…"

Darius half smiled. "Have you any idea how many people are employed by this agency? Young people, with after-hours habits similar to yours?"

"Which they discuss with you the morning after?" She tried to picture the receptionists chatting him up over cheese Danish in the GAA kitchen.

"My business is my clients. Knowing their predilections, who's capable of sustaining a TV series or six months on location, who needs rehab. Useful information, don't you think?"

"Yes, I suppose." Were the assistants on the clock after midnight as spies?

"And why do you think I invited you to come and see me today?" he asked.

"Well, in light of what you're telling me, I'm guessing that you were worried about me."

"That would be incorrect."

She felt as if this was a job interview and she was flunking. "Okay, to be honest, I was hoping that you were interested in representing me. As an actress."

"I am not."

That stung. "You know what, Darius? You could be a little kinder."

Once again the eyebrows went up. "Why?"

She hesitated. She'd painted herself into a conversational corner. "Okay, never mind. I have no idea, my esteemed godfather, why you've asked me here today. I am all ears."

He smiled. "That's better. There is, I believe, a Council meeting of the Elven Keepers scheduled for today."

"Yes."

"Time and place?"

"Don't you know?"

"I do, but I want to make sure that you do, after your all-night adventures."

"Three o'clock this afternoon, at the home of Charles Highsmith."

"Which home? He has several."

"Lake Sherwood."

"Yes, his ranch. Do you know how to get there?"

"I can operate a GPS, Darius. Even hungover. Which I'm not, by the way."

"Thank you for sharing," he said, dryness creeping into his voice. "This will be your first closed Council meeting, if I'm not mistaken?"

"Yup, first one." Now that she knew there was no chance that her godfather would become her agent, her best behavior was slipping.

"May I offer you a piece of advice, my dear?"

"I'll take several pieces, if you've got 'em."

Darius frowned. "First, in Council meetings, as regards talking, less is more. Unless you're using it for misdirection, or to encourage others to speak about themselves, talking gives away information, when the objective is to acquire information."

"Okay, makes sense."

"In other words, Sailor, keep your eyes open and your mouth shut. Strive for a ninety-five-to-five ratio of listening versus talking. Anytime you're tempted to speak to impress someone, don't. Your fellow Keepers have been at this a long time and are, generally speaking, cleverer than they look. You will not be the smartest person in the room. Try not to be the most stupid."

"Thanks for the vote of confidence, Darius."

"I have a great deal of respect for your father, what in a normal man would be called affection. I've always found it curious that I was his choice of godfather to his only child. Rafe put a lot of store in the position."

"Yes. You're supposed to oversee my spiritual development."

"But not your professional development, which is why I have thus far resisted your requests for representation."

The words *thus far* raised her hopes. "You could make me a star, you know. If you chose."

"Stardom would do nothing for your spiritual development."

Hopes died. Sailor stood. "Okay, then. Talk less, listen more, make it through the meeting without displaying my ignorance. I think I've got it."

"Sit."

She sat.

"You understand the power of alliances?"

Sailor thought of the pact she had with Rhiannon and Barrie. And Declan. "I do."

"Good. There will be more to this meeting than Robert's Rules of Order. Observe alliances. There are two major players on your Council, Highsmith, and a woman named Justine Freud. They loathe each other. Everyone else will line up behind one of those two. See if you can figure out the teams. That should keep you from falling asleep. If all else fails, amuse yourself by determining who's sleeping with whom. Finally, make your own alliances. Base your decisions not on pleasantness but usefulness. You're friendly by nature, but this is business, so there must be a quid pro quo." He reached for a pen. "I'd like a full report by the end of the day."

"Excuse me?" Sailor said. "I'm to report what goes on at a confidential meeting?"

"Yes. Will that be a problem?"

"Yes, that could be a problem. It's *confidential*."

"You'll find a way to reconcile things with your conscience," he said. "These are exceptional times for your species. You're walking proof of that."

"And one of the dead girls was a junior agent here."

He nodded. "Yes."

"Did you know her?"

"I don't socialize with junior agents. The question is, how badly do you want to find the killer of your Elven, and what are you willing to do? There are those who would consider me a powerful ally, arguably more valuable than anyone on the Elven Council. Perhaps you're not one of them."

"No, I am. Of course. But—"

"But?"

"But what's the quid pro quo? What's in it for me?"

At last, a slow smile from her godfather. "The satisfaction of knowing you're in my good graces," he said. "And that is preferable to the alternative."

He stood, walked to a mahogany-paneled door and opened it, and pulled out a jacket. "And now, my dear, I have a lunch date and you may go."

"One moment, please," she said. "Why is it so important to you that I do well in the Council meeting?"

He looked at her, his eyebrows raised. "You're my godchild. Your performance reflects on me, whether you do well or poorly. So far, it is the latter. You are twenty-eight years old, and you have to date exhibited no interest, no ability and no real understanding of what it is to be a Keeper. In short, you are something of a disgrace, Sailor."

She felt ill.

"Fate has tossed you an opportunity," Darius continued. "Thanks to your encounter with the Scarlet Pathogen, you've got people's attention. Members of the inner circles. The question is, what will you do with this opportunity? You may choose to waste it." He shrugged. "If so, I wash my hands of you."

He turned his back on her by way of dismissal.

Sailor stood, put her sunglasses back on and left. She tried not to feel envious of the people on the hard couches she saw on her way out, actors who came here to meet with their agents and not their godfathers. Godfathers who had the ability to make them feel very small.

Sailor had been driven to Beverly Hills by Barrie, who'd offered to pick her up, as well, but Sailor chose to walk to the Snake Pit. It was less than two miles and a typical Los Angeles lunch hour, which was to say perfect. The temperature was seventy-two degrees, the sky cloudless, and she hoped that movement would somehow dispel her feeling of shame.

Because of course Darius had a point. She *had* been a poor excuse for a Keeper. She couldn't blame it on her inexperience, because Barrie and Rhiannon were in the same boat, and they were pulling it off. Rhiannon had dealt masterfully with a recent crisis, saving Sailor's life, among others, and earning the respect of the entire Otherworld community. Barrie loved being a Keeper, and even her choice of a civilian career—journalism—was in service to her work with the shapeshifters. Compared to both her cousins, Sailor was a slacker.

Or had been a slacker. She could change. She *had* changed. And she would change more.

She walked faster, heading north on Santa Monica Boulevard. A car honked at her, whether because she was on foot, which was unusual in L.A., or because she'd dressed with care today. She wore a white sundress, backless, but high in the front to hide her damaged chest, with a patent leather shoulder bag, and a pair of cinnamon-colored sandals with ankle straps that had set her back two nights' tips. They were not only beautiful, but she could actually walk in them. She'd picked up the New York City pedestrian habit in college and found it funny that in her own hometown, with the world's loveliest weather, so few people walked anywhere unless dressed in athletic gear or exercising a dog.

Another car honked at her, which annoyed her. But when it happened again two blocks later she found it less annoying. Her temperature was rising, and suddenly Beverly Hills looked postcard-beautiful, palm trees swaying, the purple of a jacaranda just beginning to bloom. It was a full-on Scarlet Pathogen moment, she realized, recognizing the wave of sensual energy and, with it, a pressing need to connect to people, express herself, maybe even burst into song.

She checked her watch to track how long the wild feeling lasted. Dr. Krabill would be interested in that. Another car honked, and this one actually pulled over in traffic, twenty feet ahead of her. Sailor approached, feeling reckless, and then realized it was the spaceship, Declan's Lamborghini Aventador. Heart racing, she bent down to look in the open passenger window.

"Get in," Declan Wainwright said.

"Hey, there," she said.

"Get in," he repeated.

"What are you doing here?"

He laughed. "Holding up traffic. Get in."

Sailor looked at his face, his lovely black hair, his un-shaven, raffish quality, his absurdly blue eyes, and got in. Her heart was thumping wildly, but even as she clicked her seat belt she could feel her temperature drop. She checked her watch. Two minutes, forty seconds, and this wave of whatever it was had abated. She looked around and, sure enough, the world looked ordinary once more.

Except for Declan Wainwright, who still looked extraor-dinary.

As he eased back into traffic, she asked, "How did you find me?"

"Barrie. She said you'd be either at GAA or else on your way to the Snake Pit. On foot. I thought she was kidding. How many hours of sleep did you get?"

"Four, five, something like that. I feel fine." She paused. "Or at least I did until a half hour ago. I had a meeting with Darius."

"Darius Simonides is also your agent?" he asked.

"No—not that I'm bitter—he was giving me a godfa-therly…talk. About the upcoming Council meeting."

"How are your eyes?" He glanced at her, and she re-moved her glasses. She saw a softening in his expression as he looked at her, and she felt herself melting, the bad feelings washing away. She wanted to kiss him. She wished he would kiss her. But maybe it was too early in the day for kissing, because now he was looking businesslike again.

Oops. She was too transparent, gazing into his eyes at this range. She turned her attention to the car's upholstery. And, just peripherally, his black jeans, then his white T-shirt, which revealed a great set of biceps.

"I'm eager myself to hear what goes on at that Council meeting," Declan said.

"Uh…"

He looked at her. "'Uh,' what?"

"Well, it's confidential. Right? Isn't that the whole point of a closed meeting?"

"Yes, but I'm your partner."

"Okay. But ratting out my fellow Keepers, that wasn't part of the deal."

"Actually, it was," he said. "You told me last night I needed a friend on your Council. That was part of your offer. What else would you mean by that?"

Damn. She'd forgotten. "I guess I meant—I don't know. A friend. In a general way. Not a spy. Not 'Oh, here you go, here's the full transcript of this very confidential meeting.'"

"Afraid I'll sell information to the *L.A. Times?*"

"No, that's not the point. Do you plan to tell me what happens in your shifter Council meetings?"

He shrugged. "It wouldn't be useful to you. What happens in the Elven Council today will affect all the species."

"But it's an Elven issue, the victims are Elven, I'm an Elven Keeper, I'm not supposed to be blabbing confidential information to everyone and his dog!" Her voice was rising, and she abruptly stopped talking. It wasn't Declan she was mad at, it was herself. Declan wanted a report, and Darius wanted a report, her cousins would probably want a report, and she'd just made a promise to herself to turn herself around as a Keeper and do the right thing. She stole a glance at Declan. He met her look, then turned away once more, keeping his thoughts to himself. She took a deep breath. "I'm sorry," she said. "It's not your fault. I'm having a professional crisis. I keep discovering just how lousy a Keeper I am."

"'Lousy' is a strong word. You haven't been at it long enough to be lousy."

She smiled. "Thanks."

"What do you suppose your father would do if he were here?"

"I've been asking myself that very question," she said. "And the answer is, I don't know. On the one hand, I think he'd say that confidential means confidential. On the other hand, Darius is expecting a full report of what goes on at my Council meeting. And my father trusts Darius."

"And then there's me. Who your father doesn't know well enough to trust. Or not trust. Just like you."

"Oh, I wouldn't say that I—"

"Stop. No lying, remember?" He looked at her and smiled. "Yeah, you like kissing me, that's true. And you're happy to work with me—to a point. But you're not sure you trust me, and that's okay. I have a tough skin, I can handle it."

"All right," she said, unnerved by his reference to kissing. And how well he could read her. "Do I have to give you an answer about the Council meeting right now?"

"No, but you realize your value as a partner is dropping."

"Well, that's harsh," she said.

"True. But other than your blood samples, to put it bleakly, what have you got?"

"Research," she said, pulling a notebook from her bag.

"The girl from Cal Arts who died, the acting student? She was Cyffarwydd, and her name was—"

"Ariel MacAdam," he said. "She came into the Snake Pit a few times. My bartender had to card her. She looked about fifteen, but very Lolita, if that reference means anything to you."

"Yes, I've read Nabokov." She opened her notebook. "And the fourth victim, the agent from GAA. Did you know her, as well?"

"Yes. She was Rath."

"And beautiful."

"Very."

"How well did you know her?"

He threw her a look. "Well enough. You're not telling me anything I don't know."

Well enough? Did that mean he'd been intimate with her? A pang of jealousy shot through her, sharp and unpleasant. *Get over it,* she told herself. *Because his list of intimate "acquaintances" is a long one.* She flipped a page in her notebook. "The first two victims, our celebrities, Charlotte Messenger and Gina Santoro…aside from the usual PR blather, here's what I found. They both got around. Lots of ex-lovers. Of course, that means nothing if the sex with their killer was nonconsensual."

"Well, which was it? Consensual or non?" There was a challenge in his voice.

Sailor sighed. "All right, I'll try Brodie." She took out her cell and a moment later was talking to her soon-to-be cousin-by-marriage. Thirty seconds later she ended the call. "Yes, they were murdered. No, they weren't raped. Yes, they both had sex with the same man before they were killed. The case was just reassigned to Robbery/Homicide, as we expected."

"Looks like Brodie trusts you with confidential information," he said. "And no one's calling him a blabbermouth."

"All right, point taken. But Brodie said not to make a habit of asking." She looked at her notes. "As for their recent boyfriends, Gina had just been dumped by Alexander Cavendish, last year's Sexiest Man Alive. Charlotte is—was—dating Giancarlo Ferro up until her death."

"Your sources?" Declan asked.

"Who'sDatingWhom dot-com. But both of those men are mortals, as far as my cousins and I can tell, although either one could be a shifter. Barrie's never met either in person." Shifters were notoriously difficult to spot if they didn't want to be spotted.

"I have," he said. "They're not shifters."

"Okay, so we cross them off the list," she said. "What this tells us is that whatever common lover the two women had, it was secret. Which suggests he's the murderer."

"No, it doesn't."

"Sure it does."

Declan shook his head. "Plenty of men have could have slept with Charlotte and Gina without ending up on some website run by fans in Iowa. Your reasoning is flawed."

"No, though my research *is* limited. But I had only fifty-five minutes to devote to it. Anyway, never mind. It seems reasonable to me that Gina and Charlotte's mutual secret lover infected them with the Scarlet Pathogen, then went on to seduce and murder the other two victims."

"Huge leap in logic," Declan said. "First, we have no idea whether the other two victims had sex before dying, let alone a common sexual partner. Second—"

"Hey, it's a theory," Sailor responded. "How else do you solve crime?"

"Go on."

"Okay. First, Gina Santoro. Very talented actress—in

my opinion underrated. Just back from Romania, where she was shooting *Technical Black,* a big action-adventure pop-corn movie, which explains the theory reported in *Variety* that the Scarlet Pathogen was picked up overseas. *Technical Black* is back in town shooting in a mansion in Malibu Can-yon, where Gina died last week in her trailer. They're fin-ishing the film without her, and I want to get onto that set."

"Anything else?"

"Yes," Sailor said. "Charlotte Messenger, she'd been filming a romantic comedy at Metropole Studios as well as on location around town, but she'd just wrapped before she died, lucky for them. The film's got another week of shooting, so I want to get onto that set, as well. As for Char-lotte herself, what can you say? A-list. A-plus, even. Gor-geous, but overrated."

"In your opinion."

"Of course my opinion. No range whatsoever and dread-ful at accents— did you see that Restoration swordfight thing she did two years ago? No. Because it was unwatch-able. I looked at some scenes this morning, but it hasn't im-proved with age. Okay, now as to tribes, Charlotte's Déithe, trying to look Cyffarwydd with the nose job and the cheek implants. Like I said, the true Cyffarwydd is Ariel Mac-Adam, the acting student. Her school's up north somewhere. Fresno, Bakersfield, someplace. Her Facebook page is heart-breaking." Sailor's throat tightened.

"What?" Declan said.

"Nothing. The girl was a knockout. There was a You-Tube thing, she was doing Cordelia in *King Lear,* and—" Sailor stopped again.

"It's okay to get upset about the deaths," he said. "Cry if you want."

"I don't cry."

"Ever?"

"They made me work on it in acting school so I can if I have to, but it's very difficult. Something about my tear ducts. The Elven never cry. Ever see an Elven cry?"

Declan had pulled into a gas station. "I can't say I ever noticed," he said, getting out of the car.

Sailor got out, too, and kept talking. "You haven't and you won't. If Gina or Charlotte cried in a movie, the 'tears' were glycerin, artfully applied by their makeup artists between takes. So, anyhow... Last, we have Kelly Ellory. I took this from GAA twenty minutes ago."

She produced a flyer announcing a memorial service, with a photo of a huge-eyed woman with a short bob. Declan paused at the gas pump and looked at it. He nodded. "That's Kelly. Pretty girl."

"Beautiful," Sailor replied. "The receptionist gave it to me when I asked her about Kelly. Hard worker, loved being an agent, loved live music and avant-garde theater, had an MBA from Berkeley. Quintessential Rath, with eyes like that and the high cheekbones." She picked up the squeegee from the water trough and started to clean the windshield. "So, all Elven, but different tribes. All in show business, but different levels, different jobs."

"And then there's you," Declan said. "And you're not Rath, or Cyffarwydd or Déithe. Or Elven. But you were attacked. And you didn't die."

"I know. I fit the pattern, and then I don't fit the pattern. But I *am* in show business—at least, I'm in show business when not squandering my life away in the food service industry."

Declan smiled. "You don't have to clean my windshield, by the way. You're not my servant."

She moved to his side of the car, feeling his eyes on her. "It's not every day I get to squeegee a Lamborghini. I bet you do have people who wash your cars for you."

"Yes."

"What else do people do for you? Everything, right?"

"Not quite everything." He caught her by the hand as she went by and pulled her close. And once more he was kissing her. It lasted only three or four seconds, but it left her weak, her arm limp by her side, the squeegee dripping water onto her sandal. Weak, and ridiculously happy.

"You should always do that particular chore yourself," she said. "Keep up your skills. Because you're very good at it."

"You have a lot of talent yourself, Sailor Gryffald," he said, and gently removed the squeegee from her hand. "You're a very distracting business partner."

"Maybe you're just easily distracted," she said, and stood on tiptoe to kiss him again, very lightly.

He smiled, wiped a smudge of soapy water from her shoulder and set about cleaning the other windows. "If you're convinced we're looking for a common lover among the victims," he said, "you're overlooking an obvious point. How many lovers have you had that were either Keeper or Other?" When she didn't answer, he turned, raising an eyebrow.

"I'm counting," she said, and laughed at his expression. "Come on, you can't be serious. You want to discuss my sexual history?"

"Only the nonmortals," he said.

"That winged thing that attacked me yesterday was not an old boyfriend, I promise you," she said.

"Unless, of course, it was a shifter. But if you're correct, there goes your theory."

"On the subject of sexual history, weren't you and Charlotte once—" She stopped. It was the wrong thing to say. They'd been in a bantering mood, and this was anything but.

"Long ago," he said, but in a quieter voice.

Sailor could have kicked herself, and there was nothing to say except, "I'm so sorry."

"Forget it," he said. But the moment of playfulness was over. There really was something tough about him. Tough and unapproachable, and she wondered if that was the real Declan Wainwright, if the one who was flirting with her, the one who had twice kissed her, was a facade. A persona he could put on and off like a change of clothes.

The thought filled her with dismay. *But what do you expect?* she asked herself. *He's a shifter. Or close enough. And a player—a notorious one at that—and only a fool would expect anything lasting from Declan Wainwright.* And she was no fool.

So why did she feel so blue?

They didn't speak much the rest of the way to the Snake Pit, which was, in any case, close by. It was unfortunate, he thought, her reference to Charlotte, but it appeared to bother her more than it bothered him. For him, it was just a reminder that no matter how captivated he was by Sailor, their job was to find a killer.

He did need to know what went on at the Elven Council meeting, but he would deal with that later. There was more than one way to extract information from a woman, and intimidation was rarely the best tactic.

At the Snake Pit he retrieved her purse and keys, then walked her to her Jeep. "When your Council meeting is done, call me," he said. "Don't go running off to Fresno or Bakersfield or God knows where. Blood test first. Among other things, I want to know whether you're getting better."

"For the record," she said, "I have no intention of going to Fresno, ever, in this lifetime."

He watched her drive off, thinking how fetching she'd looked in that sundress, with her bare shoulders and back, her golden skin making him want to touch her, feel the warmth of her, run his hands down her spine.... He wondered how many men she would encounter in the next few hours who would be thinking along similar lines. The degree to which this bothered him *bothered* him.

Declan was used to women fawning on him. Along with a reasonable amount of money, looks and an accent that for some reason Americans drooled over, he knew he had charm. Even when he'd been living on the streets, there had been women, even when he was too young to know what to do with them. Eventually he'd done everything with them—except marriage. That was the shifter in him: the concept of "settling down" held little appeal. He was always clear about that to the women he got involved with, that he wouldn't be giving up his freedom. Most were fine with it. The innocents weren't his type anyway.

But now there was Sailor Ann Gryffald, and he didn't know what to make of her or the feelings she aroused in him, or how far he should let those feelings lead him. He'd originally written her off as—well, as she'd once described herself—an actress-slash-waitress, a commodity as common in Hollywood as the lemons falling off trees and rotting on sidewalks. And yes, an innocent. He was revising that opinion. She might look like a starlet, but her ambitions ran deeper. She was waking up to her destiny as a Keeper and seemed determined to educate herself. And by the time they got through this crisis, he reflected, she might not have much innocence left.

That bothered him, too.

He took his cell from his pocket and phoned Harriet. "Cancel my calendar for the day, love. And get Darius Simonides on the phone. And Antony Brandt, the coroner."

Chapter 7

Charles Highsmith didn't actually live in his own Keeper district. People with that much money, Sailor figured, couldn't be expected to have just one home. So while Charles maintained a residence in Bel Air, he apparently preferred to live with his polo ponies, which was why she now found herself driving to Lake Sherwood.

Just south of the Conejo Valley, Lake Sherwood was old, man-made and beautiful. It had originally been called Potrero Lake, but in the 1920s, after Douglas Fairbanks had filmed *Robin Hood* there and in the surrounding forest, the name had been changed. Sailor had learned all this from Merlin, who'd been telling her Hollywood history since her childhood, long before she appreciated it. The terrain was rugged, Old West and ruinously expensive to maintain if you wanted to grow anything other than desert plants. Charles Highsmith did. As she drove up the long road to his house, she marveled at the huge rolling lawn, with grass as green as a golf course. His water bill had to be as big as his mortgage.

The house looked new and devoid of personality. Sailor was greeted at the door by a uniformed maid and led across a circular foyer dominated by a sweeping staircase and endless marble, then through double doors to a library. Even though she was on time, the room was filled, and she had the sensation of entering a party in progress. Had everyone else been given an earlier arrival time?

"Sailor, welcome." Charles Highsmith was dressed, improbably enough, in cream-colored jodhpurs and a polo shirt, with glossy riding boots that she was certain had never mucked out a stable. "Let me introduce you." He seemed to have forgiven her for the night before, for which she was grateful. She'd been ready to tough it out, but it was daunting to be the newcomer in a group this tight, their closeness born of years together and countless Council meetings.

She knew most of the Keepers either by name or reputation. Of course, they all knew her father, but Rafe had socialized with only a handful outside of meetings, and the meetings themselves were closed to non-Keepers and heavily guarded. She tried to gauge her fellow Keepers' degree of friendship with her father by the way they reacted to her. It wasn't easy. These people, like Charles Highsmith, were political animals and rigorously polite.

Everyone must have been curious about her sunglasses, but only one remarked on them, the woman named Justine Freud. In her seventies, Justine was fragile but straight-spined, the oldest Keeper. Sailor wondered why she wasn't the head of the Council. "My dear, do you have a problem with light?" Justine asked.

Highsmith responded before Sailor had a chance to. "Let's wait for the meeting to begin, Justine, and then all questions will be answered. Our newest member needs to mingle before you bear her off for one of your indoctrination lectures."

This was said in a pleasant cocktail party tone, but Sailor felt the underlying ice, and Justine said, "Of course, Charles, we must all defer to your wisdom and leadership," in a replica of his tone. Clearly Darius had been right and there was little affection on either side, but she wondered how she would ever figure out the web of relationships if all animosity was hidden under a veneer of courtesy.

A man entered the room, with an "Am I late?" expression. Highsmith, noting him, said in a resonant voice, "Reggie has finally joined us, so we can adjourn to the library. Oliver, perhaps you'd do a closing spell?"

Oliver Kent was one Keeper Sailor knew—tall, black, somewhere in his golden years—and she watched him move to the windows, making hand gestures and whispering quick incantations. The Highsmith estate was no doubt already well-secured via traditional methods against the average burglar or even assassin. The Keepers were more concerned with espionage by Others. Considering what Sailor planned to disclose about this meeting, they were right to be worried. Justine Freud joined Oliver, chanting in a soft soprano, an eerie and dissonant counterpoint to his baritone.

"Hello," said a voice behind her. "You're the new kid. I'm Reggie Maxx, Coastal Keeper."

"Sailor Gryffald, Canyon Keeper." She turned to shake his hand, happy to see someone around her own age. And smiling, no less.

"How much trouble am I in?" he asked. "How mad was Charles?"

"Not mad at all, that I could tell. But you weren't that late. I would have been late, too, because I always am, but because it's my first meeting I thought I'd try making a good impression and got here on the dot."

"Smart," he said. "Everyone here is old-school about stuff like that. Punctuality."

"Of course they're old-school," she said. "They're *old*."

He laughed. "Don't let her—" he gestured toward a well-preserved brunette "—hear you talking like that. That's Jill. She's only fifty-three. Our resident sex kitten, until today."

"I think that's a compliment, so thanks. Please assure her that I never seduce people old enough to be my father. Or grandfather. Which leaves—" she glanced around "—you."

He nodded. "I try to hide from Jill, out of self-preservation, but I'll pass her a note."

"Good. Can you sit by me?"

He could not. Charles Highsmith believed in assigned seating. The meeting was held in the library, a huge book-lined room with a long oak conference table. Sailor made a complete circle, reading the silver nameplates before finding her own name, to the left of Highsmith. There would be no passing of notes. The table could probably seat fifty, and there were thirteen Keepers, evenly spaced. Would they be given microphones?

Charles called the meeting to order with all the gravitas that would precede a State of the Union address, and hearing aids were adjusted. Keepers, like British monarchs and Supreme Court Justices, rarely retired. Most had to be carried away in coffins—or urns, in the style of their Elven charges, who preferred being scattered to the wind and earth to being stuck in a coffin. They were not, after all, vampires.

"Due to the emergency," Charles said, "after the reading of the minutes we will launch into the single item on our agenda. We will also dispense with our customary speakers' lists, unless things get out of hand."

Good God, thought Sailor, listening to Jill the sex kitten read the minutes from the previous meeting. Could she sit through these things for the next sixty years? How had her father stayed awake? When Jill finished, Highsmith took the floor once more.

"Sailor Gryffald, whom you have just met," he said, "has had an unfortunate experience, which she will now recount. Sailor?"

Her boredom fled. All eyes were upon her. Hundreds of years of Keeper experience, all waiting. She remembered something one of her acting teachers had told her. "Never sit when you can stand. Standing gives you power." She stood. She told them everything she remembered of the attack and her subsequent rescue by Alessande Salisbrooke. And at the key moment, she unbuttoned her sundress down to her scar and showed them the marks of the winged creature. Then she took off her sunglasses.

The faces of her fellow Keepers showed shock, concern and anger.

"Are your eyes painful, my dear?" a woman asked. Sailor had forgotten her name, but she was Keeper of the Inland Empire, including the prestigious Palm Springs.

"No," Sailor said. "It's probably more painful for you to look at them."

"Not at all," the woman answered. "They're lovely, in an unusual sort of way."

A strapping man, totally bald, stood. Howard Zane, Downtown district. "Let's focus on the attacker. Any chance it was an actual bird? Something predatory, maybe rabid?"

"No," Sailor said. "It was Other. The air quality changed seconds before the attack. And whatever else I've got, it's not rabies."

"Then our problems are a lot bigger than four dead

women," Howard said. "Shifter or vampire, which would you say it was?"

"I can't say," Sailor said. "All I registered was Other—you know the feeling. And a rush of wind. And then there were wings all over me, and I was just reacting, protecting my face, closing my eyes."

"Either way, this is serious," Howard said.

"Either way it's a tragedy." This was the Anaheim Keeper, Sailor remembered, a man named George. "But am I the only one who's relieved? If what we have is a walking, breathing killer, then he can be found and stopped. A biological hazard spread in some mysterious way, that's a lot scarier to me than one man who has it in for a couple of beautiful actresses."

"George," said Justine Freud, "first, it's not a 'walking killer,' it's a flying one. And second, are you implying that as long as only women are being killed, things aren't so serious?"

"Justine, not everything is a feminist issue," George said. "I only meant that a serial killer is a lot easier to deal with than an airborne virus. Has the young lady been examined by a doctor?"

Sailor opened her mouth to speak, but Highsmith answered for her. "My physician will examine her this afternoon."

She was about to contradict him, but more strident voices overrode her, three people talking at once.

"Can we get back on point?" Oliver Kent asked loudly. "Because once word gets out among the Elven that a vampire or shifter is killing their women, all hell will break loose. This Council has to come up with a plan that shows we're on top of it or our charges will take matters into their own hands."

"Exactly," Charles Highsmith said. "Which is why secrecy is of the utmost importance."

"Excuse me," Sailor said. "I think speed is a bit more important than secrecy."

"True," Justine Freud said. Next to her, Reggie Maxx nodded.

Charles Highsmith stood. "You may take your seat, Sailor. Speed encourages carelessness. What I propose," he said, putting up a hand to quiet a few voices of dissent, "is that within our individual districts, we make quiet inquiries among the most trusted Elven. There are bound to be rumors of blood feuds, talk of vampires or shifters with whom our charges may have had disagreements."

"Disagreements?" Sailor said. "Four dead women would seem to indicate a bit more than—"

"I have the floor," Charles said sharply.

She felt herself blush, her face growing hot. But being spoken to like an errant schoolgirl couldn't override anger at Highsmith's muted reaction to the crisis. She recalled Darius's advice: Talk less, listen more. She made herself look around the table now, to see if she had any allies. No one met her gaze except for Reggie Maxx, who actually winked.

Reggie was cute, she noticed: broad-shouldered, but also boyish, with freckles and curly, reddish blond hair— *Damn!* she thought. *Here we go again.* The telltale flush of heat, the racing heartbeat. And Reggie wasn't the only one looking appealing. Charles Highsmith himself, patronizing though he was, had the kind of leadership qualities that made General Patton get a movie made about him. And George from Anaheim, bald-headed and potbellied, was so at home in his own body that she couldn't help feeling comfortable around him. Justine Freud? The picture of ancient wisdom. *Focus,* she told herself. *You're missing the meeting.*

George was speaking, asking if it was necessary to stick

to his own district. "Say you follow up on a rumor," he said. "It starts in Anaheim but then ends up in Studio City. I think we need to be talking amongst ourselves, number one, and number two, we need to be able to go into other districts without worrying about stepping on another Keeper's toes. Also, some Keepers are less experienced than others, and we don't want their districts given short shrift."

Great. That was aimed at her. She was about to respond when she was struck by the fact that George himself had a certain magnetism. Especially if one liked grizzly bears. Distinguished grizzly bears with hearing aids.

"George, speak to whomever you please," Highsmith said. "You don't need my permission. But phone and email are out of the question, particularly now, and being seen together will draw the attention of the Others, so significant travel is out of the question, too. In a perfect world the law enforcement authorities will find the murderer. This being the world it is, law enforcement will need our help. Dividing L.A. into districts is what we have done since the 1930s, and with over four thousand square miles in Los Angeles County, simple logistics dictate we continue to do that. The challenge we have is tough enough without taking on one another's districts. Now, if there are no more questions, I'd like to—"

"This isn't a monarchy, Charles," Justine Freud said. "Do you really propose that each of us remains sequestered, with no exchange of information as a group—"

"We will absolutely share information, at a meeting that will be called as soon as we have sufficient information to make sharing worthwhile. Let's not forget the debacle that occurred during the Malibu fires, when excessive communication and the use of cell phones created a security breach that—"

"What do brushfires in Malibu have to do with this?"

Sailor said, her fever making her both restless and talkative. "Were Others the targeted victims? Were Elven the only ones whose homes burned down? And that was forever ago. My God, I was in high school."

"Easy as that is to believe," Highsmith said, "it's perhaps best not to remind us of your extreme youth."

"Given my extreme youth," she shot back, "maybe you can enlighten me. What do you suggest? Going door to door, questioning Elven, and sowing seeds of suspicion about vampires and shapeshifters? Why not start with the obvious, these four women?"

"Because we're not the police, Ms. Gryffald. Let our people in Robbery/Homicide do their jobs. And which of those victims lived in your district?"

"None of them. But it's clear that—"

"None of them. Three of them, however, lived in mine. One of them, Ariel MacAdam, lived in Phaedra Waxman's district. Do you think Phaedra needs your help?"

Sailor glanced at Phaedra, who reminded her of the high school volleyball coach who'd made her teenage years hell. "You're missing the point. I—"

Highsmith continued as though Sailor weren't speaking. "What we don't want is to add fuel to the fire of panic already spreading, creating more death and destruction on top of the four victims already dead. Every military campaign begins with a reconnaissance mission, and that's our obvious first step. Now, each of you has a piece of paper in front of you, and a pen. A yes vote agrees with my plan. A no vote disagrees. I will abstain."

Sailor scrawled "NO," folded the paper and put it into a lead crystal bowl being passed around. Charles read the votes aloud. Six and six.

"As the tiebreaker," he said, "I vote yes. We investigate within our own districts and pool information in a meeting to be announced shortly. As for Ms. Gryffald," he said quickly, seeing Sailor once more on the verge of interrupting him, "her district is large and she herself is new, and especially in light of her current disability, assigning her a mentor strikes me as an excellent option."

"I'll take her district, along with my own," Phaedra Waxman said.

"No, you won't," Sailor said, finding her voice.

"I'll help her, Charles," Justine said.

"I think not, Justine," Highsmith said.

"I'm happy to team up with Sailor," Reggie said. "Our districts are adjacent, so it makes sense."

"Fine," Sailor said, before she got stuck with the volleyball coach. Her body temperature had dropped, and all thoughts of affection and goodwill had been replaced by anger and frustration. She pushed her chair away from the table and walked away and out of the mansion, not trusting herself to even say goodbye without exploding.

"Wait up, Sailor!" she heard, and turned to see Reggie Maxx running to catch up. "My God," he said, "was that unbelievable?"

"Which part?" she asked, heading toward her car. "Me getting stuck with a babysitter? Or Highsmith's stupid, ineffectual nonplan?"

"I'm talking about the attack on you," he said, "but yeah, that was classic Highsmith. Listen, I'm glad we're working together, and it's not babysitting as far as I'm concerned. My district is Malibu, and we can pool our resources."

"Okay, thanks. And sorry," she said. "I'm just really pissed. And disappointed. I expected…I don't know what. Some kind of big mobilization, kicking into high gear. Something."

"Then we'll kick *ourselves* into high gear," Reggie said. "Here's the deal about Malibu. There aren't any Elven living on the beach. None of them will set foot west of Pacific Coast Highway. They're all in the mountains off Las Virgenes and Kanan Dume, all the hermit types. If it was a Unabomber we were looking for, those are the first people I'd check out, but I doubt if most of my Elven have even heard of Charlotte Messenger or Gina Santoro. That said, if we can get them to talk, they may know things, so say the word and we'll start interviewing them. Tomorrow, say?"

Sailor looked at him, and he looked back unflinchingly, not bothering to block his thoughts. *I like you, you're pretty, you're hot, I'd like to be your friend and Highsmith's an ass, but we can make this work to our advantage,* he said. Not in so many words, but in thought patterns. It wasn't as clear as if he were an Elven, but she could understand him, the way she understood French after having had three years of it in high school.

She nodded. "Thanks."

Reggie glanced toward the house. "As for the Keepers, some of them will share information with us, help us out— especially given who your dad is. But the others will go right to Highsmith if you deviate from the plan. And if he thinks you're doing an end run around him, he'll make your life on the Council hell. So, you know, be careful."

Sailor flashed on Darius Simonides, whose advice she'd all but ignored. "Can you fill me in on who's who?"

"Yeah, I can." Reggie looked at his watch. "Only not now, because I have to go show a property in the Colony. I'm a Realtor. Tomorrow?" He handed her a business card.

"Tomorrow," she told him.

Sailor was in her car and halfway to the 101 Freeway before she got a good cell signal. She called Declan.

"Sailor," he said, instead of hello.

"I'm ready to tell you anything you want to know.

About—" *speak in code*, she thought "—how I spent my summer vacation."

There was a pause. "Change of heart?"

"Yes."

"That's good news," he said. "And what's it going to cost me?"

"I'll tell you when I see you."

"Provocative answer. And when will that be?"

Her first impulse was to say "the sooner the better" because she wanted nothing more than to see him again. But she hesitated. What did she have to report, really? That the Elven Keepers as a whole were doing essentially nothing. But she herself was no different, either. What was she bringing to Declan, to their partnership, other than her own blood samples? Where were her investigative skills, her resourcefulness? She had to step it up. The afternoon had been a waste, but the day wasn't over yet.

A billboard image of a cupcake flew by, and Sailor had an inspiration. "I'll see you," she said, "after I run one quick errand."

"Kimberly Krabill wants another blood sample. She's free for an hour, and then she has rounds at the hospital."

"It will take a little longer than that, given the traffic."

"Sailor, that's not going to work for me."

"I'll call you when I'm done. Bye, Declan." She hung up. Her next call was to the morgue.

Chapter 8

Sailor weaved in and out of traffic heading east, growing more indignant with each passing mile. Except for the elderly Justine Freud, Reggie, Sailor herself and maybe three others, the Council was apparently willing to be dictated to by Charles Highsmith. And her own performance had been nothing to write home about. She'd been outspoken but not persuasive, passionate rather than strong. She'd forgotten the "listen instead of speak" dictum until the end, which in any case would have been hard to pull off because of the feverish episode, which made her excessively chatty. And she had only one alliance to report to her godfather, with the second-youngest and probably least-powerful Keeper, Reggie.

Halfway to downtown, Highsmith's assistant called to set up the threatened physician's appointment, and Sailor managed to say, "No, thank you," rather than "Over my dead body." She was proud of her restraint.

An hour later, turning off her phone so she wouldn't have to ignore Declan's calls and making a stop at a bakery, Sailor pulled into the crime lab, on the campus of California State University. The parking lot was thick with RESERVED signs and warnings of dire consequences if a vehicle even paused there without a permit. But it was the end of the workday and dozens of spaces were empty, so she decided to take her chances.

In the lobby area, she pretended to admire a wall display of the top brass in the LAPD and the Los Angeles Sheriff's Department while scoping out the joint. To her left, a receptionist sat in a glass-enclosed cubicle, probably bulletproof, reminding Sailor that criminal evidence passed through here and uninvited civilians did not. Beyond the receptionist Sailor could see her destination. No point trying to talk her way in, especially as the man she'd come to see wasn't expecting her. Sometimes a woman's best bet was magic.

Sailor closed her eyes, took a deep breath, held it for the count of five and slowly exhaled. She inhaled again, and this time, when she exhaled, she let her mind fall behind her eyes, the weight of her body slide away, and then she willed herself into the far hallway.

When she opened her eyes she was a bit unsteady but satisfied. The glass-enclosed reception desk was on her right, and in front of her were the elevators.

She had to ask three people before she found Tony Brandt in the chemical analysis department, in conversation with a lab-coated technician. He turned even as Sailor approached.

"Sailor! What are *you* doing here?" he asked. Tony was a large man, structurally sturdy, with a center of gravity that was low to the ground, typical werewolf. "Did my office tell you I was here? I'll fire them all. And how did you get past security?"

Instead of answering, she strode over to him and kissed him on the cheek. "Here," she said, and handed him the box. It was white and tied with string.

"What's this?"

"A bribe."

He grunted and opened the box to reveal three giant red velvet cupcakes with cream cheese frosting. He sighed heavily. With the proprietary attitude of one who'd known her since her infancy, he said, "Did you teleport? You must be practicing if you can bring along baked goods and purses now. Just like the damn Elven. Take off those sunglasses and show me your eyes."

She glanced at the man in the lab coat, and Tony said, "It's all right. This is Fergus MacIntyre. He works here in chemical analysis. Fergus, Sailor Ann Gryffald."

"I've heard so much about you," Fergus said, shaking her hand.

"Really?" she said. She looked at him more closely. "Vamp?"

"Yes. I'm a fan of your uncle Piers."

Sailor removed her sunglasses and let Tony examine her eyes.

"Have you seen Krabill today?" he asked.

"Not yet."

"We can take a blood sample here. Save you the trip. I don't suppose it's occurred to you to take it easy?"

"I get restless, stuck in a petrie dish."

"So you sneak into the crime lab." Tony shook his head. "I don't recall your father resorting to trespassing."

"Know what, Tony? I don't know what my dad would do if he were new on the job, infected with a killer virus and faced with multiple murders. And if he didn't have friends like you. I'd give a lot to know. Unhappily, my dad's half a world away and incommunicado, and a stickler for security measures that prohibit cell phone use. What I *imagine* he'd do is whatever it took to protect his own."

Tony gave her an unexpected smile. "Okay, no need to get huffy. You people keep hounding me, I won't get any work done, that's all I'm saying. So what can I do for you?"

"Wait, what do you mean 'you people'?"

"Keepers," Tony said. "Declan Wainwright came to the morgue earlier today. You show up here now. Might as well put on a pot of coffee and wait for your cousins to arrive."

Declan. Interesting, Sailor thought. Why hadn't he mentioned he'd seen Tony? "Then I'm sorry to ask you to go through it again," she said, "but I'm an Elven Keeper, and those women are my responsibility. Anything you told Declan Wainwright, you can tell me."

"Which would be exactly nothing. He came by, but I was in a meeting with the mayor."

"Then what you *didn't* tell him, you can tell me," she said. When Tony didn't respond, she added, "You want my blood samples? I want information."

A bushy eyebrow went up. "Pushy, aren't you? All right, but only because you brought cupcakes. First thing is, none of what Fergus and I tell you goes any further. I drove all the way over here from the morgue to talk to him because we can't have a paper trail or an e-trail, because none of this goes into the official report. So if what you're about to hear gets out, I'll know who to blame. You. Fergus knows if he talks I won't just kill him, I'll fire him. So that's the first thing. Tell nobody."

"Except my cousins, of course."

"Here we go," Tony said, exasperated.

"And Declan Wainwright, with whom I'm working. But only if it's absolutely—"

"Oh, the hell with it!" Tony threw up his hands. "Tell the whole world." He lowered his voice, even though the three of them were alone in the lab. "Cause of death was exsanguination. Each girl bled out, the first one from a cut that wouldn't have required more than a bandage in the normal course of events. The underlying cause, of course, was the Scarlet Pathogen. Because the blood wouldn't clot, minor cuts proved lethal. It's possible, too, that the blood flowed unnaturally fast. In case you're wondering about your own health, your blood's clotting, so you're not dead. Congratulations."

"Were each of the cuts the same kind?" Sailor asked.

"No. Charlotte Messenger's was no more than a paper cut, source unknown. If we knew where she'd been killed before she got dumped on the beach, we might be able to tell, but then again, we might not."

Sailor shuddered. "I knew she wasn't on that beach by choice." Her own fear of water was bad, and Charlotte had all her sympathy.

"She wasn't. That's where they found her, but that's not where she died. Cops are still looking for the primary crime scene. The scratch, I'm guessing, was accidental, maybe self-inflicted. Second victim, though, Gina Santoro, bite mark on the shoulder."

"A bite sharp enough to break the skin?" Sailor asked.

He nodded. "It gets worse. The killer was rougher with Gina than with Charlotte, and he didn't move the body this time. Still no indication he forced her to have sex, though. No drugs or sedatives, only the pathogen. No ligature marks, no restraints of any kind, which would be the first thing you'd do to an unwilling Elven."

Sailor nodded. Tying up an Elven prevented them from teleporting.

"Also," Tony went on, "there were signs of romance at the scene of the Santoro murder. Mood music on the CD player and wine, that kind of thing. The next one, the bites were on her breasts. That was Kelly Ellory. The last one, he bit her all over."

Sailor winced. "Can you match the bite marks? Are they the same for all the victims?"

Tony nodded. "Working on it."

"Fingerprints?"

"Lots of them, but nothing to match them to. The guy has no record. Nothing in the databases we have, anyway. So there you go. No sign of a struggle with any of them, beyond what might be consistent with active sex. What's clear is that the perpetrator became increasingly violent. My guess is, death aroused him. One theory is that he didn't know the first one would die, but when it happened, that became part of his thrill with the subsequent victims. In each case there was blood all over, beds, floors—in the case of the last one, outside on the ground."

"Wait," Sailor said. "The victims were actually having sex *as* they died?"

"Yes, or close enough. The blood evidence suggests intercourse was under way and continued even as the bleeding progressed."

"If there was that much blood," Sailor said, "the sexual partner couldn't be a vampire, right? Because it would be hard not to feed on the woman if she was bleeding."

"In the throes of sexual arousal?" Tony growled. "I'd say damn near impossible. And no one fed on those women. I know the difference between human teeth and fangs."

"So they weren't sleeping with a vamp," Sailor said. "How long until you determine what kind of Other the partner was?"

"First of all," Tony said, "it could still be a vampire Keeper, who might be turned on by the blood without needing to drain her. Second, we only know that Messenger and Santoro had a common partner. We're waiting for test results on the other two. Fergus, how long on that turn-around?"

Fergus took out his cell phone and hit some buttons. "All right, here we go. Hot off the presses. The DNA matches. All four women had the same sexual partner at the time of death."

Tony nodded. "All right, there you have it. We sent the fluid samples to our private DNA lab—not the one the department uses—so what you now know, no one else does. So what we have is—"

"Male," Sailor said. "Caucasian, and not a vampire, unless it's a vampire Keeper."

"And not a werewolf," Fergus said. "There's a sequence in weres' blood that's not in those samples. And not leprechaun, either. Possibly ogre, though."

"What else? What does that leave?" Sailor asked. "Shifters, pixies, vamp Keeper but not a vamp, other Keepers... When will we know if it's a Keeper versus an Other?"

"Maybe never," Tony said. "We've got one guy working on it, one lonely vampire in a lab in Denver, and he's not well-funded. Hard to raise money when you can't talk about your research."

"If we can't wait for the science," Sailor said, "we'll just have to do the detective work."

"What's with the 'we' stuff?" Tony asked. "When did you join Robbery/Homicide?"

"Tony, you know my dad's philosophy, that Keepers have room to maneuver that cops don't. I have no legal authority, but I also don't have to worry about things like probable cause, search warrants, all that. Now, let's talk about the Scarlet Pathogen." She walked over to Tony, and unbuttoned the top buttons of her sundress. "See any cuts on your victims that looked like this?"

Tony and Fergus both stepped closer, looking with professional interest at her chest. "No," Tony said. "The others were made with a single slicing agent in the case of Charlotte Messenger, and human teeth in the case of the other three. Here you can clearly see three marks. A hint of another just here." He gently touched her chest. "Animal, not human."

"And can you tell, from the talon marks, what kind of bird?" Sailor asked. "Or could it be a bat?"

"I'd have to bring in some birds and some bats, and start excluding the ones that didn't fit. And because there are fifty different kinds of bats in North America and God knows how many birds, we won't be getting around to *that* this week. But, Fergus, take a photo of her chest anyway. Let's get some measurements."

"Dr. Krabill already did that," Sailor said.

"And now we're doing it," Tony said.

They moved to another room, where Fergus photographed the wound with equipment that was more sophisticated than Kimberly's had been. "So why is it," Sailor asked, "that my blood clotted and the victims' didn't? Is it that I'm not Elven?"

Tony frowned. "Normally Elven blood clots as well as human blood, but the pathogen messed with their coagulation process. Fergus?"

"Among other things," Fergus said, "the victims' blood had a complete absence of prolactin. Of course, the Elven regulate prolactin differently from mortals anyway, being unable to cry or sweat. Anyhow, when I looked at your blood samples from last night, I checked for prolactin right away. You had plenty—in the second sample anyway. In fact, the levels were consistent with someone who's just had, well, sex."

"Excuse me?" Sailor said.

"Or any highly pleasurable experience. Gambling, chocolate, whatever. During your, er, episode, with the rising temperature, there were elevated dopamine levels. In the second sample, post-episode, dopamine dropped, with a corresponding increase of prolactin. And oxytocin and other stuff."

"I have no idea what that implies," Sailor said, buttoning her dress back up.

"The good news," Fergus said, "is that your neurotransmitters are working as they should. Most important, your blood's coagulating. And your other symptoms are mild, relative to what we know of the four dead victims, despite the pathogen being delivered directly into your bloodstream."

"How was it delivered to the others?" she asked.

"They swallowed it," Tony added, "which slowed its absorption, and even so, the effects were obviously far stronger than anything you're experiencing. Which is good news for you. So far. The other good news? It's very unlikely that the disease is airborne. Not that an Elven couldn't catch it by inhaling a large, undiluted batch of it, but you're unlikely to infect them by normal interaction."

Sailor nodded, relieved. It was the first good news she'd gotten about the Scarlet Pathogen, but thinking of the victims disturbed her. "The killer made them drink it?" she asked.

"Mixed it into their drinks," Fergus answered. "Champagne for the first two—Cristal, if you're interested—red wine for the fourth, and the agent from GAA had diet cola. We found traces of the pathogen in all four glasses and in their stomachs."

Sailor stared at them. "So he was friendly enough to have drinks with them. But wait. You said all four glasses. If you don't know where Charlotte Messenger died, then—"

"She was working on a film," Tony said. "And they were

shooting at a house near Benedict Canyon. She left her Mercedes there the night she disappeared. And her trailer was just as she'd left it, they hadn't cleaned up. Which is how we were able to test the champagne glass."

"How do I even know," Sailor said, "that the attack on me came from the same person, when everything about it is so different?"

Tony said, "You don't. If I could have swabbed you as soon as you were clawed—well, even then, there's no guarantee we would have gotten anything from it."

"And how do we find the antidote?"

"Fergus is going to take another blood sample from you right now," Tony said. "We're hoping it will be like the flu, which just runs its course and leaves your body. And if that's the case, we'll see some indications of it. In the meantime, even though we don't think it's airborne, lie low. It's better not to take chances, and half the Elven population would still look at you like you're Typhoid Mary."

On that happy thought, Fergus stuck a needle in her arm, after which Tony dismissed her, recommending she use her feet rather than her superpowers to see herself out.

When she returned to the parking lot, she found Declan Wainwright leaning against her Jeep.

The sun glinted off his mirrored sunglasses. His arms were crossed, and he watched her approach with neither a smile nor a greeting. Her heart was beating fast, alternating between happiness and apprehension. Would there ever come a day when she could set eyes on him and feel completely confident?

Not with him looking at her like that.

She cleared her throat. "Hi," she said. "What are you doing here?"

"Turned off your phone, did you?" His voice was neutral.

"Left it in the car," she said.

"While you did a quick two-hour errand. While illegally parked." He plucked a citation from her windshield and handed it to her. "Good job."

She stared at it. "Forty-eight *dollars?* Man, talk about a crime, and in full view of the crime lab." She looked at him and repeated, "What are you doing here?"

"You didn't answer my calls. I got impatient. The question is, pet, what are *you* doing here?"

"But how did you find me?"

He shook his head. "You first."

"I—" She stopped. A pair of LAPD officers passed by them, quite close, moving toward a squad car parked in the next aisle. She knew this wasn't the place to talk.

Declan knew it, too. He took the parking ticket from her and stuck it back on her windshield. "Come on," he said, gesturing toward the main campus. "Let's walk."

He took her arm, and the feel of his skin against hers was like a jolt of electrical energy, pulling her into his force field, the scent of him, the way his body absorbed the heat of the sun. It made her unsteady on her feet. "Let's walk toward a vending machine," she said. "I need water. I teleported into the crime lab."

Teleportation looked easy to anyone watching—here one moment, gone the next, or vice versa—but it was hell on the one doing it. Her short jump inside the building had been the equivalent of a 5K run, uphill. She'd minimized the aftereffects with Tony Brandt and Fergus, but now she was feeling dehydrated, headachy, extremely thirsty and mentally fuzzy. Declan steered her across the parking lot toward the campus. He let go of her arm, but stayed close, his hand straying to touch her back at one point, sending another jolt through her. Soon they were at the food court.

Somewhat to her surprise, Declan gave her a break, saying nothing until he'd bought her four bottles of water—waving away her protest that she could buy her own—and watched her drink three of them almost without pausing. When she was halfway through the fourth she stopped and took a deep breath.

"Finish it," he said.

She shook her head, feeling energy return. "I'm done."

He took the bottle from her, wiped a drop of water from her chin and led her to an outdoor table.

"Okay," he said, sitting opposite her. "What were you doing here?"

"Can you take off your sunglasses?" she said. "You look like a Secret Service agent."

He complied. His eyes, piercing blue, sent another zap of energy through her. "Better?"

She nodded. "Better."

"So talk."

"I came here to see Tony Brandt," she said. "Just like you did."

"I hope you were more successful than I was."

She felt a twinge of triumph. "I was."

"And why the big mystery? Why not tell me on the phone you were coming here?"

"Because you'd have told me to forget it, to just drop everything and get to Dr. Krabill."

"I did tell you that," Declan said with a wry look. "And?"

"And…" Sailor sighed. "Look, Declan, I'd like to think I bring something to this party, something other than blood samples. I'd like to think I've got some skills. And if I don't have them, I damn well better develop some."

"So this is your on-the-job training."

"Yes."

He nodded. "And what did Tony Brandt say?"

She hesitated. "Not to repeat anything he told me, for one thing."

"Lucky you're the girl who doesn't do as she's told."

"I'd like to think I'm the girl with some integrity," she replied.

Declan smiled and reached for the bottle of water she'd left unfinished. "Not when it comes to your partner, love."

"If you'd talked to Tony," she said, "would you have shared everything you learned with me?"

"Yes." He looked right at her before taking a long drink of water.

But was that true? He wasn't shielding his thoughts from her, but shielding wasn't the only technique against Elven telepathy. There was also a trick called actualizing: if a person could convince himself of the truth of what he was saying, then that was how it would appear to the Elven—or Elven Keeper—who "read" those thoughts. It was a kind of self-hypnosis, hard to sustain, but some people were quite good at it. They were the kind of people who could lie and pass polygraphs. Sociopaths.

And now, she realized, he was reading *her* thoughts.

"We either trust each other or we don't," he said. "The fact that I can beat a polygraph doesn't mean I'm lying to you."

"My God, you're good," she said.

He shook his head. "Not me. You. Completely transparent sender."

He was right. She was a pretty fair receiver, but her real strength was sending. With enough effort and focus she could even do it without eye contact—meaning long distance—provided the intended recipient was open to nontraditional communication. But it meant she needed to guard her thoughts with Declan.

"C'mon. Enough," he said. "If information's what you

bring to the party, you'd better share, or it's not much of a party."

"All right." She filled him in on what she'd learned in the crime lab, starting with the confirmation that all four victims had been killed by the same male.

"A male with a penchant for biting," Declan said.

"Not in Charlotte's case," Sailor said. "There was an escalation in the violence, possibly because he discovered he liked it. It's possible that he was surprised when she bled out. He might not even have realized the pathogen was lethal. If so, that means his reason for infecting them with the pathogen was something other than murder."

"The biting thing—that would indicate a vampire."

"Yes, but it wasn't a vamp. Teeth aren't fangs."

"And if I'm not mistaken, vamps don't leave behind DNA," he said, and took another drink. She found herself watching him. Such a prosaic action, but it made her want to touch his face, run her fingers along the rough darkness of his five-o'clock shadow.

"Declan," she said, leaning in, "the key to this, as I see it, is figuring out what man had access to all four of them. He'd be someone with sufficient, well, charm, I suppose, to persuade them to have a drink with them. That's significant, given that Charlotte and Gina were major movie stars. They wouldn't drink with just anyone."

"I'm not saying you're wrong," he said. "Starting with the victims makes sense, but that's exactly the course the cops will take. The 'opportunity' part of the means, motive, opportunity equation. Who had the opportunity to get to the victims and win their trust? That's where the cops will devote their energy and resources. Let's leave it to them. I'm suggesting you and I look at the means, the Scarlet Pathogen. That's where the cops can't go, because it reaches too far into our world. Tony Brandt? He can't tell them what he just told you, he's going to have to give the public *and* the police force some cleaned-up version of what happened. So now you and I have an edge."

"Then what do you suggest we do?"

"Research. Where does this pathogen come from, how is it transmitted and who managed to obtain it? It's the pathogen that makes this killer unique."

She jumped up from the table. "Then let's do both. My way and your way. Let's go."

Declan stood. "Where? The doctor's office?"

"Tony Brandt's a doctor," she said, setting off. "He already examined me."

"Brandt's not Krabill," he said, catching up to her.

"What's the big deal? Isn't Tony on our side?" she asked.

"Tony's a were. He's on his own side. And he's an autocratic bastard, doling out information on his own terms. Your going to him directly cuts Krabill out of the loop, so now she's got to beg him for news, rather than vice versa."

"We'll tell her what we know," Sailor said, walking faster. Once again her conscience chimed in, telling her she was saying too much to too many. But at least Tony and Kimberly were colleagues.

"I'm talking about the science, the test results. She's doing her own research, and her priority is the living. Finding an antidote. Brandt's priority is the dead."

Sailor looked up at him, their long-legged strides matching one another. "But isn't our priority the dead, too?"

He raised an eyebrow. "Not entirely."

"I mean, of course I care about the potential victims, too," Sailor added. "All the Elven women I'm responsible for."

"Anyone else?"

"What do you mean?"

Because they were walking in sync, when he stopped,

she stopped, too, looking up at him. He reached for her hand, and, curious, she let him lead her off the path. They went past a large elm, into a little alcove created by the tree's branches and the side of a building.

She leaned against the brick of the building, grateful for its solidity, because she was nearly quivering at the nearness of him and the knowledge of what was coming next. She didn't have to use telepathy either. His intention was coming off him in waves.

He faced her and brushed a lock of her hair from her forehead, tucking it behind her ear. "You have no idea who I might mean? Who else is worth keeping alive?"

"Oh," she said softly. "You mean me."

"Yes, I mean you." He kissed her on her temple, and then dropped another kiss farther down on her cheekbone.

She was, she realized, shaking. "I—I should tell you that Tony told me, or actually Fergus told me, that my neurotransmitters are working, and so are the something or other in my blood, so I'm not in danger of bleeding out like— Oh, shoot, here I go, my temperature's rising. So anyhow, there's a chance the pathogen could possibly just run its course and not even— Of course, an antidote would be even better, because— Oh God, Declan…"

He'd let go of her hand and found her waist, and now his warm hands slid up to her bare back until she was caught between him and the brick wall, the literal rock and the hard place, and she pulled him in closer. He complied, his body firm against the length of hers, and he himself was hard, pressing against her until she could hardly breathe. She was glad to feel his obvious need for her. "Don't stop," she whispered. "I…don't want you to stop."

His tongue was hot on her neck, and he made a sound of deep satisfaction. She felt teeth on her throat, just briefly, and then he blew into her ear, sending a shiver down her spine, just before his lips came close to hers. "So," he breathed, "you don't want me to stop?"

"That's right," she said, her fingers digging into his back, his shoulder blades.

He undid one button of her sundress and then another and then he reached inside, reading her mind, doing exactly what she wanted him to do. The warmth of his fingers, of his palm on her breast, was more than she could bear. She wrapped one leg around his thigh, feeling the hard surfer's muscles, wanting the skin-on-skin contact so much....

His hand found her butt and he lifted her, and she wrapped her other leg around him, her thighs squeezing, causing him to groan deep in his chest. She felt the power that came from making him desire her, and wrapped her arms around him, her hands caught in his black hair, relishing the feel of it on her face....

He needed her clothes off, she knew. They were nearing the point of no return. He pushed the long skirt up her thigh, his hand finding bare skin, her hipbone, her—

A noise froze them. The sound of a door opening around the corner of the building was followed by the chatter of students being released from class. The moment was broken. In seconds they could be discovered.

Declan set her back on her feet, and she pulled her skirt back down. He stepped back and looked at her, and then, without taking his eyes off her, buttoned her sundress back up.

Sailor took a deep breath. Her temperature had dropped. She reached up and smoothed his hair, which looked as wild as she felt, and smiled.

The answering smile came immediately. He said, "I'm not finished with you."

"Not by a long shot," she said.

They walked hand in hand back to the parking lot. They

were silent, letting their heightened awareness of one another replace words, until their breathing steadied. The sounds of traffic, the songs of birds, a helicopter in the sky sounded like music to her. She was suddenly in no hurry.

But when she clicked her car keys, the little chirp of the Jeep broke the spell and brought her instantly back to the real world, where a killer was targeting Elven women.

"So here's the plan," she said. "We'll do it both ways, yours and mine. Right now I'm going to Cal Arts to talk to Ariel MacAdam's friends. Ariel's the one with the least obvious connection to the other three victims, so if we find that link, the others should be easier to—"

"Here's another plan," he said. "We work together rather than competing."

"Okay, but time is critical. It doesn't make sense for both of us to go—"

"It doesn't make sense for either of us to go to Cal Arts. That's way north, near Magic Mountain. And you want to go look for random friends of a woman you don't know? You'll be there till midnight."

"Can't. I have to be at work at nine." She sighed. "Got a better idea, then?"

"Several, but you're not dressed for them. You're half-naked." He looked her up and down appreciatively, making her blush, then opened her car door for her. "You'll be freezing once the sun goes down. Go home, change and pack your waitress clothes. I'll pick you up in an hour."

"And you called Tony Brandt autocratic," she said, getting into the Jeep. "Does everyone in your life just fall in line when you order them around like that?"

"Everyone but you, love." He closed the door.

She started the engine and rolled down the window. "Where are you parked? Can I give you a ride?"

"No. Just get home fast, but drive safely." He leaned in

and gave her a gentle kiss on the mouth. "An hour ago, I'd have said your partnership skills left a lot to be desired, Ms. Gryffald. But you're starting to win me over."

Declan was back at the club on Sunset in no time at all. Flight, for a shapeshifter, was less debilitating than teleportation for an Elven, but even so, he was drained. He had a shower in his office at the Snake Pit, and a closetful of clothes, and when he was changed he felt better. After a steak and a salad he felt better still. Harriet had done some investigative footwork, via phone and computer, with her usual stunning efficiency, and within the hour he was heading up Laurel Canyon, with the sun on the driver's side starting its slow descent to the ocean. He made phone calls until reception hit a bad patch, then hit the off button and tossed the cell aside. Only then did he allow his thoughts to take over.

All his thoughts were of Sailor.

So Alessande had been right. She generally was. Why was he so surprised? Maybe because his feelings for the girl had risen up out of nowhere and hit him with the force of a gale wind. It had begun when he'd seen her unconscious and vulnerable on Alessande's sofa. And meeting her as Vernon, unencumbered by their history of contentious encounters, had been illuminating. Sailor had been no less spirited but far friendlier dealing with his stockbroker than with himself.

And now? "Friendly" didn't begin to describe her. She had all the erotic energy of the species she was responsible for, and he wasn't going to fight his response to her. True, it was bad timing, but he was only human—well, more or less—and he wasn't in the habit of repressing his nature.

Declan looked at the darkening sky and sensed a rare

storm gathering its forces. Not tonight. Tomorrow, maybe. Tonight he and Sailor would be doing their work—and perhaps play—by the light of the moon.

Chapter 9

Gwydion's Cave was like a time capsule of the Roaring Twenties, all marble and mahogany and ornate decadence. Every time Sailor walked in she felt like a flapper. Her cousin Barrie, in contrast to her surroundings, was wearing her work uniform: sweatpants, socks and an old sweater. She was glued to her computer screen in her tiny office space, Sophie the cat on the desk next to her, with Wizard and Jonquil sharing a Chippendale chaise longue. She looked up at Sailor's entrance. "At last," she said. "I've been worried."

"Where's Rhiannon?" Sailor asked.

"Mystic Café. Singing." Barrie pushed back her chair. "Leaving me instructions to find out everything that's going on. So come on. I need food."

Sailor followed her into the Cave's small kitchen, suddenly ravenous. She hopped onto the counter and helped herself to a handful of M&M'S from an antique bowl and started talking. There was plenty to discuss. She kept eating, moving from M&M'S to potato chips as she described the strange episodes of the Scarlet Pathogen and what she'd learned about the investigation, and when the chips were nearly gone she took a deep breath and told Barrie what she most wanted to talk about, which was what was happening between her and Declan Wainwright.

"Okay, this is more like it," Barrie said, her green eyes lighting up. "Enough with disease and death. Making out with Declan Wainwright? I love it. I can't believe it, but I love it."

"Why can't you believe it?" Sailor asked. "Should I be offended?"

"It's not that you're not adorable, sweetie. But he's a friend of the family, and I thought he'd consider us off-limits. Professional courtesy."

"What do you mean 'off-limits'?"

"You know, as a—plaything."

Sailor raised an eyebrow and Barrie raised one in response. "Sailor Ann, Declan is notoriously...active. Classic shifter energy. He is not a guy to fall in love with. You know that, right?"

It was like being drenched with ice water.

"Well, right. Of course. Fall in love with Casanova? No." Sailor pasted a smile on her face. "What did we used to say when we were fifteen? 'A kiss is not a contract.' I know that."

Barrie peered at her. "Do you, sweetie?"

"Yes. Declan doesn't take it seriously. Neither do I. It's a flirtation. A circumstantial flirtation, because we've been thrown together. For a while I thought it might be these intermittent pathogen-based attacks of, well, fascination. With everyone and everything. Which I thought were winding down, but then I had one on the 101 North just now, becoming interested in everyone in the fast lane. Have you ever just looked, really *looked,* at drivers on the freeway? Spellbinding. Collectively, we Californians are a very attractive bunch."

Barrie was staring at her, so Sailor helped herself to a glass of water, dropping eye contact. "Okay, back to murder."

"Not so fast," Barrie said. "Your eyes are looking less scarlet, by the way. But maybe it *is* the Scarlet Pathogen, these feelings. On the other hand, you've had a crush on Wainwright since you were nineteen."

"Seventeen. Oh, Barrie. Has it been that obvious? All these years?"

Barrie nodded. "The tough-girl routine. Dead giveaway."

Sailor sighed. "Okay, I'm going to play it out, because I don't have enough willpower not to. But I know it's not going anywhere, I know not to trust him romantically, I know not to have expectations. I'm fine."

"Okay, right answer," Barrie said. "And I'm here if you need me to remind you. So what's next, investigation-wise?"

"I want to retrace the steps of the four victims, figure out who they knew in common. For Charlotte Messenger, I need to get onto the set of her movie, talk to her boyfriend-slash-director. How can I do that, do you think?"

"Easiest thing in the world. Don't you know who packaged *Knock My Socks Off?*"

Sailor's blinked. "GAA?"

Barrie nodded. "Writer, producer, director and female lead, all represented by Darius. He could get you onto that set in a heartbeat. Of course, getting Giancarlo Ferro to talk to you is another story entirely. He's temperamental, to put it kindly."

Sailor stood, reached over to hug Barrie and grabbed the last of the M&M'S. "You are a doll. And I've got to go."

"Sailor?" Barrie said. "Just be careful. With everything, especially your heart."

As soon as she'd shut the door of Gwydion's Cave, Sailor let the cheerfulness drop. She was sick with disappointment. Barrie was absolutely right, and she'd been stupid not to have reminded herself of that. It was going to be impossible to get through this partnership thing without heartbreak. Equally impossible to resist Declan Wainwright. The best she could do was act the part of someone in it for a fling and not the long haul. The best she could hope for was to save face and exit gracefully when it was over.

The worst-case scenario? She would never get over him. Never be the same.

Meanwhile, the object of her obsession was on his way to pick her up and she had work to do. She left a phone message with Darius's supercilious assistant, requesting that he call her. Then she left a voice mail for Reggie Maxx, a sort of courtesy call, saying she planned to visit two film sets in the next twenty-four hours if she could pull it off, at least one of them in his district. She told him she would report back in the morning. She stuffed her spare waitress uniform in her oversize bag, making a note to do laundry at some point, and was looking for her favorite jeans when she heard a particular *rat-a-tat* on the door. She called out, "Come on in, Merlin."

A dignified and delightful, if somewhat disembodied, white-haired gentleman entered and bade her good evening.

"Merlin, I would love to chat," she said, "except that I have no time, because I have to get dressed." Merlin was too well-bred, even in death, to converse with an unclothed woman, even one he'd known since her infancy.

"Just checking on your health, my dear," he said. "Your cousins are concerned. But I shall leave you."

"No, wait," she said. "There's something you could help

me with. If the spirit of a recently dead woman is trying to send me a message and I can't understand it, could you?"

"Maybe. What is the message?" he asked. "And who is the dearly departed?"

"The message is three words. 'Location, location, location.' And the woman is Gina Santoro. She spoke to me last night through a medium, a complete stranger, but that's all she said. And I have no idea what it means."

"I'm not surprised," Merlin said. "Of course I know who Gina Santoro is, although we never met in person, and I would have described her as very earthbound. For someone like that to have any facility at communicating with the living after death? That's going to take some practice."

"It didn't take you much time at all," Sailor said.

Merlin smiled modestly. "I'm not just anyone, however. I worked on it well before my death, and if I may say so, I am extraordinarily talented. Those with little natural ability, if they have a burning desire to send messages to someone on earth, must use go-betweens. Psychics, so-called ghost hunters, sometimes the mentally ill, and often animals. And, of course, inanimate objects. Freeway signs, falling tree branches, shattered mirrors. All riddles brought to you from the dead. But they are rarely able to communicate in full sentences or instructions. It's too much to ask. You must interpret their symbols the way you interpret dreams."

"But how?" she asked. "Obviously it's important or she wouldn't go to the trouble of communicating, but I need more than 'location, location, location.'"

"I shall snoop around on the astral plane and see what I can discover," he said, and left her.

"Location, location, location," she mumbled, as she started unbuttoning the two dozen tiny buttons that ran the length of her sundress, from neck to handkerchief hem. When she was three-quarters through, she stepped out of it, letting it drop to the floor. The bedroom window was open, admitting a pleasant breeze, and something drew her to it. She gazed down at the estate's garden—or what had once been a garden, terraced and well-tended. Now it grew wild with rose bushes and orange trees. No one had bothered to pick weeds since the days her mother had lived here.

An owl hooted in a tree, and Sailor's heart skipped a beat. But she was in no danger here, she told herself. No creature would attack her here at the House of the Rising Sun. She closed the window anyway, and when she saw herself reflected in the glass in her silk bikini panties, she closed the shutters, too. And then she crossed the room and reached under her pillow for Alessande's dagger. She quickly pulled on jeans and then an ankle sheath, into which she tucked the blade.

As her dad liked to say, you didn't have to understand a sensation to heed it.

Ariel MacAdam had grown up on an old tree-lined street south of Ventura Boulevard, west of Laurel Canyon. Declan parked the Aventador a block from the house. The ride from Sailor's had been short and their conversation minimal because he'd been on the phone doing business most of the way. As they approached the MacAdams' bungalow on foot, a man walked down the driveway toward them. He was middle-aged, in a checkered shirt and, as an Elven, undoubtedly good-looking under normal circumstances but currently unshaven and hollow-cheeked. He scrutinized Sailor. "You the Keeper?"

"Yes," she said. She didn't shake his hand, Declan noticed. She was being careful, in case she was contagious.

"This one," the man said, nodding to Declan, "says you two are working together, but I'll talk to you, if you don't mind. I have no love for shifters. I'm Hank MacAdam."

Sailor said, "I'm very sorry about your daughter."

"I don't care about your sorry," Hank said. "I care about you doing your job. Come on this way."

He led them into a two-car garage apparently in the midst of a packing project, with kitchenware and bedding all over the concrete floor. From a cardboard box he pulled out a scrapbook. "We've got more of these inside the house. Dozens. Ariel and her mother, they put them together over the years. Those two, they never threw away a single program, kept every play she ever did, every cast photo. It's all here. Her whole life."

Sailor said, "Thank you for meeting with us."

"Well, I don't want you bothering my wife. She won't talk to you anyway. Says an Elven Keeper should have done more to keep our girl alive."

"She's right," Sailor said. "I should have. I suppose the police have interviewed you?"

"Yeah. Worthless. They found her way out on Las Virgenes Road. Wanted me to tell them, did she have any friends who lived out there? Hell, no friend of hers did that to my girl. Slept with her, sunk his teeth into her, then watched her bleed to death? I know well enough who did it."

Sailor threw a startled look at Declan. "Who?"

"Someone on that movie shoot. Some man. Few weeks back, she was spending the night here, came home all excited, said she met someone on the movie who could help her career."

"What movie?" Declan asked.

"Some stupid thing called *Six Corvettes*."

"Did she mention the man's name?" Sailor asked. "Or what his job was?"

"If she did, it didn't stick in my head. She was always going on about the grips and the gaffers and the what-nots. All those movie jobs, she knew what all of them were."

"It wouldn't be a grip or a gaffer," Sailor said, "if he was able to help her career. Or an actor, for that matter, unless he was A-list."

"No, he wasn't an actor. I think he was more in the business end of things."

"Where was the movie shooting?" Declan asked.

"Hold on." Hank walked over and called into the house, "Gigi, you want to come out here a minute?" He turned back to them. "That was the tough part for her. It was on the beach. Not anywhere near the water, of course, or she wouldn't have been able to do it. Ariel was in the beach-volleyball scene with the star. She was a good little athlete. Said the people were real nice to her, not like you'd expect, treated her real good. Especially the guys. That I can believe."

The screen door opened, and a young African-American woman came bounding out of the house. Vampire. Early twenties, Declan guessed.

"This is Gigi," Hank said, putting an arm around her and giving her a squeeze. "She was Ariel's roommate. Drove all Ariel's stuff down from Cal Arts this afternoon. All the stuff she and her mom bought for her dorm room three years ago." His voice wavered. As tough a guy as he was, everyone had his limits, Declan realized.

"Gigi," Sailor asked, "did Ariel talk to you about the guy she met on *Six Corvettes?*"

"Yeah, of course. And the cop who came to talk to us on campus, I told him they should look for this guy and the cop was like, 'Yeah, yeah, sweetie, whatever,' blowing me off. Stupid were."

Sailor visibly winced, no doubt at the girl's casual prejudice, but only said, "He blew you off? That's crazy. If the victims were all in the film business, that's probably how this guy met them. What did Ariel tell you about him?"

Gigi took a fast look at Hank, and Declan could see her calculating how much or little to say in front of a grieving father about his little girl. She turned back to Sailor.

"The guy sat next to her at lunch on the set, and they went out for drinks that night. Which she needed. A drink, I mean, because of having to work that close to water, you know? And the guy was really sweet, she said, and at first she thought he just wanted to do something nice for her, get her some auditions. But then he was calling her like three or four times the next day, wanting to date her."

"But she didn't tell you his name?" Sailor asked.

"No. She didn't want me to Google him. We had this thing where we'd tease each other, like I threatened to call him up and say, 'Dude, she's just not that into you' if I heard her talk about him one more time. So what I think happened was, the night she died, I think she agreed to meet him for a drink, just to let him down gently. And then, you know, he—did what he did to her. That's what I *think* anyway, but I was out all day at a rehearsal for *Jumpers,* the play I was doing at school, so I have no proof, plus I don't even know the guy's name. So that's why the cops blew me off."

Declan looked at Hank to see how he was taking all this, but his attention was on a pair of small, well-worn pink skates lying in a shoe box. He put his hand over one skate, covering it completely, and Declan could imagine him putting the skates on tiny feet, lacing them up with big beefy fingers, tying double knots. *Be careful,* he would have told the little girl before sending her off onto the ice.

A few moments later Sailor was saying her goodbyes, and she and Declan walked down the street in silence. After a time he said, "You did well. That wasn't an easy interview."

"That sucked," she said. She was as subdued as Declan had ever seen her. "How did you find Hank?" she asked.

"The tabloids found him. I know people who own the tabloids. It wasn't hard." He paused for a moment, then said, "Want to tell me what went on in the Council meeting?"

"Give me a few minutes. I don't want to think about those people now."

"There's a surprise."

"Don't be sarcastic with me just yet, Declan. I'm too sad to put up a fight."

"All right, we'll fight later."

The daylight was dissolving, growing less harsh. A smell of orange blossoms hit them as they walked. The old neighborhood was filled with citrus trees, the branches reaching out over picket fences to the sidewalks. Sailor dodged one, leaning into Declan, and he put his arm around her without thinking.

"I'm imagining Ariel on the beach all day," she said softly. "Ten, twelve, fourteen hours, no trailer to escape to because she's just an extra or a day player. But she's an Elven, so the sound of the surf is terrifying, and no one understands except another Elven, but maybe she's the only one, so she hides how hard it is for her. She tells herself how exciting it is to be working on a movie set, how cute she looks in her bikini. She thinks, 'It's just one day's work, but it could lead to something bigger. I just have to be the absolute best, brightest beach volleyball player there ever was. It's what I've dreamed of all my life.' But time moves so slowly on a film set, and no one cares about the comfort of a day player. And when they say, 'Moving on' or even 'That's a wrap,' she's so relieved she can barely stand it. And some nice man, some Other, he offers to buy her a drink, he recognizes her as Elven, he knows what she's just been through. And she's so happy to be able to tell someone just what it was like, and he understands, he knows what it is to dream of the movies, to want to act so badly you'll do anything. You'll hide your terror of water, you'll do things that are dangerous, bad for you. And he becomes her friend just by listening to her, and then telling her what she wants to hear, that she's good, she's special, she's got the look, the talent, he could see it right away, she's destined to be a star, and he can help her."

Declan pulled her in close, and she didn't resist. It seemed the most natural thing in the world to be walking down the street together. The feel of her skin, the warmth, the shoulder blades under her T-shirt…he felt a strange familiarity, a possessiveness that he couldn't understand. This wasn't erotic, this was simply—

"Declan?" Sailor looked up at him suddenly, her distress evident. "My Council is doing essentially nothing. We're supposed to gather information within our own district but not cross into others. To listen for gossip, rumors of bad blood between the Elven and the shifters or vamps. And not to talk among ourselves, much less to anyone else. And we're supposed to keep the entire pathetic plan strictly confidential."

He nodded. It was what he'd suspected. And it was frustrating, but for the moment he was most concerned about Sailor. Despair was an emotion he'd never seen from her before. "And what do you plan to do?" he asked.

"Me?" She looked at him, her eyes green with a trace of scarlet. "I'm going to cross borders and break rules. I am going to find the killer. And when I do, I'm going to cut out his heart and bring it to the Council."

Okay, that was more like her. "How?"

"By talking to anyone who'll talk to *me*. And yes, I may be contagious to the Elven, so I'll be careful, but I've been thinking about it, my approach and your approach. And while yours is valid, mine is, too. I don't care if the cops are already covering this ground, because I have something the cops don't have."

"What's that?"

"Insight. Insight into the minds of the dead women. I'm a woman, and I'm an actress, and I'm part Elven. And I have the disease. I'm exactly the person to do this. I'm the *only* one. There's no one else."

She had a point, he realized.

"I want to retrace their steps," she continued. "There has to be a way to walk the path they walked, until it takes me to the man who killed them."

A chill went down his spine.

"Maybe," he said, "but you're not doing any of it alone."

As they reached the car, Sailor got a call from Darius's assistant, who patched her through to her boss.

"I am finishing dinner at the Water Grill," Darius told her. "I'll be in the courtyard of the Mark Taper Forum until seven minutes before curtain. I suggest, my dear, that you arrive prior to that, prepared to deliver the report I requested. I'm not known for giving something for nothing, so please make it worth my while." He hung up.

Sailor checked her watch. The Mark Taper Forum was in downtown L.A. She was in Studio City. Driving from one to the other would take anywhere from thirty minutes to two hours depending on traffic, and another fifteen minutes to find parking. Damn.

"You won't make it," Declan told her when she repeated the message.

"I have to. I need him to get me onto the set of Charlotte Messenger's movie. Also *Technical Black,* Gina's film."

"I can do *Technical Black*. I know the producers."

"Seriously? How about tonight? I'm off work at midnight."

"Tonight? Are they shooting?"

"They are. I checked. And how about Charlotte's movie?

He shook his head. "I was asked to invest in *Knock My Socks Off,* but I didn't like the director. Or the script. Word got back to the director, who already didn't like me. So no, I wouldn't be welcome on that set."

"Then I'd better be nice to Darius."

"Yes. I'd drive you downtown, but I've got a meeting at Universal. A band from Dublin I'm hoping to sign. I can't skip the meeting because they're heading back to the airport this evening."

"Lend me your car and I'll drop you, then pick you up afterward. It's on the way, and I'll save a half hour."

He looked at her, stunned. "Lend you my car?"

"Yes."

"My *car?*"

"Yes, your car. It's not like I'm asking for a kidney."

He continued staring.

"So that's a 'no'?" she asked.

"That's a 'hell no.'"

The sun had set and the moon had risen by the time Sailor found Darius sipping espresso. He sat at an outdoor café in the plaza that joined the Mark Taper Forum to the other three world-class stages that made up the Performing Arts Center of Los Angeles. His elegant assistant, Joshua, was sitting across from him. Upon seeing Sailor, Darius dismissed Joshua and gestured to the chair he'd vacated.

"In the interests of time," Darius said, "we'll dispense with the pleasantries. I'd like your report on the Council meeting."

"And I'd like entrée to the set of *Knock My Socks Off,* and access to someone highly placed enough to answer some questions and help me out," she replied.

"Then let's hope your report is sufficiently interesting."

She nodded. "Charles Highsmith is an egomaniac. He proposed a plan that consists of 'asking around' about the Scarlet Pathogen, sticking strictly to our own districts, and then called for a vote. It was a tie, with Highsmith himself being the tiebreaker. I don't know how he pulled it off, but I have to assume he's bribed or blackmailed half the Council, creating a coalition of minions. I have no idea how my father tolerated it."

Darius gave her a half smile. "Highsmith's coalition of the bribed and blackmailed must be a recent phenomenon. He never would have tried it with your father here."

"Great," Sailor said. "So Dad left town and it all went to hell in a handbasket because I'm considered a half-wit."

Darius's half smile grew. "Well said. Tell me who you believe to be on Highsmith's side."

"Everyone who had nothing to say in opposition, I'm guessing. Jill, the resident sex kitten. Maybe George Fairweather. A woman who reminded me of my old basketball coach. And others whose names I forgot because they weren't memorable. I assume the ones who spoke up are lined up with Justine Freud, his nemesis."

Darius nodded to Joshua, who was standing a little way off, gesturing at his watch. Around them people hurriedly paid their checks and moved toward their theaters to make an eight-o'clock curtain. "Did you remember my advice?" Darius asked.

"Perfectly," she fudged. After all, he hadn't asked if she'd followed it. "Listen, don't talk. Oh, I have an alliance of sorts with Reggie Maxx."

His eyebrow went up. "The Coastal Keeper?"

"Yes."

"Does Highsmith know about this alliance?"

"Yes."

Darius sighed. "Too bad. Alliances function best when they're under the radar. Ah well. Perhaps you'll improve with age."

"Yeah, sorry. Anyhow, that's all I have, Darius, and I hope it's enough, because I spent a whole lotta energy getting here."

"Teleportation?"

"Yes. I was late, plus out of gas, so I stopped at a parking lot three exits away, which is a personal best, distance-wise, and it wore me out."

"Then have some water before you start back. And I suggest taking a cab. There will be a drive-on pass for you at Metropole Studios tomorrow, and the director himself, Giancarlo Ferro, will speak with you. Don't waste the opportunity."

Declan, in the guise of a red-tailed hawk, watched Sailor materialize next to her car. He'd seen Elven dematerialize many times, but it was rare to catch one appearing out of nowhere. And he'd never seen a Keeper do it. It was a thing of beauty.

He'd almost missed it. After his business meeting he'd tracked her Jeep, thanks to a spare cell phone he'd placed inside it earlier that afternoon. When he saw it had stopped short of the Music Center, he grew concerned and flew over to check. Less than three minutes later his attention was caught by a glow of light, subtle and mystical. He watched the light shatter into particles, and the particles rearrange themselves to become Sailor.

He was mesmerized. One moment there was space, and the next that space was filled with a tall woman, hair streaming behind her, sexy and tough in jeans, boots and a black T-shirt. He understood how it was that mortals, witnessing it, would simply disbelieve their eyes. They had no frame of reference for a person appearing out of nowhere, and so their brains would persuade them that the person had been there all along.

He watched her get in her car and followed her to a gas station, and when she was back on the 101 North, he flew to the Snake Pit, shifted back into himself and phoned her.

"How did it go?" he asked.

"Fine, but I had to, uh—" she was searching for a word other than "teleport," he knew, conscious of the cell phone taboo "—arrange transport for the last few miles. Let's just say I'm worn out. And I have to work."

"Call in sick."

"I could be fired."

"Quit your job."

She laughed. "Spoken like a multimillionaire. But it's a short shift tonight. Three hours." The most he could get from her was a promise that he could pick her up after work and she would have one of her cousins drive her back to pick up her car tomorrow. He was literally afraid to let her drive home alone.

The House of Illusion was hopping, leaving Sailor with a sense of déjà vu. She was as exhausted as she'd been the night before, but not from the Scarlet Pathogen. Rearranging molecules took its toll. Why, oh why, hadn't she listened to Darius? It had been insane to try a teleportation round-trip, especially on top of the earlier incident at the crime lab. Julio noticed immediately. He was bussing a table in her section and gave a low whistle when he saw her.

"You still don't look so good," he said. "You need more of last night's magic."

And why not? she thought. She'd already given a blood sample today, so she didn't need to worry about skewing the lab results. Declan might have a problem with it, but

Declan wasn't here, and she wasn't interested in getting high, just getting through the shift. "Julio," she said softly, aware of Kristoff nearby, "do you have any more *siúlacht?*"

"No," he said. "No, I'm all sold out. I got some nice mushrooms. Organic. But not good if you're working."

"Mushrooms? Are you nuts?"

"Tell you what, let me make a phone call."

Twenty minutes later Julio showed up in the kitchen as Sailor was garnishing a pair of entrées. "Here," he said. "It's only half a pill, but it's the best I can do until later."

"Thanks." A thought occurred to her. "Julio, the person you get the *siúlacht* from, is it the person who actually manufactures the pills?"

He shook his head. "No. My supplier, he gets it from... I don't know, some woman in Topanga, I think. I don't sell a lot. The people who love it, they love it. Me, I tried it, it didn't do much."

Sailor nodded. Probably you had to be Elven to feel its full effects, just as only the Elven were susceptible to the Scarlet Pathogen. "Can you find out this woman's name for me?" she asked.

He frowned. "I don't think so. Even if I could, that's bad business practice."

"It's important, Julio," she said. "And I don't need to buy anything from her. I just need a bit of her knowledge." Alessande had said that *siúlacht* was hard to make, so anyone who could do it well enough to manufacture pills from it had to have considerable expertise.

"I could make a few calls," he said, doubtfully. "You get off at midnight, right? Meet me in employee parking."

She went back to work. Business was slow, and that was a piece of unexpected luck. The half pill revived her just enough to take the edge off her fatigue. At one point she went into her purse and dug out the business card printed with Reggie Maxx's phone number. Although he was called the Coastal Keeper, his territory included canyons, too, the ones to the west of hers. She left a voice mail asking if he knew of any healers particularly adept at creating *siúlacht* or in any of the healing arts. It was a borderline kind of message, suggesting Elven business while not actually saying anything outright.

She then checked her own voice mail, hoping to hear Declan's sultry voice. Her body had developed a craving for his British accent, and just a few words coming through her cell would keep her going, she knew. But there was nothing. Only a curious message from Justine Freud, the Valley Keeper, asking Sailor to phone her. The call had apparently come in hours earlier, but in the incomprehensible ways of voice mail, she was only just now hearing it. She made a mental note to phone the elderly woman tomorrow.

After a few dozen hours of sleep.

At midnight, dressed once more in her street clothes, she found Julio leaning against her Jeep. "One *siúlacht,*" he said, hopping up. He put the little pebblelike pill into her hand. "One is all I could score. It's not exactly a popular item."

"One's all I need. And I'm definitely paying you."

"No way." Julio shook his head. "But listen, that information you wanted? No luck. Nobody likes to give up their sources."

"Thanks for trying," she said, hiding her disappointment. She popped the pill, chasing it with a bottle of water she'd brought for the purpose. She gave Julio a hug. "You look as exhausted as I feel. You should go home. Get some sleep."

"Can't. Gotta finish my shift. Besides, my car's in the shop, so I have to wait for Tafiq to give me a ride, and he's closing tonight." Tafiq was another busboy.

She tossed him the keys. "Here, take mine. I've got a ride. I'll figure out how to pick the Jeep up in the morning."

He thanked her, and went back inside, leaving her alone in the moonlight.

But not for long. Four minutes later she turned to see the Aventador entering the employee lot. She smiled and walked toward Declan, feeling as if her life were about to begin.

Chapter 10

"Where are we off to?" Sailor asked, leaning back into the black leather depths of the passenger seat.

"Home," Declan said. "You must be exhausted."

"Nope," she said. "I got a second wind."

"How is that possible?" He peered at her in the dark.

She shrugged. "I'm young, I'm healthy and I have no choice. *Technical Black* is a night shoot."

"You still want to go?"

"You said you could get us onto the set. Well, tick-tock." She could feel his incredulity and said, "Honest, I'm fine. I drank a lot of coffee at work. So do you really know the producer, or was that just a pickup line?"

He smiled. "Ask me nicely."

"Please."

"Could you put a little more sincerity into it?"

"No. That's my best performance."

"No wonder you're waiting tables."

She laughed. "You can't do it, can you? Admit it."

He picked up his cell phone and hit a speed-dial key. "Carolyn, call the production office of *Technical Black*," he said. "See where they're shooting tonight, and then get me Gary Kiel on the phone."

Two minutes later he got a return call, talked briefly and made a U-turn.

"Okay, I'm impressed," she said. "I could get used to that, having a staff at my beck and call, even at midnight. Also, your car is growing on me. I used to think only jerks drive supercars. How much did it set you back, if you don't mind my asking?"

"I won it in a poker game. I'd never buy a car like this."

"How come?"

"Only jerks drive supercars."

"Plus, it's a gas guzzler," she said. "You should trade it in for a Honda."

"I could trade it in for twenty-two Hondas. And I have a Honda. It's in the shop."

Sailor studied his profile. He had a strong nose, one that looked as if it had been broken once. Obviously he could have fixed it. She liked that he'd kept it. "You were born wealthy, weren't you?"

He laughed shortly. "Where did you get that? Who'sDatingWhom dot.com?"

"Really? Are you saying you grew up poor?"

"On-the-streets poor."

She blinked. "What did your parents do?"

"My mother was a hooker. I never met my father."

That wasn't what she was expecting. Something stirred deep inside her, and the preconceptions she'd had about him began to shift and fall away.

He turned to her. "And what about your own mother?

I know your father well enough, but what's the other half like?"

"Hold on a sec," she said. "I'm mentally revising ten years of looking at you as a privileged rich guy."

He laughed. "I *am* a privileged rich guy."

"But I thought you just said... Never mind."

"Come on. Tell me what you thought I was like. I can take it."

"Arrogant. Out of touch with the working class. All those stereotypes." She felt him looking at her but didn't look back at him. "And then I had this serious crush on you, and I didn't like that I had this crush on you because I thought you were this arrogant, born-rich, out-of-touch stereotypical jerk. So I got in a big argument with myself every time I laid eyes on you."

"You had a crush on me?"

"From the first time I snuck into the Snake Pit and the bartender carded me and then called you and you threw me out."

"I threw you out?"

"Well, escorted me out. Told me to come back when I was of legal drinking age. You don't remember any of this?"

"Do you know how many people I've thrown—excuse me, *escorted*—out of my club in the past decade? No, I'm sorry to say I don't remember. And you still had a crush on me?"

"Oh, yeah."

"Why?"

She turned to him. "Have you ever looked in a mirror?"

He smiled and turned his attention back to the road. "Well, I'm glad you took my advice and came back when you were legal."

"Oh, I came back before that. With a better fake ID. And a wig."

"You shock me, Ms. Gryffald."

"I doubt that, Mr. Wainwright."

They drove for a while in companionable silence. Then Sailor said, "My mother was Pamela Sailor, a concert violinist. My father saw her play one night at Royce Hall, fell head over heels in love with her and followed her around the country like some crazy deadhead until she married him and came back to L.A."

"Pamela Sailor. Hence your name."

"She loved that Dad was a visual effects supervisor, didn't mind the crazy hours or his being gone on location, but she never liked his being a Keeper, the whole Otherworld thing. When I was born with the birthmark, she named me Sailor to remind me of the distaff side, my human lineage. She was determined that I would not inherit the Elven water phobia."

"And did you? Inherit it?"

"Yes. I hate water, lakes, the ocean. Drove my mom mad, even though she wasn't much for water herself. But anyhow, she encouraged me to ignore the destiny thing, fostered my love for theater, she wanted me to go away to college, be normal. For her sake, my father downplayed my Keeper education."

"And now you're playing catch-up."

"Yes. I did have a lovely childhood, though. And I'm good at teleportation, by the way—always have been. Dad's constant refrain was 'Don't teleport in front of your mother, it upsets her.'"

"Are you still close to your mother?"

"She died of cancer when I was seventeen."

He didn't respond. She was grateful for that. Saved her from her automatic responses of "Oh, that's okay" or "She lived a very full life" or "I had a wonderful family, they took very good care of me." All of which were true, but not the deepest truth. That one she rarely said aloud: *I had her for seventeen years, and it wasn't nearly enough.*

Maybe it was the same for him.

They drove through the night in silence, but a mile later he reached across and put his hand on hers. She wrapped her fingers around it and held on.

Production trucks, trailers and generators told them they were approaching a movie set. Security, too. Thanks to the murder, the general public was now obsessed with *Technical Black*, so guards—probably off-duty cops—were everywhere. Declan gave his name to one, and after a walkie-talkie exchange, a production assistant appeared.

The PA led them across the set, and Declan watched Sailor work her charm on the kid, learning his name (Pete), old high school (Malibu High) and career aspirations (indie film director).

"It must be hard on everyone, Gina's death," Sailor said. "Were you here when it happened, Pete?"

"Yeah, but it wasn't me that found her, it was transportation." He sounded regretful about that. "And man, it's crazy trying to replace her. Casting sent over every Gina look-alike in town. We're using four. One has her hair, one's got her body and another one's got her exact profile. And we have a girl who can sound just like her, so we can loop the lookalikes in postproduction. Just two big action sequences to shoot and we can wrap. It's like *Game of Death* after Bruce Lee died."

Pete delivered them to Gary Kiel, the producer, at the craft services truck. Declan watched Sailor give both Gary and the craft services guy the same attention she'd just given Pete, and after a round of cappuccinos were made and handed round, Gary led them toward a ranch house. "If we can get an audience curious about Gina's last picture, we may break even," he said in response to one of Sailor's questions. "But the franchise is over. This isn't James Bond, where you can recast the lead and keep on going, this was the Gina Santoro show."

"Was that common knowledge?" Sailor asked. "That without Gina, the franchise folds?"

"What do you mean?" Gary asked.

"Could some actress out there think, 'If only Gina were dead, *I* could be Veronica Slick'?"

"Yeah, if she's bat-shit crazy. Which, you know actresses, could be the case. But the killer was a guy, right? That's what the cops said."

"Well, maybe some guy's thinking, 'My girlfriend should be playing that part.'"

"This isn't *Gone with the Wind*," Gary said. "It's a big dumb movie with superb production values."

"Are Gina's hair and makeup artists still working?" Sailor asked.

"Twenty-four seven. They have to take her doubles and stand-ins, turn them into Gina."

"Can I talk to them?"

"Why?"

"I'm doing a human interest piece on the bond between actresses and their hair and makeup artists. A posthumous tribute to Gina would lend poignancy to it. I'd like to help you sell some tickets."

What an accomplished little liar, Declan thought.

"You're a writer?" Gary asked, eyes lighting up. "I took you for an actress, as beautiful as you are."

Down, boy. Declan had to stop himself from saying it aloud.

"You're a charmer, Gary," Sailor replied.

"C'mon, I'll take you to the hair and makeup trailer," he

said. "And maybe later you can join me in my own trailer, I'll show you some dailies."

"I'd love that," she said.

And down, girl, Declan added. He couldn't believe how annoyed he was getting. It couldn't be jealousy, because he didn't get jealous. Did he?

The hair and makeup trailer was a haven of warmth against the canyon air. The makeup artist was a woman named Melanie, perfectly made up but dressed for night shooting in jeans, hiking boots and a down jacket. She was putting a lip line on a girl no one bothered to introduce, but who looked eerily like Gina Santoro. The hairdresser was Hervé, a diminutive man with a goatee and hair an improbable shade of gold. Declan recognized that both Melanie and Hervé were vampires. Did Sailor?

She did. After Gary had made the introductions, Sailor turned to Declan and said sweetly, "Maybe this would be a good time for you to discuss your business proposition with Gary?"

"My what?"

"You know," she said, "the thing."

She looked right at him and let him read her thought: *Get Gary out of here so I can talk to these two without their boss listening.* He glanced at Gary, who was looking at him eagerly, probably having visions of getting his next film project fully funded.

"'Scuse me, Mr. Kiel," Pete said, sticking his head into the trailer. "You're needed on set. And we'll be using the Gina double."

Gary stood. "Back to work. Walk with me, Declan. We can talk."

"No, it's a longer conversation than you have time for now," Declan said, ignoring Sailor's insistent looks. "We'll have lunch next week."

"Sailor, here's my card," Gary said, pulling out his wallet from his back pocket. "Stick around if you can. We have dinner on set around 4:00 a.m. If you can't stay, give me a call, I'd like to keep in touch."

I'm sure you would, Declan thought, watching Sailor tuck the card into the back pocket of her jeans.

When Gary and the Gina double left the trailer, Sailor turned to Hervé and Melanie. "I know you guys are crazy busy, so I'll be quick. I'm Sailor Gryffald, I'm the Canyon Keeper of the Elven, and I'm trying to figure out what happened to Gina and Charlotte Messenger, and the other two Elven women who died."

"You're not a writer?" Hervé said, looking confused.

"That was for Gary's benefit, Hervé." Melanie closed the trailer door, which a gust of wind had blown open. "Okay, you're an Elven Keeper. Who's this guy?"

Hervé spoke up. "That's Declan Wainwright."

"Oh, right," Melanie said. "I thought you looked familiar. Shifter, right?"

"Shifter Keeper," he said.

"I know you don't know us," Sailor said, "but I know Gina was close to you."

"I'm just a makeup artist," Melanie said.

Sailor sighed. "Oh, please. She trusted you with her face, and she had the face of the decade. She spent every workday of the past five years with you and Hervé, going back to *Apples and Oranges.* I checked credits. She wouldn't work without you."

"So she trusted us," Melanie said. "But why would we trust you? I've never heard of you."

"I'm new. My uncle is Piers Gryffald, recent Canyon Keeper of the vamps, and my godfather is Darius Simonides. Sorry to name-drop, but I don't have many Keeper credentials of my own yet. I'm working on it."

Melanie nodded. Declan recognized the Hollywood veneer of politeness that hid a vast reservoir of ice, but at least she was thawing.

"Darius Simonides?" Hervé repeated. "The magic words. Ask me anything."

"Have the cops talked to you?" Sailor asked.

He sniffed. "Barely. We're below the line, darling." Meaning, Declan knew, that their pay grade was low and their status along with it. "It didn't occur to them that we knew her better than anyone. Plus, we weren't on set when it happened. We'd already gone home when Transpo found her body."

"When was that?" Sailor asked.

"An hour after wrap. They went to turn off lights and power down the trailer, thinking she'd gone home." A catch in his throat. "There she was. Ghastly."

Sailor glanced at Melanie, who had busied herself cleaning makeup brushes. "I bet you have theories about what happened," she said.

"Darling," Hervé said, "we talk of nothing else."

Melanie shot him a look. "Gina never liked Keepers, especially Elven Keepers."

"Then forget I'm a Keeper," Sailor said. "I'm an actress, so I know that you weren't 'below the line' to Gina. You were shrink, friend, spiritual adviser."

"Yeah, *were*. We were all those things," Hervé said. "Not anymore."

"Well, who *did* the cops talk to? The director? Producer? Was she even friends with the director?"

"That moron?" Melanie asked. "She was sorry she ever approved him. He was a last-minute replacement."

"And the cops interviewed him, but they didn't interview you two?" *Idiots,* her tone of voice suggested.

Hervé sniffed. "Werewolves, both of them."

"Figures." Sailor paused, then asked, "Was Gina seeing someone?"

Melanie shook her head. "Nope. She broke up with Feral Jones, the rapper, just three weeks ago."

"I thought she was seeing Alexander Cavendish," Sailor said.

Hervé held up a hand. "We do not speak that name in this trailer. Not since Christmas. And after Feral she went into an 'I'm swearing off men' phase. Romantic detox. Could barely kiss her idiot costar on camera."

"Cops interviewed *him,* of course," Melanie said. "Waste of time. Gina didn't like half the people on this set."

Hervé shuddered. "Certainly not to sleep with. No one here is in her league. If she had sex that night, then some maniac forced himself on her. And security was tight, so it wouldn't be someone off the street. It had to be an insider."

"That could be fifty people," Sailor asked.

"Fewer," Melanie said. "Most everyone had wrapped before second meal."

Meal breaks, Declan knew, happened every six hours on a film set, so "second meal" signaled a long—and expensive—shooting day.

"Unless he snuck into her trailer early in the day and stayed hidden. Transpo was supposed to keep it locked, but—" Hervé shuddered with distaste. "Teamsters."

"Was she in good health?" Sailor asked.

"Darling," Hervé said, "she was at the absolute top of her game."

"Enemies?"

Melanie said, "Jealous actresses. Jealous ex-girlfriends of her current boyfriends. Nothing abnormal."

"She drank champagne, right?"

Hervé looked as if he might weep. "Cristal."

Sailor looked at Declan. "Can you think of anything else?"

He was surprised she asked. She seemed to have forgotten his presence. "Did she know Charlotte Messenger?" he asked.

"Socially, yeah," Melanie answered. "Not enough to go the funeral."

"How about the agent?" Sailor asked. "From GAA? Did Gina know her?"

"Kelly Ellory," Hervé said. "Yes. Gina was a GAA client. Kelly visited the set. Lovely woman. Excellent hair. I trimmed her bangs for her."

"And the student from Cal Arts, the other woman who died?"

"We'd never heard of her." Henry grabbed a box of tissues and pulled out several, blotting his eyes. "You probably don't cry, do you, Miss Elven Keeper?"

"Not much."

"Lucky. I'm so tired of crying, I could throw up."

"Anything else you can think of that might help us?" Sailor asked.

Melanie looked at her. "I'll tell you something I heard from an old vamp actor. This disease they say they died from? It isn't new. It's been around for centuries."

Sailor glanced at Declan. "But we've interviewed doctors—Others—and they never mentioned anything like that."

"Well, they're not going to find it in their medical journals," Melanie said. "Maybe you should just interview someone really old."

Pete came in to say, "Hair and Makeup wanted on set," and they all walked out together, Melanie and Hervé toward an array of huge lights, Declan and Sailor toward the parking area.

The canyon was close to freezing, and Declan put his jacket around Sailor's shoulders. While doing so, he used a little sleight of hand to extract his friend Gary's card from the back pocket of her jeans.

"You didn't tell them about the attack on you," Declan said, driving back down the road. "That you have the disease."

"Why would I?" Sailor asked.

"Because they'll hear about it," he said. "Better to have heard it from you."

"Does it matter?"

He shrugged. "It's just being straight with people. You got information from them, but you didn't give them anything, even just something to make them feel like insiders. Once they realize that, they'll feel used."

"I didn't want to get into it. I'm feeling pretty healthy right now anyway."

He glanced at her. "If the killings continue, the Elven will take action. You talked about finding the killer and cutting his heart out of his body. That's not just a myth. Your Elven will literally do that. The most civilized among them can turn primal when threatened. I've seen it. Things are going to get ugly between the species, and now there are two vampires who have less reason to trust the Elven or their Keepers tonight than when they woke this morning."

She'd been focused on what she could get from Melanie and Hervé, and from Gary, the producer. It had been shortsighted, she realized, and not particularly kind. Her father never would have taken that approach. "Damn. I wasn't thinking."

"Next time you will be."

"I don't know, Declan. Sometimes I think I'll never get the hang of this. I'm not sure I have the instincts."

"Because you've been at it for what, a day? Thirty-six hours? Maybe you could cut yourself some slack." He glanced at her. "Okay, sum it up for me. What have we figured out today?"

"That all four women were on film sets in the weeks before they were killed. That's the connecting thread. They must have met the killer there."

"Three different films, though," he said. "*Technical Black* for Gina and Kelly, *Six Corvettes* for Ariel and *Knock My Socks Off* for Charlotte. So the question is, what kind of movie professional works several jobs simultaneously?"

"Actors can," she said, "but Ariel's dad said the man wasn't an actor. Publicity people, or agents or managers with clients on all three films. Agents love to visit sets. Gets them out of the office, makes the actors feel loved."

"I'll buy the agent theory, but not the publicity team. Gina and Charlotte's films were with competing studios and would have in-house publicists. *Six Corvettes* was low-budget. I doubt they even have a publicist."

"Animal wranglers?" she asked. "On-set schoolteachers?"

"No kids in *Technical Black,*" he said. "No animals in Charlotte's movie."

Sailor leaned back in the passenger seat. "What else? Fight coordinators, dialect coaches, stunt teams? Maybe tomorrow, when I'm on the set of *Knock My Socks Off,* it will come to me. Because I'll be on the lookout. You know how there are dozens of jobs in a movie but you only really pay attention to the ones that are directly working with you?"

"No, Sailor. I'm not an actor. Also," he said, "I'm not sure I like the thought of your wandering around *Knock My Socks Off* without me."

"Why not?"

He shrugged. "What if you have one of your…episodes? By the way, were you having one with Gary Kiel?"

"Nope. I'm feeling normal, in fact. I think my eyes are returning to normal."

"I've been noticing that." He paused. "But you were awfully friendly with Gary."

Was Declan…*jealous?* she wondered. Aloud, she said, "That was just me being me. You know, using people. Exploiting them. Shamelessly."

He smiled. "When did you last have one of these pathogen moments? Because you haven't told me how handsome I am for an hour at least."

"Missing it?"

He shook his head. "Not really. A shifter can look like anything he pleases. Compliments about looks…they don't mean much."

"Or maybe it's that you're a man."

"Possibly."

"I, however, am not a man."

"True enough. And no one would mistake you for one."

"And I am not able to shift."

"Your point?"

"A compliment once in a while would be okay with me."

"Good God." He turned the wheel and pulled onto the shoulder of the road. "Have I been stupid? Have I not told you what a beauty you are?"

"No."

"What I'd like to do with you?"

"No."

"*To* you?"

"Uh-uh."

"What a wanker I am." He looked into her eyes, and by the light of the nearly full moon he let his convey to her everything she could imagine wanting to hear from him and a few things she hadn't thought of.

She felt herself blushing. "I don't think you're a...wanker, whatever that is. And I want to do all those things with you. To you. And it's got nothing to do with the Scarlet Pathogen."

Declan peered at her in the darkness. She could hear him breathing, even feel it, feel herself breathing along with him. Finally he said, "What do you think we should do about it?"

"You could kiss me," she said.

He smiled, then looked in the rearview mirror and pulled back onto the road. "Oh, I will," he promised. "But this time we're not starting something we can't finish."

"Then maybe you should drive faster," Sailor said.

He did.

Chapter 11

Inside the Snake Pit, Declan took Sailor by the hand and led her through a door she'd never seen, through the back, down a hallway and up a private stairway to a loftlike room. His office, she realized. It had a waist-high wall, like a box at the opera. He showed her the vista below, of the Snake Pit in full open-for-business mode, crowded with people dancing and drinking. A blues singer crooned something into her microphone, a song in a language Sailor could only guess at—Portuguese?—but understood nevertheless. She was singing about love. Or sex. Or love and sex. And possibly heartbreak.

Declan stood behind her and wrapped his arms around her, holding her tight. The sensation of his hands on her abdomen sent a thrill through her. Then one hand slid up and found her breast, and the effect was so electrifying she could hardly stand still. He kissed her neck, her shoulder, her ear. She turned her head so he could kiss her cheekbone, and then he pulled her back, out of sight of the crowd below, and turned her so that they were face-to-face, six inches apart, the air between them pulsing with the need to touch.

They looked long and deep into each other's eyes, seeing how long they could go telling the truth, revealing exactly how they felt about each other. Waves of heat and telepathy vibrated between them. When she couldn't bear it any longer, Sailor moved closer until she couldn't see him clearly, until there was nothing to do but close her eyes and find his mouth. And then his tongue. His teeth. He bit her lip and she bit him in return, and then the pent-up feelings of the day overcame them both and their hands took over, gripping, feeling the heat through their clothes, shoulders, backs, arms....

The craving for skin was too much. Sailor unbuttoned his white shirt until he grew impatient and pulled her hands away, then grabbed the hem of her black lace T-shirt and pulled it over her head. She pushed his hands away and pulled his shirt off without bothering with the last of the buttons. His bare torso was far more muscled than she had imagined, and she ran her hands over his shoulders and biceps wonderingly, hardly believing he was hers to touch. His abdominal muscles caused her to gasp. She'd never touched anything like them.

He seemed to be feeling the same way. His hands were on her waist, then her rib cage, his eyes on her body as he reached the black lace of her bra. Her own eyes closed, and she let out a sigh that turned into a shudder. And then she couldn't stand it anymore.

She grabbed his belt buckle and undid it, then unsnapped his jeans and pulled down his zipper. He was about to be more naked than she was, and she could see him register that. He immediately slipped his fingers through her belt loops and pulled her close enough to unsnap her jeans. She tried to kick off her boots, but she'd forgotten about the ankle sheath and the knife. And then he'd apparently had enough of the vertical striptease because he picked her up and carried her across the office, into the darkness.

He had more strength than she had any idea he possessed.

Sailor was tall, and she hadn't been lifted off the ground by a man since her childhood. She felt herself blush all over at the sensation of helplessness, and she resisted, her body tensing until he said, "Get used to it," his voice low. She didn't know how he could read her mind in the dark, but she *did* relax, and then she was being carried through a doorway into another room, lit by low, sultry lights. The next thing she knew she was on a bed, on her back, looking up at the ceiling, the voice of the Portuguese singer giving way to a saxophone.

He pulled off her boots, one by one, tossing them on the floor. Pulled out the knife and placed it on the bedside table. Ripped off the sheath and tossed it alongside the boots.

Pulled down her jeans.

His hands were on her hips now, on the silk of her panties, and she put her knees up so he could slip them off. And then the bit of lace that was her bra was gone, and she didn't even know how he'd done that, but she was naked now. Her eyes adjusted to the darkness, and she watched him push his own jeans down and off, his swimmer's body naked now, too, as he moved onto the bed, straddling her, that gorgeous chest above her. She reached up and pulled him down to her, and the whole of him covered her with warmth and skin and muscle.

His arms tightened around her and crushed her to him, and they were as close as it was possible for two people to be. In a moment she felt him between her legs, the hardness of him, and she snaked her legs around his back and reached down to guide him into her, gasping as she found him and felt his answering gasp. And then he was deep inside her, and her gasp turned to a cry. She didn't recognize her own voice.

He stayed silent, looking at her, moving rhythmically inside her, and she knew he loved making her cry out with pleasure at the feel of him, loved making her lose control, and she decided there were worse things in life than letting a man take over and rule the world for a few minutes. And as the Portuguese singer raised her voice in a crescendo of passion, Sailor rose with her and then, at the high note, let go. Let the world come crashing down beautifully around her, let him take her for his own pleasure, his own crescendo, his own loss of control.

Their arms were still wrapped around one another and stayed that way for a long time, as if they were alone in the world and did not dare to let each other go.

Some time later, Declan didn't know how much later, a phone rang somewhere on the floor next to the bed. Sailor's phone, not his. He reached for it and held it to her ear as she smiled up at him.

He watched her smile fade, listening to the urgent words that he could hear, too.

"Sailor, it's Rhiannon. Where are you? The police are looking for you. Your car was at the House of Illusion, and someone set off a bomb in it. And, Sailor, there was a man inside."

The crime scene was chaos, and Sailor couldn't get closer than a half block away, even with Brodie there, alongside Rhiannon.

"They won't let you near, Sailor," Brodie said. His tall, commanding presence would have been reassuring, were it not for his grave expression. "Bomb squad's in there. When the detectives need to question you, they'll come get you."

"But I need to see him," Sailor said. "Or at least try to help—"

"Sweetie, you're blaming yourself, I know you are," Rhiannon said. "And it's not your fault."

Sailor said nothing. Standing outside the crime scene with her were cops and civilians of all kinds, even at four in the morning, and a fair number of House of Illusion staff, customers and magicians. She was engulfed with guilt and grief, and couldn't do anything but stare in the direction of the mess that had once been employee parking, that had once been her Jeep.

Had once been Julio.

He had a mother, she knew. And probably siblings. A girlfriend. But most of all a mother. When would they show up here, his family members? Would she witness their cries? She could hear them in her imagination, and she couldn't bear it. She'd hardly spoken as Declan had driven her here. He'd understood and dropped her off as soon as she saw Rhiannon waving at her from the street, then gone to hunt for a place to park.

He joined them now and put an arm around Sailor, pulling her close. There were no sexual overtones in it, but it was territorial, and she saw Rhiannon take note of it.

"Sailor!" A woman called. It was Lauren, her fellow waitress. "Did you hear? God, isn't it awful? I can't believe he's dead." She came running over and hugged Sailor in the strange way of people who aren't on hugging terms until tragedy hits.

"Is his family here?" Sailor asked. "Do they know about it?"

"I don't know. I heard about it from Tafiq."

Eventually a detective escorted her to a squad car to interview her. She threw a glance over her shoulder at Rhiannon, Brodie and Declan. They were all, she knew, worried about what she might give away, emotional as she was. But emotional didn't equal stupid.

She studied the detective, using her powers of perception to see if he was were or shifter, but he had none of the telltale signs. Vampires and Elven were so obvious, she didn't even have to wonder. He wasn't a Keeper, either. When she gave her name, he merely asked her to spell it. A Keeper would recognize "Gryffald" the way the residents of Hyannis Port knew the Kennedys, and he would have indicated in some way that he was a colleague.

But he was merely mortal.

His name was Grant Mulligan, and she played it straight with him or as straight as she could, given that she was withholding information like crazy. No, she had no idea why anyone would plant a bomb in her car. No, she had no enemies. She'd hardly been back in town long enough to make any. She couldn't imagine anyone wanting to harm Julio, either. Everyone had loved Julio.

Ironically, the most difficult thing to explain to Mulligan was that she'd given Julio her car keys simply out of friendship. This, she could see, he found suspicious. He was also staring at her eyes more than she thought necessary, which meant that they were changing color again. He was probably thinking "drugs," so she told him that she had a rare optical condition, which he could verify with her physician, Kimberly Krabill, who was probably working the graveyard shift at Cedars-Sinai.

After taking her contact information and advising her not to leave town, he gave her his card and a copy of his preliminary report for her insurance company. "The bomb squad will keep your car, what's left of it," he said, "but you can get started on your claim." With that mundane advice, he let her go.

By now the sun was rising. Brodie had gone off to inform the detectives working the Scarlet Pathogen murders that this was a new development in their case, and not some random car bomb. Rhiannon explained that while sitting on the curb with Declan and wearing his jacket, obviously freezing. Sailor herself was immune to the cold, her physical sensations subordinate to her emotional distress.

"How did it go?" Rhiannon asked, and Sailor told them she'd gotten through it well enough, mentioning Mulligan's curiosity as to why she'd given Julio her car keys.

"Yes, why did you?" Declan asked.

Sailor felt a spasm, a kind of retroactive horror at what she'd done, the part she'd played in Julio's fate. But there was no question of covering up with these two as she had with the cops. She plunged ahead, telling them about the *siúlacht* that Julio had given her in the parking lot.

"You took a pill tonight?" Declan asked, frowning.

"*Siúlacht,* yes," Sailor said, "Look, I teleported today more than I've done in the last year, I was truly worn out, and—"

"But you didn't mention to me that you'd taken something," Declan said. "Why?"

"Because I knew you'd disapprove and—"

Rhiannon, looking from one to the other, said, "But *siúlacht,* surely it's—"

"As legal as aspirin," Sailor said. "And as innocuous."

"Not if you've got any Elven in you," Declan said. "Then it's powerful. Enough to repress the symptoms of the pathogen."

"You make it sound like I do drugs, Declan," Sailor said. "I don't. Alessande Salisbrooke gave it to me, Kimberly Krabill said it was a good choice, and—"

"The point is, you didn't tell me."

"I'm telling you now. I gave Julio my car keys because he's my friend. Was my friend," she amended, and felt an intense pain behind her eyes. "I thought I was helping him out. I didn't know."

Declan looked at her steadily for another long moment, then turned to Rhiannon. "Can you take her home?"

"Of course."

"And activate your security system?"

"It doesn't work," Rhiannon said. "We didn't pay the bill."

"It works now," he said. "Your bill is paid."

"*You* paid the bill?" Sailor asked.

"We'll repay you, Declan," Rhiannon said. "And don't worry about Sailor. Barrie and I are there, and Brodie will be back, too, once he's off work tonight. We have weapons, and we're all well-trained in their use. We'll keep her safe."

He nodded. "Okay. She shouldn't go running around tomorrow, either."

"Stop!" Sailor said. "'She,' as you put it, can take care of herself and—"

"You're doing a hell of a job," Declan snapped. A spark had ignited between the two of them and it had nothing to do with the fire they'd felt an hour earlier. "That car bomb was meant for you. Those body parts scattered around that lot? That was supposed to be *you*, Sailor."

Rhiannon held up a hand. "If I may just say something here?"

"Sorry, no." Sailor, to her horror, found she was about to cry. It was so unusual that the prospect further upset her. "What would you want me to do about it, Declan? Don't you think I wouldn't undo it all if I could?"

"I want you to take this seriously."

"I'm completely serious," Sailor said. "I couldn't be more serious. Do I seem casual?"

Mulligan approached and Sailor stopped. Mulligan looked at the three of them and said to her, "The bomb technicians found a cell phone they believe came from your Jeep. What's left of Julio's was in his pocket. Yours?"

"No, I've got mine."

"Any idea whose?"

"No idea at all," Sailor said. "Could it belong to the person who planted the bomb?"

"Could be," Mulligan said. "I'm a little concerned about your safety. We should talk about protective custody."

"No," Sailor said.

"She's got family," Rhiannon said. "We'll be looking out for her."

"You change your mind, call me," Mulligan said, and took off.

Declan held out his hand for the police report. "May I?" he said. He'd calmed down, Sailor thought, but he still wasn't looking anything like the man who'd made love to her that night.

He read the report and said, "Rhiannon, if you see Brodie before I do, tell him not to worry about the cell phone. It's mine."

"Yours?" Sailor asked. "No, it's not. You've got yours."

"I have several. I put one in your Jeep this afternoon."

"Why?"

"Easiest way to track you."

She gasped. "You put a tracking device in my Jeep?" She felt herself growing hot with anger. "Why the hell would you do that?"

He turned to her. "Isn't it obvious? I can't trust you to take care of yourself."

She drew herself up to her full height. "I'm a Keeper,

Declan, like you are. I'm not a kid. I thought you knew that."
She walked away, throwing over her shoulder, "Rhiannon,
I'll meet you at your car."

"I'm coming with you," Rhiannon called back.

To reach Hollywood Boulevard, where Rhiannon's Volvo
was parked, they had to walk down the long drive, passing a
handful of House of Illusion staffers gathered on the drawbridge. Those on the closing shift who hadn't left the prem-
ises prior to the explosion were now stuck there until their
cars were released when investigators were done. Some
people were crying. Others greeted Sailor, but she was too
distressed to stop and chat. When someone touched her
arm, she jumped.

"Sorry to frighten you." It was Dennis, the bartender.
"You okay?"

"No, not even close. This is a nightmare."

"Is it true? It was your car that blew up."

She nodded.

"Are you guys parked on Hollywood?" he asked. "Come
on. I'll walk with you."

She was glad of his company. She'd worked with Dennis for months and never had a conversation outside of
work, but he'd known Julio, and that was all that mattered
right now.

"You have the sickness, don't you?" he said, as Rhiannon left them to talk and headed more quickly toward her
car. "The Scarlet Pathogen."

She looked at him. "You know?"

He nodded. "Your contact lenses tipped me off. Rumors
have been running rampant among my people."

Sailor often forgot Dennis was a gnome. Gnomes were
notoriously well-connected and incorrigible gossipmongers.

Bartending was a natural profession for them; tabloid journalism was another. She needed to watch herself with him.

"Yes, I have the pathogen," she said.

"And Julio needed the *siúlacht* tonight for you."

"Yes," she said. "But I'd appreciate you keeping that to yourself. I didn't mention it to the cops, for obvious reasons."

"I won't either." They walked past a few onlookers; there weren't many, due to the lateness of the hour, but she was surprised there were any at all. "I wanted to talk to you," Dennis continued, "because Julio came to me a few hours ago. He'd sold me a couple of *siúlacht* pills earlier today and wanted to buy one back. I figured it was for you."

"Why would you buy *siúlacht?* Does it have an effect on gnomes?"

Dennis shook his head. "I have an Elven girlfriend. She gets migraines. Hey, you're shivering." He took off his jacket and put it around her.

"No, I'm okay," she said, trying to understand what Dennis was telling her. "But what does this have to do—"

"Here's the thing. Julio asked me if by any chance I knew who made the *siúlacht*. Said it was important to him to find out. So I figured that if the *siúlacht* was for you, it was you who wanted the information."

"Right, I did. *Do.* What did you tell Julio?"

"I told him I had no idea who made the stuff, that he should ask his supplier."

"Maybe the supplier made them," Sailor said. She recalled what Dr. Krabill had said. "If it's hard to make *siúlacht* as a tea, it would take someone very good to make it into a pill."

"'Very good' doesn't cover it. Genius. And not just genius, but genius with access to the recipe, which is hidden away in some document as old as the Dead Sea Scrolls.

We're talking the stuff of myth and legend. My girlfriend says it has to be an Ancient."

"A *what?*"

"Ancient. Like the underground, they support themselves dealing in what we'd call the black market. Off the books. Herbs, magic, healing potions. Nothing the IRS would ever see."

"What underground? And what's an Ancient?"

"You don't know?" Dennis asked.

Sailor thought of Great-Aunt Olga's window ornament. The symbol of the Ancients, Aunt Olga had called it, but she had never explained the term and Sailor had never thought enough about it to be curious. "No. Tell me."

A police officer approached, and Dennis waited until he had passed. "There are those who don't subscribe to the laws of the Councils," he explained. "Some are outlaws. For some, it's a political philosophy, to remain independent of Keepers. That's the Underground. A fringe element is the Ancients, Elven who shun technology and progress—and mortals. They live in the canyons, for the most part. Everything between here and the ocean."

"My God, why am I just hearing this for the first time?" Sailor asked.

"Well, you're new on the job," Dennis said. "And they don't ordinarily cause trouble, because their whole mission is to be left alone. But the thing to know about the Ancients is this—they keep the old texts. They're the historians, the librarians. They have ancient manuscripts, brought across the sea from the Old Lands, and they keep a tight grip on them. Word on the street, or at least at the bar, is that there are mentions in those texts of the Scarlet Pathogen. That it's a disease that's made the rounds before."

She nodded. "I've heard rumors of that. How do I find these Ancients?"

"Well, that's the problem. Except for a precious few—the drug supplier, for instance—they don't want to be found. According to my girlfriend, it would be dangerous even to look."

"It's also dangerous to start a car," she said, shivering. "But, Dennis, you're not suggesting Julio knew any of this."

"No way. But his supplier might."

"And who is that?"

Dennis looked around and lowered his voice. "You never heard this from me, okay? Julio buys—bought, I mean—from Magdy, the guy in the kitchen."

"Who?" Sailor asked. "Oh, wait. The werewolf dishwasher?"

Dennis nodded. "Magdy didn't work tonight. I'm guessing Julio called him at home, couldn't reach him, whatever. So he came to me. But now I'm coming to you."

"Why?"

"Because someone's killing Elven women, and that needs to stop. And now someone just blew up your car hoping to kill you and got Julio instead. All this secrecy, all these little separate factions among the Others, everyone holed up, nobody talking to anybody—that's just adding to the problem."

"Okay. So I have to go deep into the woods," Sailor said, "and track these people down, then get them to talk to me."

Dennis nodded. "Just don't go alone and don't go unarmed. You have no idea what lives in your canyons."

An hour later Sailor was home, with her cousins sleeping in the bedrooms down the hall, unwilling to leave her alone in the house. She put on her pajamas, called Jonquil, who was euphoric to be allowed up on the bed, and crawled under the covers. Soon Jonquil was snoring, but Sailor lay in the dark, desolate. Her body retained the memory of

Declan, the feel of him on her, in her. His smell, his sounds, all hers now. It had been the best night of her life, and then it had become the worst, every beautiful thing overridden by the sounds of crying, the smell of smoke.

And apart from the horror of Julio's death was another kind of shock, much smaller, but plaguing her nevertheless. That Declan had tracked her. Without her knowledge. It made her feel like an animal. It touched something primal in her she knew was part of her Elven nature: the terror of being trapped, watched, spied upon. This man to whom she had given herself without reservation, what else was he keeping from her?

She realized she shouldn't have trusted him nearly as much as she had. For all the reasons Barrie had given, she should not have let down her guard with him, shouldn't have let herself dream.

Because now she felt utterly bereft.

She got out of bed and opened the door to her room, quietly, so as not to wake her cousins. "Merlin," she said softly. "Merlin, are you around?"

He was in front of her almost immediately. "Yes?"

"Come in, please," she whispered, and invited him into her bedroom. He stood in his polite and formal way until she was back under her covers, then seated himself on an old mahogany armchair.

"You've had a difficult night," he said.

"The worst possible," she said. "Merlin, what should I do?"

"About your young friend who crossed over tonight? Nothing, child. His passing was quick and painless. He has made peace with it, and you must do so, too."

She shook her head. "I can't."

"You will. Give it time."

"And what about the four Elven women?"

"Ah," he said. "They suffered a different sort of death. Much more personal, face-to-face with their killer. Those women are urging you on, wanting to help, but they are unskilled in communication. They're still traumatized, which is not uncommon in the case of violent death, especially murder. Also, where there is illness involved, there can be confusion and disorientation. They haven't, well, *settled* yet. It's particularly hard on Elven, who tend to live much longer lives. There is something so unfinished about the young ones who die. One thing seems clear. If I understand them correctly, the words 'location, location, location' are shared by all four of the dead women. It is what they had in common."

"But they *didn't* have it in common," Sailor said. "They were killed in different places. Except maybe in Charlotte's case, because we don't know where she was killed."

"Nevertheless, that is the connecting thread. They repeat it like a chorus. And they chatter at me, they send me…orders. 'Look for the cap,' 'Return the call.' One of them screams, 'Listen to the messages!' which is presumably what you're attempting to do. Another insists, 'Don't go near the water!' which I don't expect you ever to do."

Sailor sat in bed, hugging her knees to her chest. "But this is crazy," she said. "None of that means anything to me. Is the Spirit world always so chaotic?"

"Not always, no. But consider with whom we are dealing—three actresses and an agent. While I love theater as much as anyone and more than most, thespians can be a bit high-maintenance and very dramatic. I should let you sleep, dear."

"Yes, but would you—would you mind staying?" she asked. "Until I doze off?"

"Not at all," he said kindly.

She thought she was too upset to sleep, but her body decided otherwise, and as the moon was setting she began to dream of cars on fire, of eyes glowing red and crows flying outside her window.

Chapter 12

The next day began with a ritual the cousins called the Morning Report. Over coffee and whatever passed for breakfast—the three of them were idiosyncratic in their eating styles—they discussed Keeper business, which usually devolved into girl talk. Today, though, their mood was uniformly somber.

"I realize it's a cliché," Barrie said, picking at a cheesecake Rhiannon had brought home from work the night before, "but you really can't blame yourself, Sailor. You didn't kill your friend, and you're not responsible for the actions of some madman simply because you were his target."

Rhiannon, flipping an egg in a skillet, shuddered. "I can't even imagine what his family is going through. Brodie hasn't been home yet. He spent the night with the investigative team. What an unholy mess."

Sailor told them what Dennis had told her. "Have you

ever heard of this Underground movement?" she asked, peeling an orange.

"Oh, yes," Rhiannon said. "The Underground's a coalition of the various species. We're talking very small numbers. Dad said the Councils take no official position, as long as they stay off the radar, which is usually the case. As for the Ancients, I remember Great-Aunt Olga mentioning them, but I thought it was something she made up to scare us with. Keep us in line."

Barrie shook her head. "No. They're real. Or at least they were in the sixties, according to my research. They kept to themselves, lived off the grid and avoided mortals. It could be they've died out since then."

"No, Dennis says they're alive and I believe him," Sailor said. "I think they know more about the Scarlet Pathogen than anyone else does, except maybe the killer himself."

"I don't suppose," Barrie said, "that you'd consider staying home and letting Rhiannon and me use our resources to find these Ancients for you?"

"You know I can't." Sailor held up a hand as Rhiannon prepared to object. "I have so many leads to follow, so many pieces of this puzzle to figure out, and mostly I feel so awful about Julio. So, no. Staying home would be hell. If you're willing to hit me over the head with a hammer, go for it. Otherwise, I have to be what I should have been for months now—a Keeper."

"That is just crazy," Rhiannon said. "At the very least, one of us has to be with you at all times."

"I have to be in Pasadena at two," Barrie said, "for a shifter Council meeting. This morning I'm interviewing Scott Donner, who Kelly Ellory worked under at GAA. It's a story for the paper. I can try to change the appointment."

"No," Sailor said. "You blow off Scott Donner, he'll never reschedule. And you may learn something important. Anyway, what I'm doing this morning is a one-woman operation."

Rhiannon reached over to give her arm a shake. "Sailor, someone is trying to kill you."

"It's harder to hit a moving target," Sailor said.

"Look," Rhiannon said sternly, "I have a Keeper meeting of my own this afternoon, an emergency meeting, and I think it's vital that we all attend our Councils—"

"It is," Sailor said.

"But if one of us can't be with you, you *have* to be with Declan. Or Brodie."

Barrie shook her head. "Declan will be in Pasadena with me. At the shifter Council. He won't miss that."

"He will if he thinks Sailor's off roaming the city on her own."

"Then don't tell him," Sailor said, gathering up her purse and cell phone. "And Brodie's got plenty to do without babysitting me. I have about three hundred friends in this town, I'm sure I can—"

"Reggie Maxx," Rhiannon said. "He called here last night, returning your call."

"Perfect. There you go. We talked about pooling our resources, so we may as well do it in person. The only question is, what do I do for a car?"

"The only question," Rhiannon retorted, "is what we tell Declan when he asks where you are and how you're doing."

"You tell him," Sailor said, "that I will be in touch once I have something new to report."

"No," Barrie said, handing over a set of keys. "We tell him that Sailor's driving my car while I drive the Caddy. And then he'll tell us how to put a tracking device on a Peugeot."

Barrie's Peugeot was smaller than the Jeep but still big enough for Jonquil to ride shotgun. Given his temperament, he would be useless in a fight, but he looked tough, and he was good company. And Sailor wasn't leaving him alone in the house. If a killer could find out what she drove and where she worked, he would have no trouble finding where she lived—but he wouldn't find her dog there, not if she could help it. Barrie, meanwhile, was driving her own father's beloved antique Cadillac, a car Sailor wouldn't touch. The Peugeot was Uncle Owen's car, too, but the Caddy was more like a member of the family than a vehicle, and Sailor would rather face a serial killer than Uncle Owen should she damage it.

She headed to Echo Park. Back in the silent era, it had been the center of the film industry, but she saw no signs of its former glory on the street where Magdy lived. She'd found the address through Lauren, her fellow waitress, who'd dated the sous chef who'd hired Magdy. Because of the tragedy, people were going out of their way to help one another. She hoped that this trend would continue when she talked to Magdy, but she doubted it would extend to his neighbors in the ratty apartment complex she pulled up to. At least a large dog in the car would be a disincentive for anyone looking to steal the Peugeot's tires.

It was reassuring, in a place like this, to have a weapon, and she had brought along Alessande's dagger. She was growing fond of the knife and suspected it was charmed. The Elven tended to do that, layering spells and incantations into their tools and weapons. She'd added a tactical vest to black jeans and a white T-shirt so that her dagger was more accessible than it had been in the ankle sheath. So far the attacks on her had been stealthy, not face-to-face, but that could change. Later she would go home and dress in something more feminine for Kelly Ellory's memorial service. But for now, the tougher she looked, the better.

The intercom for Magdy's apartment seemed to be broken, so she pressed random buttons until someone buzzed her in. She walked down a hallway, following signs out a door to a courtyard, into another building and up a floor to a steel door. She knocked.

A little boy wearing shorts and nothing else answered. A littler boy, in a T-shirt and diaper, came up behind the first one to stare at her. Then Magdy appeared. Sailor almost didn't recognize him, as she was used to seeing him in kitchen whites, not a muscle shirt. His hair was matted and tangled, and he needed a shave and some sleep, but it was him. He was shorter than she was, but far stronger. He met her gaze with an unspoken *What do you want?* and she simply removed her sunglasses and looked at him, letting the scarlet of her irises register on him. "I need your help," she said. He spoke sharply in another language to the boys and they ran back into the apartment. Magdy, too, disappeared, but only briefly. Then he came out and closed the door behind him. Wordlessly, he walked down the concrete stairs. Sailor followed.

In the courtyard, they sat on a stone bench facing patchy grass decorated with a used intravenous needle, a deflated soccer ball and a tiny broken flip-flop. Magdy pulled a cigarette from his pocket and lit it. "So?" he said, exhaling and looking at her.

"I need to know where you get your *siúlacht* pills."

"Why would I tell you?" He had a rough vocal quality common among were. The dishwashers were their own subculture in the bowels of the kitchen, so she'd never spoken to him, but now she could see that he was as physically powerful as he was socially insignificant.

"Because I'm trying to find a killer."

He shrugged. *What's it got to do with me?* his eyes said.

"Julio was murdered last night. Did you know that?"

Nothing to do with me, Keeper.

She opened her purse and counted out five twenties. "I can pay you. Not much, but it's all the cash I have."

"A hundred dollars." He gave a short, derisive laugh. "It's not much, period, to a dead man."

"Are you saying someone would kill you if you gave me a name?"

"It's what I'd do."

"Then I have a problem." She had more than one problem, she realized, because her temperature was rising, and Magdy was shimmering in the sunlight, looking less dicey and even friendly. She let him see it, knowing her eyes were pulsing and red, and might accomplish what her own powers of persuasion couldn't. Especially as English was not Magdy's first language and she didn't know what was. Something she didn't speak anyway.

Magdy's large brown eyes peered into hers. "So this is it, the sickness?"

"Yes, in part. My body grows hot, I feel my blood flow faster."

A thought struck her. With a sudden intuitive surge, she understood exactly what had happened to the Elven women. The Scarlet Pathogen had entered their bloodstream and made their blood circulate far too quickly, producing in them not just the warm and fuzzy feelings she experienced, but something much stronger: a fever pitch of passion. The sensations that came over her intermittently were for them a deluge. If Magdy looked appealing to her in this moment, then for an Elven woman he would have looked utterly irresistible.

"I have to know what it is the Ancients know about my sickness," she said. "Can you just tell me, this source of the *siúlacht,* is he or she from the Underground?"

Above her, a crow called out.

Magdy looked at the sky. "She's Elven, but she won't talk to you."

An opening, Sailor thought. "Where does she live?"

He took a drag on his cigarette. "Canyon."

"Somewhere between four and seven hundred Elven live in the canyons, more if you count the multiracial," she crooned into his ear. "Which canyon?"

"Lost Hills."

Outside her district, Sailor thought. Reggie's territory. And vast. "Narrow it down."

"And what do I get?" he said, with a sidelong glance.

"What do you want?"

His face grew more wolfen. He grinned. It was an answer of sorts.

Sailor's temperature was dropping, and he no longer looked friendly. She thought of the knife she carried and told herself to stay calm. "I'm just asking for a name. No one will ever know it was you who gave it to me."

"The woman is Rath."

"I need a name."

"And what do I get?" he repeated, the words now a snarl. He could change, she realized. Right here, in broad daylight.

And then, in one swift movement, he moved in and pinned her arms against her sides, then started to suck on her neck. *Shit,* she thought. That was going to leave a mark. She couldn't reach the dagger because he was holding her too tightly. This was twice in two days she'd let a guy in too close. The dagger could piss him off anyway, and that could bring on the transformation. And even armed she was no match for a full-on werewolf.

He kept nuzzling, and she looked around, belatedly thinking, *situational awareness.* She could scream, but that didn't mean help would come. This looked like a courtyard where screaming women were routinely mauled by men.

"Magdy," she said, summoning up all her bravado, "are you crazy enough to kill me? Because you mess with me, you better kill me, or I will make your life hell. Maybe you'll lose your job, maybe your visa, but you *will* lose your balls one night while you're sleeping, because I know where you live and I'm good with a knife. You wouldn't mess with an Elven woman, and I'm an Elven *Keeper*. Think about it."

He stopped nuzzling and looked at her appraisingly, and she put all the force of her anger into her stare, knowing her scarlet eyes intensified the effect. It was something a werewolf respected, sheer stupid courage. Sometimes.

His nostrils flared, but his grip relaxed, and relief coursed through her. She pulled away from him with as much grace as she could muster and stood, moving out of reach.

"You better get out of here, Keeper."

She wanted to bolt. She was shaking. But she made herself stand her ground and open her purse. She pulled out the twenties for a second time and held them out.

He was silent. Then he stood and looked at her, fixing his eyes on her in a way that demanded her attention. She saw what he was doing, and she took a deep breath and from his mind to hers came the answer she sought. It was as though he spoke it aloud, though he never opened his mouth.

Catrienne Dumarais.

He plucked the money from her fingers and sauntered toward the building with an insolent swagger. When he reached the doorway, she called to him, "Can you spell that?"

But Magdy entered the building without looking back.

Reggie Maxx answered his phone on the second ring. He'd already heard about her car and Julio's death. "What can I do to help?" he asked.

"I thought maybe you could give me a tour of some real estate I want to check out in Lost Hills."

"You got it," he said. "And I've been doing some research of my own. Where should we meet? I'll be in Beverly Hills in an hour to get some documents signed. That should take another hour, hour and a half. Then I can be anywhere."

"Three hours, then," Sailor said. "Let's meet at the Mystic Café."

Brodie McKay answered *his* cell on the first ring, sounding both grim and tired. Sailor was driving east, toward Crescent Heights, with Jonquil in the passenger seat, his long ears flying behind him in the wind from the open windows.

"I'm fine, Brodie," she said in response to his questions. "Yes, I'm alone, but it's broad daylight and I have my briefcase with me." In other words, *I have a weapon.* At least, she thought that was what it meant. Those Keepers addicted to telecommunication talked on their cells in code. Unfortunately, the codes changed weekly and she rarely remembered to study them, something that would have to change. "Listen, I'm driving and there's a deli up ahead. I know you're worn out, but could you…meet me there?"

"Give me a street address."

Less than a minute later she pulled into a parking space to see an extra-large Elven already coming out of the sandwich shop with an extra-large drink in hand. Brodie gave her a hug and indicated an outdoor table.

"Sorry to make you teleport," she said, "when you're already exhausted."

"Not a problem. I was close by. What is it you can't talk about on the phone?"

"The Ancients."

He frowned. "What about them?"

"I'm not asking you to go into the details of the investigation, but can you just tell me if you've interviewed any of them?"

He shook his head. "No reason to interview them."

"I've heard they have a bunch of really old documents that might reveal something about the Scarlet Pathogen."

He leaned forward, his voice low. "Sailor, we have our hands full pursuing every credible lead we get. Is it possible the Ancients know something? Sure. Anything's possible. It's a question of priorities. We have a limited number of Others on the force, and I can hardly send a mortal into the woods looking for a tribe of antisocial fundamentalists who may or may not have an old book somewhere on a shelf with some reference to a plague reminiscent of this pathogen."

His tone was kind, but she could see the stress he was under, signs of the all-nighter he'd just pulled. "Okay, Brodie, I get it," she said. "I know you know what you're doing, and that you're doing everything you can. Can you just tell me, have you heard of a woman named Catrienne Dumarais?"

He stopped, his cup halfway to his mouth. Then he knocked back at least ten ounces of ice water and set it down. "I've met her once," he said quietly. "And it was a long time ago. I don't know if she's still alive. If she is, and still living where she lived then, there's no way in hell you could find her."

"Lost Hills, though, right?"

He shook his head. "It's been twenty years at least. Somewhere in the Valley, that's all I remember. But you can't go wandering around looking for her. I mean it. Hey—" he glanced at the Peugeot "—why *are* you alone? And Jonquil doesn't count."

"I'm heading to the Mystic Café," she said, "to meet Reggie Maxx."

"Okay. I know Reggie. Once you're with him, stay with him until one of your cousins gets back. Promise me."

"Promise." It was an easy promise to make. What Brodie didn't need to know was that en route to the Mystic Café, she was going to make a stop. One that wouldn't take more than an hour or two.

The problem was, no drive-on pass awaited Sailor at Metropole Studios.

"No," the guard said. "Nothing for Gryffald, nothing from GAA, nothing from Darius Simonides. And sorry, but you're holding up the line. You'll have to make a U-turn. You can't come onto the lot."

She snarled under her breath. A drive-on pass was the gold standard, allowing a visitor a parking space inside the studio lot. For lesser mortals, including auditioning actors as low in the food chain as she was, there were walk-ons. With those, a visitor had to find her own parking and enter the lot on foot. Even then there was a guard gate to get past, which meant being on a confirmed appointment list and providing photo ID.

And now Darius wasn't returning her calls, and at this point his assistants were as sick of hearing from her as she was of talking to them. She could hear the trained politeness in Joshua's voice reaching its outer limits. No, Mr. Simonides hadn't left instructions; no, Joshua had not arranged a pass of any sort for her at Metropole; yes, it was possible Mr. Simonides had forgotten his promise. Joshua couldn't really say.

Sailor found a parking place two blocks from Metropole's south entrance gate. In the shade. After a twenty-minute walk Jonquil was happy to return to the Peugeot and work some more on his beauty sleep. The sun was still hidden by clouds and thus not beating down on the car, so

Sailor opened the sunroof, cracked the windows halfway to let air in and kissed him goodbye. "I'll be back soon," she promised him. On impulse, she left Alessande's dagger in the car, too. She couldn't say why, only that her sixth sense told her to, and when it was that strong, she listened.

As she walked toward Metropole, her thoughts turned to Declan. All morning she'd wondered how to avoid his calls, and now she wondered why he hadn't called. It was starting to seem silly how angry she'd been at him....

Why hadn't he called?

Surely he wanted to. You couldn't fake what they'd done in bed, or resist thinking about it afterward and reliving it over and over. Of course Julio's death had changed everything, but even so, Declan had to be thinking about her. Because she sure as hell couldn't stop thinking about him. Lying with him in the most intimate conceivable way had been like a mating ritual. She and Declan were very different people. He was older and, by all social and economic standards, more powerful, but on a fundamental level they were equals. And having mated with him, there was no going back. That hour in his bed had changed her, changed her dreams. She had sometimes wondered if she was a woman whose primary passion was her art, a woman for whom romance would always be a distant second, one who would be happy with a succession of lovers kept in the background of her life. She now knew the answer: no.

Which was a problem.

Declan had felt it, too, the intensity of their coupling— she knew that. But maybe for him it happened all the time. He was notoriously, famously single, always linked to women, never staying with them, never living with them. Never marrying them. His spying on her wasn't an expression of love but simple intelligence gathering, along with some control issues. She wasn't angry about it, as she'd been last night, but she wasn't fooling herself, either. It showed a lack of trust and a lack of honesty, both of which troubled her.

But why hadn't he called?

She reached Guard Gate #3, the Melrose entrance. She could try talking her way in, but she knew she would be turned down, that any cover story would prompt corroborating phone calls, and the whole thing would end badly.

She looked at the sky, the clouds racing by, a hawk circling high above, and she pictured herself in a bungalow inside Metropole Studios, one of the old flat one-story buildings that had been built in the 1940s. She knew exactly how they looked from auditions, five in the past six months, and also from a film job she'd gotten once as a teenager. Only a day's work, but she'd memorized the whole place, the tiny streets, the big soundstages. Everything.

For teleporting, that was what mattered: the ability to picture the destination.

She got as close as possible to the wall around the studio, minimizing the distance she would have to travel to conserve her energy. She closed her eyes, loosened her shoulders, relaxed the tension in her face, took five deep breaths and let herself dissolve as she pictured just where she wanted to be.

And then she was there.

Chapter 13

Metropole was bustling with activity. Sailor knew, from having checked the trades on line that morning, that two features were currently shooting there, along with another three TV shows.

Two hefty guys moved a wall-sized flat on wheels across a cobblestone street, and she asked them if they knew where *Knock My Socks Off* was shooting. One said, "Never heard of it," which was probably a lie, but whatever. A block later she asked a Goth-type girl she took for an actress or maybe a designer, who said, "Follow me. I'm headed that way." The Goth girl turned out to be in the accounting department. Sailor considered asking her about Charlotte Messenger, but the chance of the film star being friends with someone in accounting were so remote as to be nonexistent. The Goth pointed to a building marked 51 and then peeled off to a bungalow.

"And…action!"

Sailor heard the words but couldn't see their source because they were amplified. She stopped so as not to inadvertently walk into a shot.

A few minutes later she heard "And...cut" and resumed walking, circling Building 51 to find the film crew in an alley they'd created behind the huge soundstage.

She'd done her research, so she knew what Giancarlo Ferro looked like. And she'd grown up around movie sets, so she understood the working/not working phenomenon. A movie crew was a huge group, everyone doing different jobs. Someone's job was to maximize the number of people working at the same time, so that while a shot was being set up by the camera department, actors were in Makeup and Hair, and sets were being constructed for an upcoming scene. Still, at any point there were people who weren't working. And when someone wasn't working, they were killing time, which meant they welcomed diversions.

Giancarlo Ferro wasn't working; he was waiting. It was now or never.

"Excuse me, Mr. Ferro...Giancarlo," Sailor said, walking right up to him. "My name is Sailor Gryffald. Can I talk to you for just a minute? It's about Charlotte Messenger."

It was a risky approach, and the minute the words were out of her mouth she realized how crazy they sounded, how unprepared for this she was. Stupid, stupid.

Giancarlo's face clouded over. "Who are you? What are you doing on my set?"

"I'm not a journalist or anything."

"What are you, then?"

"I'm—" She could hardly tell him she was a Keeper; Giancarlo was entirely mortal and unaware he'd been dating an Elven. Saying she was an actress was also not an option. Unemployed actors were Hollywood's Untouchables.

"I have information you might be interested in." She took off her sunglasses.

He looked at her eyes and blanched. "What's wrong with you? What are you, some kind of freak?"

"I have a mild version of the illness that killed Charlotte."

"Get away from me." He backed away from her, looking around wildly. "Get her away from me! I can't get sick! I have a film to finish!"

Immediately, three or four people converged on Sailor, crew people with clipboards and headsets, and demonstrating varying degrees of belligerence, either real or for the benefit of their boss. She put up her hands. "All right, all right. I'm not contagious, and I'm not here to make him sick or upset him, I just want to—"

"What's your name? How did you get on the lot?" a man asked, his voice shrill, and another one yelled, "Security! What the hell kind of preschool operation are you people running here?"

"I'm here because of what killed Charlotte Messenger— Okay, look, never mind, I'm leaving right now," she said, backing up when the heftiest man there moved forward threateningly. "I don't want to cause problems."

But before she could break free of the crowd, a studio security guard had her firmly by the arm and was pulling her away from the alley.

"I'm going, I'm going," she told him, working to hold on to her temper. "There's no need to manhandle me. Let go, okay?"

Instead, his grip tightened, and he jerked her hard, making her trip and fall against him. That angered him, and he jerked her again.

But if he was angry, Sailor was livid. "Get your hands off me!" she yelled. "Let go of me!"

Instead of acquiescing, he jerked her a third time, at which point she turned and hit him with a right hook.

He let go.

She was as shocked as he was that she'd actually hit him, especially with a hook, which wasn't her best shot. Clearly those boxing classes had paid off. The thing she was supposed to do now, she knew from her boxing coach, was to take off running, and she did, but three guards were approaching from different directions, and even with great hamstrings, quadriceps and calves, she had no chance against them.

From somewhere she heard a siren, and she had a bad feeling it was coming for her.

The jail at the LAPD's Hollywood Division wasn't the worst place in the world, Sailor told herself. It wasn't like Men's Central, where prisoners were known to die before being charged with anything. And the list of celebrities who had been brought here was illustrious.

Or so she told herself. But what she felt was that she might start screaming any second.

She had just enough Elven in her to abhor being locked up. Elven were creatures of earth and could not be separated from it for more than a day without growing weak. Three to four days and they died. That was why they hadn't come to America from their native British Isles until the arrival of transatlantic flight in the 1920s. They were incapable of teleporting over such a vast body of water as the Atlantic, and ships took too long to cross the ocean. In the late 1800s, if the tales were true, there were Elven who tried to sail across the sea, only to experience a yearning for earth so desperate that they threw themselves overboard to reach the ocean floor. Sailor had found those rumors too fantastical because the Elven terror of water was truly pathological. But she was beginning to see how panic could override sanity.

The cops weren't brutal, not like the Metropole security guards. But neither were they interested in Sailor's protestations that she was at heart nonviolent and breaking the guard's nose had been mostly accidental, possibly because people had watched her throw a nice right hook when she had no legitimate business on the set, and the gate guard had no record of her coming through, which suggested trespassing.

So here she sat in a cell. She'd used her one phone call to try Rhiannon, but she'd gotten voice mail. At least the cops had let her try again. She didn't call Barrie, who would still be doing her GAA interview and didn't need to be bothered by a cousin in the slammer. Plus, if news of her behavior reached Darius's ears—which it was pretty much bound to eventually—it would be a disaster. Nor would she call Brodie. He wasn't quite family, not yet, and she'd blithely disregarded his advice, which would probably irritate him. Instead she called Reggie Maxx, who, God bless him, answered his phone.

"I'm running a bit late for our meeting," she told him. "And I have a small favor to ask."

Reggie, God bless him again, said he would spring her ASAP. She congratulated herself on having found the one person in her life willing to help who wouldn't be either hopping mad at or deeply disappointed in her. She was also grateful that she'd persuaded a kindhearted officer to send someone to rescue Jonquil from the Peugeot.

"What you lookin' at, bitch?"

The voice came from the cell next to her. A wall separated the cells, so Sailor couldn't see the speaker. As she was wondering if the question had been rhetorical, it came again. "Bitch! I'm asking you a question! Who you lookin' at?"

The woman was clearly having a bad day, and Sailor didn't think this attempt at conversation would improve things. The woman apparently felt otherwise. "I'm askin' you for the last time, bitch!" she yelled. "What the bitchin' hell you lookin' at?"

Sailor sighed. "If you're talking to me," she called, "what I'm looking at is a phlegm-colored concrete wall with a steel toilet attached to it. What I'm not looking at is you, which you'd know if you were looking at me, which you aren't, unless you can see through walls."

This did not stop the woman from responding, but Sailor put her hands over her ears so it turned into a drone of words, every fourth one being "bitch." She wanted to teleport in the worst way. Any Elven who found herself jailed faced the primal urge to simply relocate her physical body, and it was a Keeper's responsibility to bail her out before that happened. Sailor could recall her father getting calls in the middle of the night and running out with his checkbook. Not only did teleporting make the perp a fugitive from justice, but it also alarmed the cops to have people simply vanish from their jail cells. "Bad for business," her father would say, whenever a Keeper failed in his or her primary objective, which was to hide the very existence of the species. Yet it happened. At any given moment there were several Elven on the lam, and that made things stressful for the community at large.

"Bitch!" The scream penetrated despite Sailor's hands over her ears. "What you lookin' at? I'm not asking you again!"

"I would love to believe that," Sailor yelled back, "but you're not making it easy."

The problem with teleportation in her case, in addition to

being a bad idea for the usual reasons, was that she wasn't Elven. The least talented among the Elven could teleport fifty miles; many Keepers couldn't penetrate a few inches of drywall. She was a prodigy in this respect, but the most she could do was a few miles, and she had to be completely relaxed, which at the moment she was definitely not. For that matter, an Elven wouldn't be here, because they would have teleported away from Metropole the minute they sensed danger, an impossibility for Sailor, who'd been filled with too much adrenaline.

"Location, location, location," the woman in the cell yelled. "Shifters aren't the only shifty ones! Beware the winged ones! Check your messages!"

Sailor blinked. "What did you say?" she called, but now there was only silence.

Okay, she knew what this was about. She was being sent help from beyond. It was just as Merlin had said: spirits used anyone receptive to them as channels. They chose those with few defensive mechanisms: mediums, meditators, children, animals, anyone who was high or had mental problems.

"Did you hear me?" the woman called. "Listen to your message!"

"I *am* listening to the message," Sailor called back. "If only I could *understand* the message." This was what she found maddening about the spirit world: it was never straightforward, never "Here are this week's winning lotto numbers." No, it was all real-estate clichés and "beware the winged ones." And people wondered why ghosts got such a bad rap.

Okay, so what would happen next? What was the penalty for assaulting someone? How could she afford a lawyer? What on earth was the matter with her? These things never happened to Rhiannon or Barrie. They had adventures, they did good Keeper work, they were great people and they stayed out of jail. The only smart thing she'd done was leave her dagger in the car.

"Quit lookin' at me, bitch! Just quit it!"

"Listen up!" Sailor called. "I'm doing my best to make lemonade out of lemons over here, but I am just about done being chipper, so if you want to have a screaming contest, bring it on because I am the queen of catharsis. I went to a top-tier acting school, I played Medea—who murdered her children and fed them to her husband for dinner—I can scream for eight shows a week without even straining my voice, and if—"

The door opened. Sailor stopped screaming and jumped up, praying it was Reggie coming to rescue her.

Instead, it was Declan Wainwright.

Declan nearly laughed, watching Sailor go from hopeful to shocked, apprehensive and finally sheepish, all in the course of thirty seconds.

She wisely kept quiet as the police went through the release procedure, probably gauging his mood. When she'd last seen him, he realized, he'd been bloody angry, but his fair-mindedness had long since reasserted itself. Sailor was who she was: impulsive, occasionally reckless, a rule breaker. It was part of her charm. But he was hypervigilant on the subject of drugs; his mother, whom he had loved with the wholehearted devotion of a ten-year-old, had died of an overdose. She hadn't meant to, but she was dead nevertheless, leaving him with the knowledge that he must never fall in love with a woman with a drug problem.

But Sailor didn't have a drug problem. He knew it as soon as he'd calmed down. She had a pathogen problem. And a crisis requiring her to burn the candle at both ends.

Siúlacht was to the Elven what a triple espresso was to a mortal. Or a couple of triple espressos.

But she hadn't told him about it, and that had pissed him off.

Once outside the Hollywood station, she headed for a skinny stretch of grass and took off her shoes and socks, letting her feet sink into it. The sky was overcast and she looked up and breathed deeply. A squad car pulled up, and a policeman hopped out and opened the back door. Jonquil, his leash flying behind him, bounded over to them, knocking Sailor onto the grass in his enthusiasm. She thanked the cop and retrieved her keys, then hugged Jonquil. Finally she stood and for the first time looked at Declan.

"Thank you," she said.

"You're welcome. Come on, I'm parked the next block up."

She fell in beside him but kept a bit of distance. "How did you find me?" she asked.

"Reggie Maxx. He didn't have the cash to bail you out."

She threw him a sideways glance. "Why would Reggie call you?"

"He and I are doing some business together. He knows I'm a friend of yours, and knows I have money."

She went back to not quite looking at him. They headed toward Hollywood Boulevard with Jonquil now between them in the manner of a chaperone. "I'll pay you back," she said.

"Why? You plan on skipping bail?"

That got a smile out of her. But she was being uncharacteristically quiet.

"How bad was it for you, being locked up?" he asked.

"You mean the Elven aspect of it? Bad. But I don't suppose anyone loves jail."

"But you didn't teleport out. You must have wanted to. So that took discipline."

Sailor shrugged. "It would have been stupid. And getting arrested used up my quota of stupid for the day. For the week, in fact. Actually, getting my friend Julio killed—"

"Sailor." He touched her shoulder and could feel her resistance, but she let him stop her, facing him there on the sidewalk. Jonquil, looking up at them, sat.

"What?" she asked.

"We all have our time to die. Julio's was three o'clock this morning. Yes, you can let that bury you in guilt and grief. Or you can accept that it's part of life as a Keeper and move on. And maybe save someone else from dying."

"I *am* moving on."

"You're taking crazy risks. Breaking the nose of a security guard."

"That wasn't a risk. That was just me getting mad. He was physically restraining me." She looked pointedly at his hand on her arm.

He smiled and let go. They reached his car a minute later and with difficulty persuaded Jonquil to squeeze into a space not intended for a human, let alone a large dog. Sailor told him where she'd parked the Peugeot, and he pulled into midday traffic. "I talked to Brodie twenty minutes ago," he told her. "They lifted prints off your car that match prints found in Gina Santoro's trailer."

"That's not much of a surprise, is it?"

"Not to us," he said. "But now every Other in law enforcement knows about the car bomb and that it's connected to the celebrity deaths, which means every Other in the general population knows, too. There's a spate of emergency Council meetings coming up today. Everyone but your Council, presumably, because you met just yesterday. Rhiannon's already at hers, and I need to be at mine in half an hour, along with Barrie. We're going to be devising a contingency plan in case the Elven turn against us."

Sailor stared at him. "Is that likely to happen?"

"It could. The clues are pointing to a shifter. The first attack on you—"

"—could have been a vamp. It could easily have been a bat that clawed me."

"But the killer wasn't a vamp," Declan pointed out. "So shifter's a good theory. It would explain how one guy could get onto three closed movie sets, for one thing, and seduce four women."

Sailor shook her head. "Listen, I figured this out. He didn't have to seduce them, he only had to buy them a drink. And then he spiked it and let the Scarlet Pathogen do the rest, making him irresistible to them. I really believe that's what happened, that the effect was that intense. So in the case of Charlotte and Gina, he could have offered them a drink on the set at the end of the workday. Right? Gina was found dead in her trailer."

"Charlotte wasn't."

"No, but her Mercedes was left at the location. So maybe she had just enough champagne to get into his car with him after work. It wouldn't take a shifter to pull that off."

"Charlotte wouldn't be swilling champagne at work with a grip."

"No, but look, here's what I noticed when I was on the lot at Metropole. It's a closed environment. There's a social hierarchy, but it's a safe location. All the riffraff, the fans, the paparazzi, they're kept out by security—it was the same on *Technical Black*. Anyone on the set is there because they belong, they're part of the team. Charlotte's guard would have been down. Gina's, too. Charlotte might not drink with a grip, but she wouldn't think twice about accepting a glass of champagne from one. Or from a sound guy, or even a production assistant. Also, they'd have wrapped by then. There's a reason they call the last shot of the day the martini shot. It would have been the most natural thing in the world to have a glass of champagne as she's changing out of wardrobe. And when she finishes, there's the guy who gave it to her standing outside her trailer, saying, 'Come on, I know a place we can watch the sun set.' By then the effects of the pathogen are kicking in, hard, and she thinks, 'Yeah, why not?'"

She was right, he thought. He could picture Charlotte doing just that. "And with the other two victims, it would have been even easier."

Sailor nodded. "Much easier. If they met on the set and were standing around talking, they would have agreed to meet up with him at a bar later. Simple. Ariel's roommate told us as much. The only problem is, this theory opens up the field rather than eliminate anyone, so we're back to square one. What I should do is sit down with cast and crew lists and compare all three films—Ariel's included—and look for common denominators."

"All right. Meanwhile," Declan said, "our theory notwithstanding, the rumors are flying and shifters are the favorite suspects. At any point the Elven could take things into their own hands."

They'd reached the Peugeot, and he pulled into a loading zone and turned off the engine.

She got out of the car and, with his help, coaxed Jonquil to follow, her mood subdued. She would, he knew, understand the seriousness of the situation. Peacekeeping in the Otherworld was a priority among the Keepers, but they were far outnumbered by their constituents, many of whom distrusted the other species.

She looked up at the overcast sky, then at Declan. "So

we have a killer on the loose and the possibility of secondary violence. Which do we address first?"

"We have another issue to address," he said, moving to her. "The killer is targeting you."

"I haven't forgotten." She regarded him steadily, eyes green as glass, with only flecks of scarlet in the irises. She was so lovely. Even weary and tormented, she was as desirable to him as... His gaze traveled down her neck and stopped.

"Did I give you that last night?" he asked, touching the red spot in the corner between her neck and shoulder.

She pulled on the neckline of her T-shirt, as if to cover the spot. "No. A were gave me that. This morning."

It was like someone had whacked him with a baseball bat. "Are you trying to drive me bloody crazy?" he asked.

"Hey, it's not like I— It wasn't a *date*. It was a sticky situation, but I handled it."

"Who was he?"

"Don't." She shook her head, and he could see it in her eyes, the memory of something frightening. "Leave it. We have real problems to deal with. This isn't one of them."

Strong emotions welled up in him: protectiveness toward her, rage at her unknown assailant. "I should have left you in jail," he said. "At least you'd be safe there."

"I wouldn't have lasted. I would have teleported. Listen, Declan." She stopped and took his hands in hers. "I'm sorry about last night. That I didn't tell you about taking the *siúlacht*. I wanted to go on that film set after work. And even more, I wanted to be with you. To do exactly what we ended up doing, which we couldn't have done if I'd been dead asleep. So I don't regret taking it, but I'm sorry I didn't tell you. Okay?"

He thought of how she'd looked, naked, lying beneath him. He didn't regret it, either. "Okay," he said.

"And I was mad at *you,* too, for tracking me. Seriously mad. Only now, in the light of day, it doesn't seem so important. But I have to keep investigating, just like you. I won't go anywhere else alone. But I'm not sitting around waiting, either. You're going to have to live with that."

"When this is all over," he said, taking her car keys from her, "we'll talk about what we can and can't live with. For now, okay. Stick close to Reggie, who's big enough to discourage anyone who wants to harm you. Now stand back." He pressed the alarm fob, unlocking the doors.

"What are you doing?" she asked.

"Starting this car. Move back, would you?" He got in.

"Oh, so in case there are any bombs in there I can watch *you* blow up?" she said. "Like hell I will."

He could feel his temper fraying. "Will you for once just do something I ask without a fight?"

"When you ask something reasonable, yes," she said. "But if you plan to blow yourself up in my cousin's car, I'm going with you."

Whether that indicated affection or sheer stubbornness, he had no idea. "And you'll sacrifice your dog, as well?"

"Good point," she said. She picked up a rock from the ground and threw it. Her form wasn't bad, and it went sailing down the block, with Jonquil taking off after it at a run. "Go on, start the car," she said, leaning against the driver's door. "Quick."

The Peugeot rumbled to life. It did not blow up. Declan stepped out and held the door open for her. "Go meet Reggie. And stay with him—or someone else you trust—until my meeting's done. I don't want you alone until I see you again. Call it autocratic, call it what you want, but that's my condition. Promise me."

Sailor snapped her fingers, beckoning Jonquil, who came running and bounded past her into the car. "I promise," she said, and then surprised Declan with a quick kiss on the mouth.

He was calmer now. Part of it was the kiss. Mostly it was that he'd stuck another cell phone under the Peugeot's front seat. Wherever this car went, he would know about it.

Sailor found Reggie on the terrace of the Mystic Café having a cappuccino and chatting up the waitress. He looked reassuringly normal, with his freckled face and baseball cap, and reassuringly muscled, should they run into trouble. Also reassuring was that she once again had the knife. After a quick word with the proprietor, Hugh Hammond, she brought Reggie a to-go cup. "Sorry to be pushy," she said, "but we're in a hurry."

They decided to take Reggie's Lexus, leaving both the Peugeot and Jonquil at the Mystic Café. Hugh Hammond was an old family friend and Canyon Keeper of the were, half the clientele were Others and everyone knew Jonquil. Hard to plant a car bomb in full view of a dozen latte drinkers. Jonquil established himself near the door, turned in circles a few times and prepared for a long afternoon of intensive napping.

Sailor filled in Reggie on what she and Declan had learned in the preceding twenty-four hours.

"You weren't supposed to research any of that, you know," Reggie said with a grin. "You went way outside your district. Shows an alarming degree of initiative. Good job."

Her cell phone rang and she answered, after a glance at the screen, "Hello, Declan."

"Hello, love. Where are you?"

There it was again, that word he said so easily, making her heart skip a beat. *Stop it,* she told herself. *It doesn't mean what you want it to mean.*

"Reggie's Lexus, en route to Alessande's. Are you checking up on me?"

"That's exactly what I'm doing."

"Figured. Have you heard of an Elven woman named Catrienne Dumarais?"

"No. Hey, I have to go. I'll check in again. Remember your promise."

"I will." She hung up and turned to Reggie. "I don't suppose you've heard of Catrienne Dumarais?"

Reggie shook his head. "No. Should I have?"

"She's a member of some renegade group called the Ancients, who reportedly know about the Scarlet Pathogen. She lives somewhere in the canyons. Possibly Lost Hills, which would be your district."

"Wouldn't surprise me. Those canyons are full of Elven, no one even knows how many. I can probably find her. I have boxes of records in my Malibu office."

"What kind of records?"

"Old passenger manifests. Airplane lists going back to World War II. The Elven are pack rats. They save everything."

"How did you come to have these records?"

"I inherited tons of stuff from the Coastal Keeper before me. If this Elven woman came to America in the regular way, legitimately—"

"As opposed to?"

"Some of them teleported right past the immigration authorities. If they did that, then they had to get identity papers, drivers' licenses, Social Security numbers. Not all of them, but those wanting to work and become citizens. My predecessor ran that operation for them, out of Topanga. I have a house there with all his forgery equipment."

"Good grief, how many houses do you have?"

He laughed. "I flip them. It's a lot of work for not a lot of profit. I'm no Charles Highsmith."

"Thank God. Okay, searching through documents is plan B, because that could take a while, right? Plan A is an Elven woman named Alessande. That's where I'm directing you now—I have a strong hunch I'm supposed to talk to her. She has a symbol hanging in her house, a tree that forms a circle. The symbol of the Ancients."

"Your dad must know hundreds of Elven. Surely one of them would—"

"No, his friends are civilized types. Assimilated. Not the sort to whip up a batch of *siúlacht* from stuff lying around their front yards." Sailor indicated the road ahead. "Make a left when we get to Mulholland. So, what did *you* find?"

"Same rumors you've heard. The Déithe in Carbon Canyon say this disease made the rounds in Europe in the eighteenth century. Tough to find Elven who lived through it because they'd have to be really old *and* living in Paris or Berlin when it hit. But the theory is, someone kept a sample of the pathogen all these years, and now they're unleashing it."

"Sounds pretty sci-fi," she said, "but okay. The thing is, why? I mean, there have to be easier ways to kill someone."

He took the indicated left on Mulholland. "How hard is it to work with? Do we know? It's gotta have something going for it if he's gotten away with murder four times."

"Good point." She pointed to a turnout on the right side of the road. "Park there."

She led the way on foot toward Alessande's, then hesitated. "Here's where I was attacked," she said. "Give me a moment, okay?"

She stood in the spot, knowing the earth could retain the energy of the things that occurred there. But curiously, no sense of trauma or even danger emanated from the patch of ground. She had a memory of it, but there was no more evil associated with this spot than with the kind of fall she'd sometimes taken while jogging through the woods, resulting in bruised and bloody knees.

"Come on," she told Reggie, pointing to the cabin. "It's just ahead."

Alessande greeted them as though expecting them. Which, given the radar the Elven had about the earth and those walking on it nearby—earthsense, they called it—was probably the case. Sailor introduced Reggie, then wondered if she'd been summoned, if the impulse to see Alessande had been planted in her mind by the Elven woman herself.

"Yes," Alessande said, looking Sailor in the eyes. "I did summon you. I would have called, but I didn't have your number." She turned to Reggie. "Sailor and I have a meeting to attend, and you, I'm afraid, will not be welcome. They won't want Sailor, either, but in her case I'm not giving them a choice."

"Okay," Reggie said. "Then I'll leave her in your hands. You two look like you can defend yourselves."

"Where will you be?" Sailor asked.

"The Kelly Ellory memorial. Forest Lawn's ten minutes away. I'll get there early and talk to people who knew her. I'll call you when it's over." He turned to Alessande. "I promised Declan Wainwright I wouldn't leave her alone. Promise me the same?"

"Yes."

Sailor was feeling as passed around as a library book, but she kept her thoughts to herself. Alessande wasn't in a communicative mood, either. They drove her Volkswagen two miles along Mulholland, past Coldwater and then up a long steep drive to a house that had several cars parked in front.

Alessande led the way around back to a trail that led to a clearing. Two dozen people were gathered there around a fire pit. A fine rain had begun to fall, and a fire would have been welcoming, but the pit was nothing but ashes, the remnants of Beltane. Nor was there welcome in the faces that turned to them. Many were openly hostile.

And they were all Elven. A male Rath came forward but did not attempt to shake her hand. "I'm Dalazar. You're the Keeper."

"What's she doing here?" a woman demanded, palpable anger in her voice.

"She's the one," Alessande said. "I thought you should see for yourself. Sailor, take off your sunglasses."

Sailor did so, then watched the crowd back up as though she'd pulled out a sword. "For the love of God," a man called out, "get her out of here."

"Don't be an idiot," another man said, and walked over to Sailor for a better look. "You won't catch it from looking at her, or even touching her."

"How do you know?" someone else asked.

"Because I've read the texts. And because Alessande here treated her after the incident, and she's healthy enough. Keeper, where were you clawed?" When she indicated her chest, he asked, "Would you mind showing me?"

She unbuttoned three buttons and let him see the scratch marks.

"I brought her to the Elven Circle today," Alessande said, "because she's the living symbol of the disease."

"Why do we need a living symbol?" a woman asked. "We have four dead ones."

"Yes, but this one's a Keeper, Saoirse. By some standards, that's mortal. You can't look at her, at the color of her eyes, and then write this off as an Elven problem. She is not just our liaison in the outer world, but she is also the best chance we have of making our case to those who will vilify us for what we're about to do."

"What are you about to do?" Sailor asked.

"You're talking public relations," a woman said. "Not appropriate for an Elven Circle."

This Elven Circle, Sailor realized, was a far cry from the Keeper Council. There was no cocktail chatter here, no smiling. The lack of social facades was unsettling.

"This Keeper's a child," a man added. "Who's going to listen to her? Highsmith?"

"Highsmith doesn't speak for the entire Council. Yet," Alessande replied. "And if we're not to be outcasts, we need a Keeper on our side or no one will stand with us."

The woman named Saoirse said, "You're missing the point. It is to avoid war that we're taking this step, Alessande. It's the Old Way."

"The Old Way," said Alessande, "worked in the old country. I'm not confident it can work here, Saoirse."

"Already decided upon," Saoirse said.

"May I ask," Sailor said, "are you the Ancients?"

Someone snorted in derision.

"We're a coalition of all tribes, all sects," the man called Dalazar said. "The Ancients keep to themselves. They want nothing to do with governing."

"What is the Old Way?" Sailor asked. "And what is the plan?"

Dead silence ensued. Sailor looked around the circle, seeing distrust on their faces, each face more physically beautiful than the one before. Déith, Rath, Cyffarwydd...

Saoirse spoke up. "She can't know. She would give the plan away."

"The plan," a Cyffarwydd man spoke up, "does not depend upon secrecy."

"It better not," said a Rath woman dressed for motorcycle riding in a leather jacket. She addressed Sailor. "Does

Charles Highsmith know what happened to you? And the manner of it?"

"Yes."

"Then he'll be expecting this plan," the woman said. "Highsmith knows the Old Ways. He has in his possession treaties dating back to the Middle Ages. I've seen them. Our proposal has a long history of efficacy."

"It hasn't been used since the 1940s," Dalazar said. "And never in America."

Sailor couldn't contain her impatience and asked again, "What *is* it? What's the plan?"

"Tell her," Alessande said. "Try to sell her on it."

"All right," Dalazar said. "Four Elven are dead. Deliberately poisoned. The perpetrator is a vampire or shifter, which we know from the attack on you. So we take four hostage—two vampires, two shifters. We hold them for three nights and three days. If the killer comes forward or is brought to us, the hostages go free. If not, we execute them in place of the killer and there's an end to it."

Sailor stared. "That's—" She was at a loss for words.

"Barbaric?" Alessande asked. "Yes."

"Not as barbaric as war," Saoirse said. "In three days we are done and honor-bound to walk away. Case closed."

"First," Sailor said, finding her voice, "the killer is not a vampire. The DNA proves that."

"Not to me," Dalazar said. "Those claw marks look like the work of a bat. In any case, the shifters and vamps will be strongly motivated to find the killer among them. You'd be surprised at how well it works."

"No," Sailor said. "I'd be surprised if there's not an all-out attack on the Elven in retaliation. These are vampires you're talking about. Shapeshifters. Dalazar's right. This isn't the old country, it's the Wild West, and I can see every kind of Other rising up against you. It's madness. It's not justified morally or practically. It's—"

"A life for a life," Saoirse said. "It's entirely practical, and it's been around for centuries. What's the alternative? Wait around for the human criminal justice system to function properly?"

"I don't know about the justice system," Sailor said, "but I can tell you that there are mortals and every other species working on this case, grieving for those dead women, determined to find their killer. Please don't do this. Don't kill four innocents. Even to avoid an all-out war, even if it worked, it's deplorable. We'll lose every friend, every scrap of goodwill we ever had." She was breathing fast, feeling desperate.

"And the Keeper Council, those purveyors of goodwill?" Saoirse said. "What's your Council doing to bring the killer to justice?"

Sailor looked around at the clear-eyed Elven, and knew that if there was ever a crowd to lie to, this wasn't it. "Very little. Yet. But I promise you—"

"Thank you," Dalazar said, interrupting her. "You are earnest, and your passion is evident. But the decision of the tribal leaders has been made. It passed by a slim majority, but it was made with the intention to avoid war."

"What about the Elven who weren't here or didn't vote yes?" Sailor asked. "You don't speak for them any more than my Council speaks for me."

Dalazar held up his hand. "The decision's been made."

"When does it happen?" Sailor asked.

"It's taboo to take a hostage on a holy day or for three nights beyond. Tuesday was Beltane. At moonrise tonight we act."

"Tonight?" Sailor asked, stunned. "Are you saying that

unless the killer is found by— What time does the moon rise? Eight o'clock?"

"Three minutes past eight," Saoirse replied.

Sailor looked around the circle. "At three minutes past eight, you kidnap four people?"

"Unless the killer is found," Dalazar replied.

Sailor glanced at Alessande. "Then with all due respect, I'm leaving."

"Keeper," Saoirse said, "I advise you to keep your mouth shut. No good will come of sounding an alarm. We'll still get our hostages, but you'll make enemies of us, and your days as a Keeper will be finished."

Sailor faced the Rath woman. "I've got better things to do than feed the rumor mill." She turned to Alessande. "Coming?"

Alessande nodded. "Let's go."

"Five hours and thirty-three minutes," Sailor said, hurrying to Alessande's car, heedless of the wild rosebushes along the path. "In the time it takes to fly from New York to L.A. this species I'm bound to protect will commit an act of war. How long have you known about this?"

"They decided this morning. I didn't know they planned to act tonight."

"I should appeal to my Keeper Council," Sailor said. "Get them mobilized."

"No," Alessande said firmly. "Highsmith won't stop this, he'll use it. He'll declare a state of emergency, then say the Council needs a formal leader, a single voice to negotiate on its behalf."

"If he can avert this crisis, he can stick a crown on his head and call himself King Charles for all I care."

"But he won't avert it. You're not listening." Alessande walked faster. "If hostages are taken and he stages a rescue attempt, he's seen as a strong leader. If the hostages are killed, it's war, and there are always those who profit from war. Either way, he takes control, and once he has the Council, he'll never let it go."

Sailor stopped as they reached the car. "You're saying Highsmith would throw four innocent people under the bus to instigate a war and profit from it?"

Alessande turned to face her. "Highsmith's playing a different game than you are. You want to stop this? Find the killer."

It sounded impossible, but Sailor couldn't see that they had a choice. "Okay. Catrienne Dumarais," she said. "Do you know that name? Do you know how to find her? Or any of the Ancients?"

Alessande looked at her curiously. "Yes, I've heard the name. No, I don't know how to find her or her cohorts."

Sailor glanced back toward the house. "Would any of them know?"

"They won't help us."

"Then I have no idea what to do."

Alessande gave her a slow smile. "In that case, you will be open to magic."

They walked a quarter mile or so until they were out of sight of the house and the Elven Circle, then found a tree that looked good to Sailor—a melaleuca, according to Alessande. Its trunk was huge, but the bark was soft and peeling. They stood on opposite sides of the tree, literally hugging it, their hands meeting on either side. Sailor was impatient and very skeptical, but Alessande assured her that nothing would come to them until they were calm and had emptied their minds.

They closed their eyes. Sailor had tried meditation many times, but without any real success. It took a minute before she could relax sufficiently to hear things like the buzzing of a fly, the chirping of birds, the very distant sound of an airplane, or to notice Alessande's cool hands, the bark pressed against her face, the smell of imminent rain.

And then, as clear as if someone had whispered into her ear, came the words.

Listen to your message.

Sailor's eyes sprang open. Alessande's eyes opened, too. "Did you hear it?" she asked.

"Yes," Sailor said. She didn't know which was more thrilling, that she'd heard the voice herself or that she finally understood, because of the exact inflection, what it meant.

She took out her cell phone, hit the voice mail icon and found the saved message she knew was the one she needed. It was from Justine Freud, who had left a number.

Sailor called it.

Chapter 14

From the 101 West, Alessande and Sailor exited the free-way at Lost Hills and made their way to a dirt road that dead-ended into a creek.

"Now," Alessande said, "I imagine we walk."

"To where?" Sailor asked. "This is complete wilderness."

"No, there's a path. Look. Once, I believe, it was even a road. Beneath all this sage and these poppies. In the winter I suspect you can see it." Alessande pointed to what was invisible to Sailor.

"But how can anyone live here? How do they get in and out?" Sailor plunged into the brush after her.

"I'm guessing they teleport," Alessande said.

As if on cue, an Elven boy appeared in front of them. He carried a water bottle that he immediately began to drink from. He was barefoot, wearing shorts and a T-shirt, and his long, uncombed hair revealed extremely pointed ears. It was so unusual to see unaltered Elven ears that Sailor had to work on not staring. But he didn't appear to notice, merely saying, "This way," and taking off down the invisible trail.

Twenty minutes of hard hiking later, they came to a property with two barns, a corral and some horses. A stone house stood in the distance, and solar panels and generators were visible everywhere. The boy pointed to the far barn, then took off in the other direction toward the horses.

In the barn, milking a cow, was Justine Freud. The elderly Keeper looked up at their entrance, pleased. "At last," she said.

Sailor and Alessande both shook hands with her, and then Justine said, "So you are looking for Catrienne Dumarais. May I ask why?"

Sailor said, "I'm told that she makes *siúlacht*. In pill form, which my friend Alessande tells me is nearly unbelievable."

"If it's true," Alessande said, "then she is some kind of pharmacological savant. With access to—"

"The Ancient manuscripts," Justine said. "Yes, that's true. That's where she learned the technique."

"And she herself is an Ancient?" Sailor asked.

Justine shook her head. "Used to be. Thirty years ago. But then she fell in love. The Ancients reject mortal society, even Keepers, so Catrienne was ostracized. Lucky for you, because if she was still one of them, she'd never talk to you. In those days, if you'd found your way here, she would have struck you dumb." She smiled. "Anger issues." Justine stood, gave the cow a pat and retrieved the bucket of milk, then covered it and carried it to a refrigerator. "Do you drink milk?" she asked.

Sailor shook her head.

"Nor do I," Justine said. "I'm vegan, except for the occasional milk chocolate, my passionate weakness. But I study milk. I'm a biologist." She glanced at them. "Yes, yes, I can see you're in a hurry. Follow me."

Justine led Sailor and Alessande down a rock-bordered pathway to a yurt. She moved to knock on the door, but while her hand was still inches away, the wooden door opened and a woman confronted them. She had stark white dreadlocks and eyes of such light gray they seemed to be part of the clouds overhead. She was as old an Elven as Sailor had ever seen, and she was scary.

"Go away," she said unceremoniously.

"Come now, my love," said Justine. "This is Sailor, the young Keeper. The one with the illness. And Alessande is your kinswoman, although she was unaware of it until this moment. So don't be difficult, Catrienne."

Catrienne turned and walked away, and Justine held the door for Sailor and Alessande.

The yurt was more spacious than it appeared from the outside, but stuffy. A standing fan was on, but it wasn't up to the task of cooling a place whose walls absorbed the day's heat. Everywhere Sailor looked were bottles and test tubes, glass jars of dried herbs and grasses, others filled with pills and capsules. The scents were overwhelming, complicated, alive. It was part laboratory, part sweat lodge.

"Catrienne is a healer, a true genius," Justine said. "I would say that even if I did not love her. She has no formal education in medicine, but is smarter than any doctor you could find. Catrienne, they're here about the *shúile scarióideach*. Tell them."

"You tell them," the Elven woman replied, her voice gruff.

Justine sighed. "A man visited," she said, turning to Sailor and Alessande. "A month ago, just before the full moon. A man we'd done business with many times, half Pixie. He deals in antiquities. Catrienne loves antiquities.

Of course, she was born in 1798, so they're not so 'antique' to her. This man, Stepanovich, brought a small vial, like a snuffbox, but with a stopper held tightly in place, sealed with wax. Inside the vial was a liquid that appeared to be blood. What was its significance, Stepanovich wanted to know, that this liquid had been preserved all these years? Catrienne is knowledgeable about such things. History and chemistry. She told Stepanovich to come back in a week."

Catrienne spoke. "I promised nothing. It took me six hours alone to open the vial without breaking it."

"And then?" Sailor asked.

"And then it nearly killed her," Justine said. "Just inhaling it."

"I felt its potency instantly," Catrienne said, as if pulled into the conversation against her will. "If Justine had not dragged me out of the yurt into the air, the exposure would have killed me."

Justine was visibly distressed by the memory. "I, however, felt none of sensations Catrienne experienced. Which suggested a substance that affects only the Elven. And that was clue enough for Catrienne. It was the *shúile scarióideach*—scarlet eyes—a plague that killed hundreds of Elven in 1712. Catrienne heard tales of it in her childhood. It was recorded in manuscripts, most of which were lost when the Elven library burned in the Great Chicago Fire of 1871. Most, but not all. We possess one such manuscript. It described the disease precisely."

"And you told no one?" Alessande asked.

Justine hesitated, and Catrienne took up the tale. "When Stepanovich came back the following week, I gave him the empty vial. I told him of its effect upon me, its danger. I told him that if he had any more of it to destroy it. He said he had none."

"But we had our doubts," Justine said, "because he wasn't Stepanovich. He was a shifter."

"During his second visit," Catrienne said, "I saw the glimmer. He was very good. I followed him down the road to see who he was when he shifted back, but I lost him."

"Such a pity," Justine said.

Sailor thought of the day she'd been attacked, of Vernon Winter, the persona of some unknown shifter. She looked at Alessande. Had she known "Vernon" was not Vernon?

Alessande's attention was on Catrienne. "So who was it and what did he—or she—want?"

"Oh, he was male. Once I recognized the shift," Catrienne said, "I could feel the energy creating it. And I believe he had more of the liquid *shúile scaríoideach* or he wouldn't have parted with that sample so easily. I had warned him that the vial as well as the contents might not survive the attempt to open it, but he cared nothing for the vessel itself, only for the liquid inside. He wanted it identified."

"I contacted the real Stepanovich," Justine said, "at his shop in Santa Monica. I showed him a photo we'd taken of the vial, and he recognized it at once as the work of a Viennese artisan, a vampire named Teodoro Lapizio, destroyed in 1797 during a religious purge. His vials became collectors' items. Stepanovich was quite excited to see it. He'd heard rumors of others being found recently."

"But, Justine," Sailor said, "you didn't say any of this in the Council meeting."

Justine looked startled. "Give information to Charles Highsmith? I wouldn't give that man a French fry if I owned a potato plantation."

"And what about Sailor?" Alessande said heatedly. "She has the disease."

"Exactly so," Justine said. "Which was why I phoned her

immediately after the meeting. She ran out so quickly that day. I wanted to tell her she was in no danger."

"The pathogen," Catrienne said, addressing Sailor, "will leave your system within the week. It was true for the Elven, as well, according to the old texts. If they avoided cutting themselves and bleeding, they survived." She turned to Sailor. "There were also Keepers infected in the past centuries, but for them it was mild, as it is for you now, and never life-threatening."

"That's a relief," Sailor said. "Thank you."

"But at moonrise," Alessande said, "there will be a hostage-taking. Unless we can find the killer."

"We cannot help you," Catrienne said.

"Then we'll be on our way," Sailor said. "I'm sorry to be abrupt, but we're in a hurry. Thank you for your help," she added, although she was far from sure what help they'd actually been given.

She and Alessande were soon navigating their way back—apparently the return trip didn't merit a guide—and Sailor said, "What was the point of that exercise, do you suppose? Not a lot of useful information. I mean, it's nice to know that I'm going to fully recover, but—"

Catrienne appeared on the path in front of them, startling them both.

"I'll walk with you," she said, her voice low. "I did see him. The shifter posing as Stepanovich. He was a young man, one I knew. A *breugair*." Her tone dripped contempt.

"A shifter for hire," Alessande explained.

"I've seen him at work before," Catrienne said.

"What's his name?" Sailor asked.

Catrienne looked at her—through her—with her gray-glass eyes. "A name? A man who can change his face for a price has many names. I don't know his name."

"Who has he worked for, then?" Sailor asked.

"Too many to count. Weres, pixies, vampires. Mortals. A man who owns Century City."

Sailor looked at Alessande in surprise. Someone *owned* Century City?

"So he was here at someone's behest," Alessande said. "But without a name, how—"

"I followed him all the way to the road, to his auto. It was a black BMW."

Sailor said, "Only a few hundred thousand of those in L.A."

"With license number 1NJC488?"

Sailor stopped, staring at her.

"I won't have Justine knowing this," Catrienne said, returning her stare. "I don't want her playing detective."

"So you kept it to yourself," Alessande said, "for weeks? Sticking your head in the sand, and hers, too, and she's a *Keeper*."

"She is seventy-five years old. How long do I have her for? Another twenty years, if I'm lucky? Her life cycle is short. Hunting killers is a young person's game, not hers, and not mine, either. I am a healer."

"But she could at least have taken it to the Council," Sailor said.

Catrienne laughed. "*Your* Council? And whom do you suppose the *breugair* has worked for in the past? Your own Charles Highsmith."

Sailor was stunned.

"You could have told someone," Alessande said, bitterness in her voice.

"I am telling *you*." Catrienne turned and walked away.

Sailor and Alessande continued hiking as fast as possible. Alessande had no trouble seeing the path they'd taken a half hour earlier and trampled the underbrush with great energy, seething with indignation. "Catrienne and her secrets. But for Justine to agree to tell no one, even what little she knew? She's been around Catrienne too long. A more antisocial creature I never want to meet."

Sailor dialed Brodie and relayed the license plate number, not bothering with encryption, because she couldn't remember how to do it.

"Can I ask what this is about?" he said.

"No," she said. "Not until I see you. But call me back as soon as you get something. All I need is a name."

She hung up and turned to Alessande. "Speaking of shifters, the man in your cabin on Wednesday when I regained consciousness—his name wasn't Vernon, and he wasn't a stockbroker. He—or she—was a shifter. Did you know? You must have known."

"I knew," Alessande said.

"Who was it?"

Alessande shook her head. "It's nothing to do with this."

"Can't you just—"

"No, because I said I wouldn't. Every vow we break weakens us. Every promise."

"My God, you Elven are annoying," Sailor said. "The secrets. The vows of silence. It's like the Mafia." She turned her thoughts to the identity of the shifter. She knew dozens. She probably knew more than she knew she knew, given how shifty they were about acknowledging they were shifters.

Her cell phone buzzed. It was Brodie. Refusing to say a name, he gave her a series of numbers, which she wrote down as she walked. Fortunately one of three basic default codes she'd memorized worked, turning the numbers into letters. The letters spelled the name of the man owning a black BMW Z3.

Joshua LeRonde. The assistant to Darius Simonides.

* * *

Back in Alessande's cabin, Sailor phoned Darius and told his receptionist that unless he called her back within the hour, events would ensue that would be "bad for business."

Then she paced.

"Are you mad?" Alessande demanded. "Why warn the man before closing in on him?"

"I'm not warning him, I'm warning Darius. Who's my godfather, who I've known my whole life. If his assistant is a serial killer, I want Darius to know first, so he can do whatever damage control he needs to. And we may need *his* help to hand Joshua to the cops."

"Sailor," Alessande said, "we're not handing him to the cops. The Elven Circle gets him first. But what if it's not his assistant who's the killer but Darius himself?"

"It's not Darius."

"Assistants in Hollywood will do anything for their bosses. Procuring drugs, hookers, covering up criminal behavior, it's part of the job description."

"You really think if Joshua was innocent, he'd organize his boss's killing spree?"

"No one at GAA is an innocent. They lose that the first day on the job."

Sailor shook her head. "The killer's not a vampire. The only question is, does Darius know what his assistant's done?"

"If he does, it's a mistake to alert him that we've figured it out," Alessande said. "He'll more likely continue to protect the *breugair* rather than turn him over to us."

Sailor took out her cell and dialed Declan. It went straight to voicemail, so she disconnected. It would be too risky to explain any of it over the phone, and she didn't have the patience to try it in code. The strange thing, she realized with a start, was that she trusted Declan's judgment, and his standards of right and wrong, as much as she trusted her own father.

And her father had trusted Darius.

Her cell phone buzzed. She glanced at the screen, and her heart sped up. She pressed the answer icon and said, "Darius?"

"Sailor."

She took a deep breath. "I need to talk to you. In person. I have news that I'm willing to share with you before taking it to our friend Brodie. But it has to be now."

There was a small pause. "I am entirely at your disposal. I am currently at Geoffrey's in Malibu. It's a restaurant."

"I know Geoffrey's is a restaurant. But I'm in Laurel Canyon, so that's not convenient for me."

"I am packaging a film. It will take an hour at least. That should give you time to get here."

Sailor ground her teeth. It was no small victory, getting Darius to return her phone call so quickly, not to mention agree to meet. Geography was another story. In L.A., power in a relationship was determined by which party was willing to drive to the other. Darius would eat a silver bullet before traveling across the Valley to accommodate an actress/waitress.

"Fine. I'm leaving now." She hung up.

Alessande was appalled. "This is all wrong, Sailor. I'll accompany you as far as Pacific Coast Highway, but I can't go any farther. I can't be that close to the ocean. I'd get so weak, I'd be a liability. So you'll be alone with him."

"Alessande, I don't need an escort, and there's no point in your coming. I think Darius will tell me the truth. Once it's confirmed, if Joshua's the guy, the next step is to find him. And we shouldn't all be in Malibu in case Joshua's in Hollywood or Beverly Hills."

"I promised your friend I wouldn't leave you alone."

"Reggie? I won't tell him."

"Reggie promised Declan," Alessande said.

Something in Alessande's voice stopped her. The way she said his name. "Are you friends with Declan Wainwright?" Sailor asked.

"Oh, yes." Alessande didn't bother to hide it. It was in her voice, and when Sailor glanced at her, she saw it in her pale eyes, as well. *Lovers*.

She looked away, stricken. Past or current? She couldn't bear to ask. Alessande had no idea that she had fallen for him, and this wasn't the time to go into it. But why hadn't Declan mentioned that he knew the woman who'd rescued her?

She glanced over again to see Alessande studying her.

"I should hurry," Sailor said, grabbing her purse. "Can you drive me down the hill? My car is at the Mystic Café."

"Take mine. It will save time."

"Thanks. Should I take Mulholland or go straight to 101?"

"Take Mulholland to Kanan. There's construction on 101. You still have the dagger?"

"Yes."

"Use it if you have to."

"I will."

Alessande handed her the car keys, then put a hand on her shoulder. "Wait."

"What?"

"Close your eyes." She made the sign of the tree on the hollow of Sailor's neck, tracing the symbol with a fingertip, as Darius himself had once done when he'd initiated Sailor as a Keeper. Then she whispered an incantation in Gaelic, calling forth from the astral plane a quality that would be needed for the journey ahead. A gift.

"Protection?" Sailor said, opening her eyes.

Alessande shook her head. "Courage. So you will do what needs to be done."

Reggie called as Sailor was crossing Coldwater Canyon. "Kelly Ellory's memorial service just finished. Finally," he said. "Everyone who ever knew her got up to speak. And half of them are actors she repped, so for them, it was like an audition. Captive audience, microphone—God save me from actors. No offense."

"I hardly remember what it is to be an actor," Sailor said. "Three days of being a hard-core Keeper has fried my brain. Listen, was there a man there named—" she hesitated, then thought, *What the hell?* No time to work out codes "—Joshua LeRondc? An assistant to Darius Simonides."

"Black hair, goatee, very thin?" Reggie asked. "He read a statement from Darius, who *wasn't* there."

"Darius wasn't there because death is no reason to postpone business. Look, new plan. I'm actually heading to Malibu to meet Darius. It looks as if Joshua could be...*the guy.* If he is, we can't let him slip away."

"He's the guy?" Reggie asked. "Are you serious?"

"He fits the profile. He could have convinced Ariel that he could make her a star, he's welcomed onto movie sets, he knew Charlotte, Kelly and Gina."

"The same can be said for Darius," Reggie pointed out.

"I'll deal with Darius."

"'Deal with Darius'? God, you're confident."

"I'm just talking to him, I'm not trying to take him down. Meanwhile, can you get to GAA and see if Joshua's there?"

"Okay, but most of the guests from the memorial are heading to Kelly's parents' house for the after-party. Or whatever that's called."

"Alessande could go to the Ellorys'," Sailor said. "I've

got her car, but she could teleport. I bet Joshua goes back to work, though. Darius would expect him to cover the office, not squander his time at a post-funeral party. So that's where you should be, ready to bring him in. But not till we get confirmation."

"I'm still worried about you. But okay, I've got the Ellorys' address, so I'll call Alessande. Give me the number. Your cell signal will get patchy as you near Malibu."

Which was just as well, Sailor thought, because she was losing battery power on her phone. She turned it off, wondering where Declan was and longing to see him. Even the knowledge that he and Alessande were lovers seemed less important than it had twenty minutes earlier. She liked Alessande, so hate wasn't an option, but she couldn't control her jealousy. She would simply persuade them both to give each other up, in the event they were still sleeping together. How, she had no idea. She would work that out later.

She felt for the knife around her waist, and then turned off the radio and did a kind of meditation that her father had taught her, an internal readying for the challenge ahead of her. She had never confronted someone as powerful as Darius Simonides. Next to him, Charles Highsmith was a teddy bear. And she hadn't done such a great job confronting Highsmith, either, she realized. But she had to give this her best shot. A lot depended on it.

When she reached Pacific Coast Highway, she felt the approaching panic that always came with proximity to the ocean. She reminded herself to breathe deeply, and kept breathing as she pulled into the parking lot at Geoffrey's restaurant, with its spectacular view of the water.

And saw Declan.

"What are you doing here?" she asked.

"This," he said, taking her in his arms. Behind her, the valet was driving off in her car and the people coming out of the restaurant had to squeeze to get by, but so what? For a moment she was suddenly, sublimely, happy.

She fit perfectly against his chest. He was bigger than she was by just the right margin, six-one or two to her five-ten and a half. Already she was becoming familiar with his dimensions, the strength of his arms, the muscles of his back, his warmth. Her hands found their way under his shirt, crisscrossing at his waist. He couldn't possibly fit this well, feel this good, with Alessande or anyone else on the planet.

He stopped kissing her and pulled back. She was about to ask about Alessande, but the look he gave her was so intense she couldn't catch her breath.

"What am I doing here?" he asked. "I planted a cell phone in Barrie's car—if you're going to freak out, now's the time, and make it quick—and it told me the car's been at Mystic Café all afternoon. So I called Mystic Café, then Reggie, then Alessande. And now I find you here. Alone."

"You and these cell phones," she said. "Do you buy them in bulk?"

"Sailor, I know about the Elven Circle. I know they're planning a hostage-taking."

She blinked. "Alessande told you? What about sacred oaths and secrecy?"

"I saw it coming. Rumors have been flying for days."

"They didn't fly by me. It was a complete shock."

"We're not letting it happen. It would set off a frenzy of counterattacks, shapeshifters would take Elven prisoners in reprisal or kill them outright. There are shifters out there just waiting for an excuse to settle old scores, and the vamps are worse. We need to intervene."

"I know."

"The problem is, it's Friday so half of L.A. is headed out of town for the weekend. Barrie's at the coroner's office, trying to get Tony Brandt to release the autopsy reports among the Others, proving the killer isn't a vamp. That may at least postpone tonight's plan."

"I hope so," she said. "But don't count on it. They looked at the marks on my chest and decided it was a bat. I think their minds are made up. What about Rhiannon?"

"She's halfway to Palm Springs to find a vamp named Zoltan, and I'm heading to Santa Barbara to see an influential family of shifters. All of them have strong ties to the Elven and a lot of influence, and they may be able to stop this. I want you to come with me."

"To do what?"

He only looked at her.

"To stay safe?" she asked. "Declan, tell me you're kidding."

"Your car blew up twelve hours ago."

"Be serious. The only sure way to avert this war is to find the killer. That's what I'm doing. I'm following the trail, and it's taken me to Darius. And his assistant."

"If the assistant is the killer, you'll need proof of it to stop the hostage-taking."

"Then I'll get proof."

"I'm coming with you," he said.

"No, this isn't the time for the buddy system. Darius may say things to me he wouldn't divulge with you there. If things pan out here, Alessande and Reggie are nearby, and Brodie's a phone call away. But you need to go to Santa Barbara, because if my plan doesn't work, yours has to." She tugged on his hand. "You know I'm right, and we can't spend time arguing. Go."

He looked at her, and she let him see in her eyes the determination she felt. She released his hand, but he captured hers and held on to it. "Okay," he said. "Tell Darius what's being planned, this coalition. If anyone can exercise some useful influence, it's him. He's not taking Rhiannon's calls, but apparently he took yours. That's the first thing. Here's the second."

From his pocket he produced a key, which he pressed into her hand. "My beach house is four miles north of here. The address is right here on the keychain. When you finish talking to Darius, go there and wait for me. If Joshua LeRonde is the killer, I will help you take him down. Don't go after him without me."

"I…can't." Sailor shook her head. "A beach house?" The mere thought caused her chest to constrict. Bad enough to be here at Geoffrey's, which was high above the surf. To be actually on the beach…

Declan touched her chin, forcing her to look at him. "You're doing fine right now, and my place is no worse than this. I'm not asking you to go swimming. Just go to the house, park in the driveway and lock yourself in. It's the safest place I know. Call me as soon as you're inside and I'll be there within twenty minutes. My business in Santa Barbara won't take long."

Sailor stared. "You can't get from Malibu to Santa Barbara and back in under three hours, not on a Friday afternoon."

"I'm not driving. I'm flying."

"In what? A helicopter?"

"I can shift, Sailor. I'll become a bird."

She stared. "Are you serious?"

He nodded. "I'm very good. I'll show you sometime. You'll like it." He kissed her quickly, stopping her questions. "Promise me," he said, "that you'll go from here to the beach house and nowhere else."

A phrase popped into her head. *The one who can fly is not to be trusted.* But it couldn't mean Declan.

"Promise?" he said.

"Promise *me*," she countered, "that you'll be back for me as fast as you can."

"I promise," he said.

"Then so do I."

Chapter 15

Sailor found Darius at an inside table in the Waterfall Room, for which she was grateful. She was sure that the only reason she was keeping her ocean aversion at bay—so to speak—was the bracing effect of having been with Declan for those few minutes. Even then, she'd had a whole building between her and the ocean view. Sitting outside would be tough.

Darius had a pile of contracts in front of him. He looked up as she approached and then stood. *And they say chivalry is dead,* she thought. Her godfather might be a cold bastard, capable of all manner of ruthless behavior, but nothing interfered with his manners. He pulled out her chair and then took his seat again.

"Well?" he said.

Might as well dive right in, she thought, before she lost her nerve. "Last month your assistant, Joshua LeRonde, had in his possession a vial of the pathogen I'm infected with."

He raised an eyebrow. "And?"

She was taken aback. "This isn't news to you?"

Darius leaned back in his chair. The blue of his dress shirt accentuated the pale perfection of his skin, his sharp cheekbones, his aquiline nose. "It *is,* in fact. Perhaps you'd care to share the source of this story."

Sailor took a deep breath. "Catrienne Dumarais. She called it—the Scarlet Pathogen—by another name."

"Shúile scarióideach."

"Yes."

He stood. "Let's take a walk."

She felt a sinking in the pit of her stomach. "No, I—"

"Not on the beach, my dear," he said, putting his contracts into a briefcase. "I won't torture you. But I've been in this restaurant quite long enough for one day. Packaging a film is tedious work. This particular director likes to eat while doing business. I kept his martinis coming and was able to talk him into some things that he would not have agreed to sober."

As he talked, he was leading her out of the restaurant so smoothly that she had no room to protest further. When they passed the maître d', Darius handed the man his briefcase. She wondered if he'd paid his bill earlier, or if he was so famous that he got to just wander off, like a pope or a president, not bothering with the mundane details of life.

He guided her down a series of steps that led not to the beach, which was some distance away, but to a residential road crowded with small, and no doubt expensive, houses. Walking here was less anxiety-producing than sitting high up in Geoffrey's, with its panoramic views. The sea smell was sharp and the surf disturbingly loud, but the latter would make audio surveillance difficult, and that, Sailor guessed, was the point of the exercise.

"This vial of *shúile scarióideach* to which you refer,"

Darius said without preamble, "surfaced recently. It was, in fact, buried treasure. Do you recall the Malibu fires of 2007?"

"Yes," she said.

"A house off Malibu Canyon Road burned to the ground. The owners, disheartened, left town. Last winter the property was sold. As the debris was cleared away, a fireproof safe was discovered, itself an antique, although not nearly as old as what it contained. I imagine the previous owners had no knowledge it was buried on their property. I learned of this discovery, I'm sorry to say, too late to acquire the safe or its contents."

"How did you learn of it?"

"My assistant, Joshua, has a cousin. Like Joshua, a shifter, but one of some…renown."

"A *breugair?*"

He smiled. "Very good. Joshua's cousin found it necessary to leave Los Angeles a year or two ago, but he returned last month and did a job for client. He borrowed Joshua's car to do it. When Joshua learned the nature of the job, he thought it might interest me. He was right. At that point I did some investigating and learned a bit more."

"From?"

"An antiquities dealer who had examined the safe and its contents. A discreet man, but upon hearing that his own persona had been, shall we say, borrowed by the *breugair,* he became irritated and then…less discreet."

"And told you what?" Sailor asked.

"Inside the safe were six vials, and inside the vials, as you learned, was the *shúile scarióideach.* The Scarlet Pathogen."

"Why would anyone do that? Save samples of a deadly disease?"

"Why does one save anything? Historical value, scientific research, a feeling it could come in handy one day. I myself have a little stash of the *shúile scarióideach*. To continue, six vials were sold to a collector. There was, in the box, room for two more, and there were signs that they had been recently removed."

"Presumably by the murderer?" she asked.

He nodded. "Who then hired Joshua's cousin to authenticate the vial."

She stopped. "Darius, can we dispense with the suspense? Do you know who the murderer is or don't you?"

"I do not."

"The collector who bought the other six, couldn't it be him?"

"That would be your colleague, Charles Highsmith, and no, it couldn't."

"Highsmith?" Sailor exclaimed. "My God. And why couldn't it be him?"

Darius raised an eyebrow. "Motive?"

She recalled Alessande's words. "Create a crisis and then exploit it for his own advancement," she said.

Darius shook his head. "Too risky, too uncertain and far too bloody. Not his style. He's too antiseptic, a man with a need to control every aspect of his well-ordered little world. Also, during the time of Gina's murder, he was in my company, along with hundreds of others, watching Gustavo Dudamel conduct the Los Angeles Philharmonic. Finally, Highsmith has nothing to do with the film industry. It's not a natural pool for him to swim in."

Sailor nodded. "And the night I was attacked, he was at Hollywood Bowl."

"Oh, the killer you're looking for isn't the same person who attacked you, my dear."

"How can you know?"

"Because that was me."

Sailor stopped walking, took a ragged breath and stared at him. She had a rare impulse to cry, which she did not give in to. When she found her voice, she whispered, "Why, Darius?"

"A wakeup call."

"What—what do you mean?"

"You were a substandard Keeper. Almost an embarrassment. And your father had asked me to keep an eye on you."

She could feel herself blushing, recognizing the truth of what he said. "And you think assault was what he had in mind?"

"I'm a vampire, not a life coach. Your father knows my methods are…effective. And you've come a long way in a few days. I knew you wouldn't be harmed by the *shúile scarióideach*. I was around in the eighteenth century. Quite a few Keepers contracted it with no more lasting effects than those from the common cold. But I thought it might get your attention."

"It did."

"And brought you, in turn, to the attention of others. I plucked you from the cheap seats and put you front and center, in the middle of this crisis. You may thank me later."

She didn't feel grateful, she felt betrayed—by a man she considered a surrogate father. "But I *was* in danger. I *still* am. A killer is after me. A friend of mine died because of that."

"Because of your investigation, not because of the Scarlet Pathogen. It's because you're stepping on toes, you're coming too close, you're a threat. And isn't that the job? Someone thinks you're dangerous to him. That's to your credit."

"You could have been straight with me, Darius."

"It's not my way, child. Don't attribute to others your own morality. Such naïveté can be fatal. You want to be an effective Keeper? Trust less."

I don't think I'll trust you *again, Darius,* she thought but she didn't make the mistake of saying so. She had no time. The light was changing. It was subtle but unmistakable, the sun starting its slow descent toward the horizon. And clouds were gathering, threatening rain. She took a deep breath. "So you attacked me in the shape of a bat?"

He nodded.

"Some Elven have decided the killer is either vampire or shifter, based on that—based on a false premise."

He looked at her quizzically. "And are they now planning a hostage-taking?"

"How did you know?"

"It's the Old Way. And I am old."

"Then you have to tell them, Darius, because they'll listen to you, that the killer and my attacker are not the same, so it might be anyone at all, any Other, and not necessarily a shifter."

"It very likely *is* a shifter," he told her. "I can't fault the Elven reasoning, although I find their faith in the Old Way childish."

"And I find it dangerous and barbaric. Could you talk to them?"

"No. An Elven Circle would no more listen to me than I to them."

Sailor stopped walking. "Then I won't waste any more of your time. I'm going back." She paused, then said, "Highsmith doesn't know the man who sold him the vials?"

"No. He says the antiquities dealer, Stepanovich, approached him on behalf of the seller."

"Then Stepanovich met the seller, who could also be the killer."

"He spoke to him on the phone. The safe was delivered by a courier, who turns out to be none other than Joshua's miscreant cousin."

Sailor stopped. "But surely he can identify the man who hired him?"

"Almost certainly. Unfortunately, he has disappeared."

"Disappeared? Or died?"

"For our purposes, there is really no difference. The trail stops with him." He took her arm, walking her back toward the restaurant. "You're doing well, my dear. Better than I expected. Swimming well for being thrown into the deep end." He smiled down at her. "I'd waste no more energy on this proposed hostage-taking. The Elven will pick hostages who are easily overcome, nobodies with little spirit or vitality, unlikely to be missed. Not worthy of your attention."

A seagull flew overhead, calling to its mate.

"You have no soul at all, do you?" she asked.

Darius sighed. "Dear child, must you always point out the obvious?"

Six minutes later Sailor pulled into Declan's driveway. She'd found the house easily, because the Lamborghini Aventador was parked on the street in front of it. Mindful of Declan's instructions, she pulled into the driveway next to a Jaguar. As she locked Alessande's car she considered how crazy it was to be here, two hours before sunset, with moonrise occurring twenty minutes after that. However, she had to recharge her phone and, for that matter, use the bathroom, two prosaic needs without which she couldn't save the world. And she'd promised Declan.

But it all felt wrong with the sounds of the ocean so close and harsh.

Declan's assistant, Harriet, introduced herself and welcomed her with warmth and smiles, although Sailor guessed she was more used to keeping people out of Declan's life than letting them in.

"Mr. Wainwright instructed me to arm the security system and wait with you," Harriet said. "He has concerns about your safety. Did you park in the driveway?"

"Yes," Sailor said.

"Good. I'm closing the gate so no one can get to your car. I'm arming all the doors, as well, except for the front, which we'll lock but leave unarmed for Mr. Wainwright. Don't even go onto the deck or the alarm will sound, and it's extremely unpleasant."

"I won't be going onto the deck. Do you have a phone charger I can borrow? I have the same phone as Declan."

"Right over here," Harriet said, leading Sailor to a kitchen, immaculate and beautiful, with gray stone counters and white cabinets. "Mr. Wainwright will be home eighteen minutes from now. He was specific about that, so you can set your watch by it. Would you like something to drink or eat?"

"No, I'm fine. But a bathroom?"

"The guest bath is being remodeled, but the master bath is one flight up. And I'll be one flight down in the office."

Sailor plugged in her phone first, looking from the kitchen into the living and dining areas, which formed one great room. The house intrigued her, and under other circumstances she would revel in exploring it on her own, enjoying a glimpse into her lover's world. It was modern and serene, and it drew her in and made her want to stay. The art on the walls enchanted her, although she couldn't say what style or period the paintings were. The Lamborghini key on the kitchen counter near the phone charger was the only thing she recognized, yet everything looked somehow familiar to her. She had the strangest feeling that she belonged here.

Except for the view. Sliding glass doors ran the length of the house, displaying the ocean. Maybe if the curtains were closed she could stand it.

She helped herself to a glass of water, and noted the land-line next to the cell charger, along with a stack of Post-its and a silver pen. On the top Post-it were her own name and number in a handwritten scrawl. Declan's, no doubt. She noticed that he crossed his sevens in the European manner. Funny that she knew him intimately, yet knew so little else about him. What a strange three days it had been, how very— Another Post-it, this one stuck to the countertop, caught her attention, this one in a different and very neat handwriting, perhaps Harriet's. She stared at it, feeling her heart thump in her chest. *Call Vernon Winter.*

Vernon Winter, the man she'd met the night of the attack. Except she hadn't met him, she'd met a shifter posing as him.

Could that shifter actually have been a shifter Keeper? Had Declan been Vernon Winter?

It was possible. There were disparities in the degree to which a Keeper shared the traits of the species. Some Keepers had many of the talents—and liabilities—of the creatures they protected, others were little more than mortal, with pale birthmarks and very mild abilities. Declan was obviously in the former camp if he could fly.

But why would he misrepresent himself, and why keep it secret later? Why listen to her account of her attack as if it were news? It was as unsettling as a flat-out lie. And Alessande, too, had been part of the deception. *Don't jump to conclusions,* she told herself. He must have had a reason. She would let him explain.

Her phone came to life at that moment, alerting her to five urgent messages. She picked it up, putting aside her train of thought.

Both Barrie and Rhiannon had called to update her on their Council meetings and confirm what Declan had told her. Reggie had called three times. Forgetting all about her need for the bathroom, she dialed him immediately, pacing the room as far as the charger cable would allow while she waited for him to pick up. His phone went to voice mail, so she left a message asking him to call her, then hung up. She hurried upstairs to the master suite, another marvel of interior design that she couldn't take the time to admire. She used the bathroom, glanced at the shower and hot tub—which brought to mind scenarios of the things she and Declan might do in them that were only peripherally concerned with getting clean—and took a look at herself in the mirror, noting that her eyes were nearly their own shade of green once again. She was hurrying back through the bedroom, wondering if she would ever lie with Declan in that vast king-size bed under that gray linen duvet, when something in the sitting area caught her eye.

It lay on a side table, a small leather bracelet studded with jewels.

Feeling a little ping of jealousy, she picked it up. On closer inspection, it wasn't a bracelet at all but a tiny pet collar.

But Declan had no pets.

And she'd seen it before, she was certain. Where, though? The only cat of her close acquaintance was Sophie, who belonged to Barrie. Sophie wore a rhinestone collar worth $7.99. This was in another class altogether. For one thing, it was Gucci; for another, it had charms on it, green gems, quite beautiful. Sailor wouldn't know a real emerald from a piece of glass, but she knew what Gucci meant: money to burn. But why was this significant? She read the tag. *Tamarind.*

She recoiled.

It wasn't a name you would forget. Tamarind was Charlotte Messenger's cat, a gray tabby she famously took everywhere with her. Charlotte had named her pet after a tree, a bit of trivia that Sailor had noted because it was a nod to her Otherness. The Elven were crazy about trees. Trees were their passion, their totem, the birthmarks of their Keepers. And Charlotte was equally passionate about her cat. News accounts of her death invariably mentioned Tamarind's disappearance.

And here was her collar.

Shaking, Sailor went downstairs to her plugged-in phone and got online, typing in "Charlotte Messenger" and hitting "images." There it was, the photo she'd remembered, taken the day before Charlotte died. She'd been photographed coming out of a Rodeo Drive boutique with Tamarind's head peeking out of a handbag, the jeweled collar clearly visible around her furry neck. The same collar Sailor now held in her hand.

Her phone rang, so startling her that she dropped the collar. She answered, praying that it wasn't Declan.

It was Reggie. "Sailor," he said. "Joshua LeRonde? He's not the killer."

"I know." Reggie had to be upset, she thought, to be speaking so openly on a cell.

"But I found something significant. I think. It's— I think I found the crime scene."

"The what?"

"Charlotte Messenger. Remember? They found her body on the beach, but they never found the place she was killed."

"Oh, my God, Reggie. Where are you?"

"Just off Kanan Dume. Are you still at Geoffrey's?"

"No, but I'm not far," she said. "Point Dume. I'll meet you."

"Okay. I'm a half mile inland from Pacific Coast Highway. There's stuff here I think could be proof. Even if we don't have the killer's—"

Her phone beeped, alerting her to a text. "Hold on, Reggie." She pulled the phone away from her ear and looked at the screen. It was from Declan.

On my way, the text read. *Home in five.*

Panic shot through her. She couldn't face him, couldn't ask him about the collar, but neither could she pretend there was nothing wrong, that she wasn't freaked out. She wasn't that good an actress.

She had to get out of his house.

"I'm coming," she told Reggie. "I'll call you from the car and you can direct me."

"If you're at Point Dume, you're no more than five minutes away."

Five minutes. The time it would take for Declan to return. And her car, Alessande's car, was behind a security gate that she didn't know how to open.

She grabbed the Lamborghini keys and ran out the front door.

Declan couldn't say what it was exactly that made the hair on the back of his neck stand up, but he knew exactly what time it was and where on Santa Barbara's State Street he was when he realized that Sailor had shut him out.

It wasn't until she closed the mental window that he was aware how deeply he'd been connected to her psychically for the past two days and nights. Psychically, physically... and emotionally.

For forty-eight hours the world had been far less cold.

He knew, because Harriet had texted him that Sailor had made it to the beach house. But after that something had either deeply upset her or...rendered her unconscious? He didn't know how to interpret this, the shutting down of the strong current between them.

The thought of her being in danger so unnerved him that he had to take several moments to calm himself to effect the change. That had never happened to him. He knew he had strong feelings for her, but until now he hadn't suspected their true depths. He texted her, in case she was conscious and frightened and needed to know he was coming. No reply.

He moved to an alleyway where he would be blocked from view. And then he shifted.

The Aventador was a bitch. Sailor realized it within seconds, starting with the crazy doors that lifted up and out. Once inside, she had to deal with a paddle shift system she wasn't used to, and then a blind spot the size of a horse combined with seven hundred times more power than a horse, which made getting out of a tight parking spot onto Pacific Coast Highway and into Friday night traffic hair-raising.

Plus, she was stealing a car. If Declan was a murderer, the theft was justified; if he wasn't, he could very likely become one, once he discovered her theft. But she'd had no choice. Getting Harriet to open the gate would have taken time and persuasion, and Declan would have returned before she could succeed. Even now there was a chance he had a bird's-eye view of his own car fleeing his own house.

She should call someone. Brodie? But there might not be enough evidence for a search warrant. A Gucci cat collar, the fact that Charlotte's body had been found on the beach somewhere nearby—was it enough?

Something about Charlotte's body and the beach nudged her memory, saying *pay attention to me,* but so many thoughts needed attention that this one would have to take a number and get in line.

Could Declan really be a killer? It wasn't possible. It made her blood run cold, then hot thinking about it. It was unimaginable. On the other hand, Darius had attacked her, torn open her chest and injected a pathogen into her bloodstream. Her own godfather, a man she'd known since birth, had done this. And she'd known—really known—Declan only a few days.

And nights.

Leave your feelings out of it, she told herself. *Think.* First, Declan had access to Charlotte, Gina, Kelly and Ariel, not only because he owned a nightclub they'd all frequented but also because he could get onto any set in Hollywood. Except *Knock My Socks Off,* but that wouldn't matter because he could have met Charlotte anywhere. He was a man who stayed on good terms with his lovers. Alessande was proof enough of that.

Second, he had the resources to acquire a vial of the Scarlet Pathogen. He had property everywhere, and money.

Third, he would have alibis. Anyone who could shift well enough to fly could make people believe he was drinking with them all night when in fact he could commit a quick murder and return to the bar by last call. She'd done it in college, party hopping through teleportation. Exhausting, but possible. The amazing thing was that Declan could fly at all. Barrie, for instance, was a very talented Keeper, but she couldn't do birds well enough to become airborne. Declan must have an immense amount of shapeshifter in his DNA, which only added to the strikes against him.

Fourth, he was undoubtedly the one who'd shifted into Vernon Winter, deceiving her both then and after.

Add to that Charlotte being found near his beach house and Tamarind's collar being in his house—not to mention the message not to trust the one who flies—and it was no wonder Darius's words echoed in her ear. Would she ever learn?

Trust less.

Chapter 16

Storm clouds were gathering overhead as Reggie met Sailor at the end of a dirt road—little more than a path really—off Kanan Dume. He was visibly upset, his friendly face lined with stress. It sent chills down her spine, imagining what he'd seen to make him look like that.

"We'll walk," he said, when she'd climbed out of the Aventador. "The car won't make it."

"Really?" she said. "I could drive on that."

"In your Jeep maybe. Not in this. And it's starting to rain. If it turns to mud, you're screwed. What are you doing with Wainwright's Lamborghini anyway?" He took the keys from her to lock the car with the remote, prompting the reassuring beep.

"Stealing it, I guess," she said. "Where's *your* car?"

"Up on the hill. Let's hurry."

The light was rapidly fading, and she could sense Reggie's urgency matching her own as they made their way toward the scene. The land was thick with springtime foliage, obscuring the view to the highway, and there was a curiously secluded feeling to the lot. There were no houses within screaming distance, she thought. It was a bad image to conjure, Charlotte screaming, and she pushed it away. "How on earth did you find this place?"

"There's a property up there that I manage," he said, gesturing to the hillside on their right. "A few weeks ago we were scouting a location for a TV show, and the director asked about this land down here. I didn't know anything about it, so I looked it up and found out the property's been on the market for years. And I noticed the shed." He pointed again. "Then I started to see lights driving up Kanan at night, and I kept thinking, 'I have to check that out.'"

"What do you mean you 'were scouting a location'?" Sailor said, feeling a small *frisson* of warning. "Do you work in the industry?"

"One of my side businesses," he said. "I have a company that rents out properties for movie shoots. So today, just now, I thought, 'Time to check it out.' I couldn't believe what I found."

In a voice she hardly recognized as her own, she asked, "What's it called, your company?"

Reggie glanced back at her, pointing to the words on his baseball cap. In small letters. "Location, Location, Location."

Sailor grew cold all over.

The strangest thing was the spark of joy she felt at the knowledge that Declan wasn't the killer, that Declan was the good guy.

And then the terror overtook her.

Facts dropped into place. Reggie had an entrée onto movie sets, any set for which he was providing the location. Including, no doubt, *Technical Black, Knock My Socks Off, Six Corvettes*.

He turned, sensing her slow down. "You okay?"

She looked away. If she made eye contact, he would see her thoughts. "Yes," she said, and wondered if she should just make a run for it. Back to the Lamborghini.

Except that Reggie had the car keys.

Keep talking, she told herself. *Don't let him know you suspect anything.* "I'm just— Reggie, I think Declan Wainwright is the killer."

"Wainwright? Are you serious? Why would you say that?"

"Charlotte was found near his beach house, you know."

"All right, come on," he said. "Maybe there's something in here that will connect him to the murder."

She stared at his back. He was big, six-four or more and rangy. What was she doing here with him? What was he planning to do with her? And how could she let anyone know that this was the man the entire community of Others was seeking?

She felt for her phone as Reggie glanced back. If she could make a call, keeping it in her pocket, even 9-1-1... But it was a touch screen. She couldn't just hit buttons, she had to see the screen. Stupid smartphone.

"Watch your step here," he said, as the path dipped just before the entrance to what looked like a construction shed, some kind of one-room prefab structure.

Don't go inside, she thought.

"Come on," he said, reaching out to take her hand, but she put it behind her back, unable to control her reflexes.

"No, I— It's giving me the creeps," she said. With her arms pinned to her sides like this, she could feel the sheath holding Alessande's knife. "I—"

"Come on," he repeated. "If any of this stuff belongs to Wainwright, we have our proof."

"Let's call the police," she said, which was a stupid thing to suggest because it was the last thing he would agree to. And she wanted him to stay agreeable.

"No. We have to deliver this guy to the Elven Circle, right?"

"Yes. True." She needed to get the knife out. She slipped her hand inside her jacket. "Okay, after you," she said.

He reached to open the door, a rickety affair, but he didn't take his eyes off her. Shit. This would get physical the moment he realized she was on to him. Her fight training was in stage combat for the most part, where the point was to avoid hurting your fellow actor.

For the most part, but not entirely.

"Come on," he said, and reached over, putting a hand on her waist. It was so intimate a gesture, and so repellent to her, that she had to force herself not to jerk away. How had she found him even mildly attractive? How had four dead women?

He was propelling her into the shed.

Once inside, she stepped away from him. She freed the knife from its sheath, keeping it inside her jacket.

A small window provided light, enough for her to make out a mattress on the floor. The mattress was bare, its patterned fabric marred by dark stains. The floor around it was also stained, and even the wall behind it. She could discern handprints. She gripped the knife, keeping it close against her rib cage, and stared, unable to look away.

The dark stains were blood, and there was so much of it she could hardly comprehend it.

Play your part, she told herself. *Stay in character.* "What—" She cleared her throat. "What kind of evidence should we be looking for?"

"Well, there's this," he said.

She turned to see him pull a vial from his jacket pocket. It was ancient, ornate, scarlet-colored. She stared, paralyzed, but also fascinated by the small glass bottle responsible for so much blood and death.

Reggie stepped forward and grabbed her.

He spun her around, and the knife fell from her jacket and skittered across the floor toward the mattress. Reggie was substantially bigger than she was and strong; he maneuvered her until he was behind her and holding both her arms behind her back. She felt him moving, and she knew he was trying to get a rope around her wrists.

Fat chance.

She lifted her knee and stomped down hard on his running shoe with enough force that Reggie let go of one of her hands. She turned toward him. He was bent over in pain, and she drove her elbow downward, onto his back. He grunted at the blow, then stood up fast, some part of him catching her on the chin.

She wasn't sure what happened next because the shadows were swirling around her, and then she was falling. Reggie came down, too, going for her hands again, but she squirmed like mad, knowing what he was trying to do, and got them in front of her, holding them against her stomach. He wrestled her onto her back and then sat on her, his weight crushing her, but she kept squirming, moving her arms back and forth to stop him from tying her up. Then he backhanded her across the face, hard, and while she was waiting for the lights in her head to stop flashing he got the rope around her wrists and knotted it.

When he was done, he stood, towering over her. Breathing hard.

"Try teleporting now," he said, smiling.

A moot point. Under this much stress she couldn't teleport three feet. What concerned her more was that bound like this, she couldn't even run, not effectively. "You over-estimate my abilities," she gasped out.

"Really? Your father used to say you were half Elven."

Thinking of her father made her want to cry. *Stop it,* she told herself.

Reggie took out his cell and walked toward the door-way to look out. He put the phone up to his ear. "I got her," he said. "She's tied up, but she came here in Declan Wain-wright's car."

Sailor was stunned. Reggie had a *partner?* How could that be? What could be in it for someone else? The person on the other end apparently began talking, and Sailor rolled onto her stomach and inched her way toward the mattress. Thank God her hands were bound in front.

"It's a fucking Lamborghini, he's gotta have some kind of LoJack system. He apparently tracks everything. I gotta get it away from here, drive it a few miles, maybe send it down a cliff."

The knife was on the far end of the mattress, out of Reg-gie's line of sight. In the scuffle, it was possible he hadn't seen it or heard it drop, wasn't even aware she'd had it.

"Not until she's in the car," he continued, picking up the conversation. "I'm not dragging another corpse up that hill. It's brutal. And she's bigger than Charlotte. Wherever she gets dumped, she's getting there on her own two feet."

Sailor reached the knife. She grasped it in her bound hands, sharp edge up, tip pointed toward her. She slashed awkwardly.

The rope held—but it frayed.

"I will if I have to," Reggie said from the doorway, "but I'd rather not. It's going to be a loud fucking noise.... All right." He was winding up the conversation. And walking toward her.

She slashed again. The rope frayed some more. Halfway there. It would have to do.

She slid the knife under the mattress a second before he reached down to pull her up by her arm, saying, "Let's go." She kept her wrists firmly together, not knowing how much force it would take to break the rope, praying his focus would be elsewhere.

"Who was that?" she asked.

"A mutual friend," he said, making her wonder who else of her acquaintance was a sociopath. He steered her to the door. Outside, the rain was coming down at last.

"What if I don't want to go?" she asked, resisting. Reggie let her go so abruptly that she lost her balance and fell.

He laughed. "Then I shoot you," he said, pulling a gun from his jacket pocket.

He was holding it wrong, too low on the grip. Random details penetrated her fog of fear. The gun was a 1911, a .45 caliber, which she knew because she'd had one as a prop in an off-off-Broadway production of *A Midsummer Night's Dream* set in 1940s Chicago. A complete turkey of a production, but at least she knew a cocked 1911 from one that was uncocked with the safety on. Reggie, she realized, wasn't a gun guy.

There had to be a way to use that. She needed to keep thinking, keep her mind on details and away from the panic that was nibbling at the edges of her brain. She got to her feet awkwardly, her legs as wobbly as fettuccine, and she wondered if she would even be able to run if the opportunity arose. Reggie might not want to shoot her until she was in the car because he didn't want to carry her dead weight up the hill, but once in the car, she was as good as dead, and it wouldn't take much expertise to put a bullet into her brain at point-blank range. And that meant she couldn't get into the car.

"I wouldn't have pegged you as a murderer, Reggie," she said, and pulled her hands apart, testing the rope to see how much strength it had left. So far it was resisting.

"Me neither. Funny what you discover about yourself. Thought I was just a sex addict with a taste for celebrities. Always going for the bitch who's out of my league." He glanced at her. "You're not much to look at right now, but with your clothes off? You'd qualify. No time for that today, though."

"But you enjoyed it?"

"Which? The sex or the killing?"

"Either. Both."

He laughed. "Are you kidding? Both! Charlotte Messenger. Charlotte *Messenger*. She couldn't get enough of me. *Me!* And then she started bleeding like crazy and I watched the life just drain out of her, and let me tell you something, she didn't even care. As long as I was on top of her, she didn't care that she was dying. It's a fan boy's wet dream. You can't even imagine."

"You didn't know she'd die?"

"I knew she might. It's in the old history books. Highsmith has a library full of that kind of stuff. But it actually solved some problems, their dying. It meant I could go on to the next one without getting caught."

Highsmith? What did he have to do with this? Was Highsmith the one Reggie had called? "You're a Keeper. It didn't bother you to watch them die?"

"It did, a little. But I was never a very strong Keeper. Can't teleport for shit. Anyway, you can overcome your instincts, you know—if you want something bad enough. Question of will. And I wanted them bad. Gina Santoro? You have no idea."

"But Ariel and Kelly? They weren't celebrities."

"I'll be honest, I have a hard time remembering which

was which, with those two. But once you get a taste for blood, you just gotta have it…." He shrugged.

"But the car bomb. The one that killed my friend Julio…"

"Charles's idea. He doesn't like you. I kinda did, up until five minutes ago." *Oh, my God,* she thought. Highsmith was a murderer, too. The thought enraged her. Reggie tightened his grip on her arm and pulled her toward him, and she thought, *now.* She turned into him and pushed with all her weight, her shoulder hitting him in the chest.

He wasn't expecting it, and he couldn't keep his balance, let alone level his gun at her. She kept hitting him with her shoulder, pushing into him, gaining momentum, and when he loosened his grip on her to stop his own backward fall, the rope finally broke, freeing her hands. She elbowed him in the face.

He spiraled forty-five degrees and fell to one knee, dropping his gun.

They both went for it, but she was faster.

She grabbed it and scrambled back out of his reach, then aimed it squarely at him, holding it with both hands and locking her elbows.

Time froze. Reggie crouched, staring at her, and then he turned and ran toward the Aventador.

She tried to find the safety, but her fingers wouldn't work properly, either from the adrenaline pumping through her or from her hands having been bound too tightly. She finally managed it, but then it took several tries before she could pull back the hammer, and by that time he had reached the car and was lifting that crazy door.

She didn't know if she had it in her to shoot a man in the back, but she could sure shoot a car.

Reggie was inside and turning the key in the ignition when she fired the first shot. It missed.

So did the second. The next produced a distinctive ping,

suggesting her aim was improving, but the car was now reversing away from her. She lost count of how many times she fired before the Lamborghini abruptly stopped.

Reggie hauled ass out of the car, then dropped into a crouch, staring at something behind her. She turned and saw, to her shock, an Elven woman coming out of the shed.

It was Alessande. She was moving slowly, almost tentatively, and Sailor turned to see Reggie take off running, not to the road, but straight down the hill, into the brush.

Alessande must have teleported. She would need recovery time before she could give chase, and even longer before she could teleport again.

And Reggie was heading for the ocean. In less than a minute he would be crossing Pacific Coast Highway. No Elven would follow him there. It was up to her, Sailor realized.

She took off after him.

Declan returned to the beach house to find both Sailor and his car gone, and Harriet as frantic as he'd ever seen her. What the hell had happened? If Sailor hadn't been taken against her will, then she'd taken his car and driven… where?

He was in no shape to shift again so soon, and with no clear intention of where to go, it would have been pointless anyway.

And then he felt her. As abruptly as it had closed, the window opened, restoring the connection. He felt Sailor's energy, her unique vibrational energy reaching out to him. Hope. Terror. He could almost hear her thoughts.

Find me.

Sailor was running well, as well as she'd ever run. It must be the relief of survival. Adrenaline. Or shecr, stupid will. But for the moment she was in her element, even in the rain.

The clouds parted at the horizon, just enough to show the sun sliding slowly toward the ocean. Another hour, she figured. She watched Reggie cross the highway during a break in traffic. She braced herself to do the same, and less than a minute later she was on the oceanside.

Being close to the sea again made her feel sick, but she told herself that after Geoffrey's and the beach house she was building up a resistance to the salt smell, the rotting seaweed, the crabs, flies... Besides, if Reggie could do it, so could she.

I'm not running to the ocean, she told herself. *I'm running to Declan.*

Reggie was leading her along residential roads and back to Point Dume, and her legs pumped hard as she tried to keep him in sight. It helped that she was a runner. They weren't even into the second mile, so if they kept on course she would run out of land long before she ran out of breath.

And exactly what, she wondered, would she do when she caught him?

Get the vial.

The vial and the Scarlet Pathogen inside would stop the war. Handing that over to the Elven Circle would be proof enough. Even if she couldn't bring in Reggie—and it was hard to see how she could—the vial itself, plus Alessande's eyewitness account of Reggie running away, would be compelling proof of his guilt. But what about Highsmith? Who would believe he had played a part in this? The only way to catch him, she was willing to bet, was to catch Reggie and convince him to turn on Highsmith.

She might run out of time, though. Moonrise was twenty minutes after sunset, and sunset was coming fast. But she had to try. The gun was safely tucked into her waistband, and she would use it to make Reggie relinquish the vial.

He was leading her along a small street crowded with

houses. He turned once to look back, and she was certain he saw her.

Running always brought her mental clarity, and even now, things started to fall into place. The knife must be enchanted, and the nature of the enchantment, she guessed, was that it could summon Alessande and had made it possible for her to teleport to a place she'd never seen before and couldn't picture, something that would otherwise be impossible.

And by now Alessande would have called someone, sounded the alarm, summoned help. Declan. He would find her. But meanwhile she had to keep running.

Reggie darted between two bungalows and over a fence, and she followed him, finding herself in someone's backyard. From there he led her through a gate to a path leading downward. Of course. Reggie was a Realtor and the coast was his turf; he knew where he was going.

He assumed she wouldn't follow him to the ocean.

Another wave of nausea overcame her as the path swerved and she saw, spread out below her, the ocean. *It's just fear,* she told herself, and remembered her mother telling her that when she was little. "It's only fear. It's not the water itself, it's our fear that keeps us away." But did it matter what it was? The effect was the same. She wanted to stop. She wanted to vomit.

How could *he* keep going?

Because he wasn't a strong Keeper. He was a strong man, but the Elven in him was weak, so he had few of their abilities and only a mild aversion to water.

The path turned into a series of wooden steps leading to the beach thirty feet below. She caught just a glimpse of Reggie as he descended. They were both forced to slow down because the way was steep and the steps slippery from the rain. The roar of the surf and the calls of the seagulls were deafening, and she was as frightened now, in a different way, as she'd been in the shack, fighting for her life. The smell of the salt air sickened her, and the crash of the waves stopped her breath, as if each one presaged a tsunami.

But she'd come this far, and her rational mind knew she wouldn't die from this, she wasn't going into the water, she was just going to follow him until—

The steps stopped.

She was six or seven feet above the beach, on a tiny outcrop of rock, and Reggie was nowhere in sight. If she jumped she would land in seafoam, at least a foot of it, maybe two, the waves and rain and tide bringing the ocean all the way to the foot of the cliff. It was a desolate place, cold and increasingly dark.

She crouched, wondering what to do, wondering where Reggie was, when a hand snaked itself around her foot and pulled her off her ledge.

She screamed. Her fall was broken by Reggie himself, and as she landed on top of him she was already fighting and kicking, desperate to scramble to her feet, more terrified of the water than she was of him. Once upright, she got the gun out and aimed it at him with both hands, shaking badly. Water was pooling around her calves, knees, soaking her legs, freaking her out.

"Gonna shoot me, Sailor?" he yelled over the roar of the surf, and he was grinning at her, an awful grin. "Because I don't think you've got any bullets left."

She backed up, as much to get to higher ground as to get away from him. But he advanced, and she had no idea how many shots she'd fired at the car and whether he was right, or even whether the gun had gotten wet and if wet guns fired.

"Let's find out," she said and pulled the trigger.

Reggie was knocked back by the force of the shot, barely

louder in her ear than the ocean. An incoming wave had thrown off her balance and ruined her aim, but his shoulder spouted blood.

He kept coming.

She pulled the trigger again. Nothing. Nothing. Nothing. She was out of ammo.

She backed up. But she was against the cliff already, so she moved to the right, away from Reggie, who was still coming for her. He was moving slowly, maybe because of his injury, the surf churning around him, and she moved faster, hugging the cliff wall. Then she glanced to the right and her heart sank. In fifty feet the cliff jutted out into the water. Deeper water. She couldn't believe her own arrogance, escaping death once and now facing it once more because she couldn't leave well enough alone, she had to try to save the world.

There was nowhere to go but up. She looked at the cliff face, treacherous and rocky and not at all climbable. Except…

Ten yards away there was an opening in the rocks, just above eye level. It was small, maybe too small for her to fit into, but maybe not.

She glanced back at Reggie, just visible in the rain, the very definition of madness, all bleeding shoulder and wild hair, trudging through the water, swaying with the surf.

She made her way toward the opening, climbing onto boulders, trying to get higher, closer. It was too much of a stretch. She looked around. To her left something stuck out of the cliff at a crazy angle, a piece of wood or rock, maybe a root. Whatever it was, she grabbed on to it. It held, allowing her to pull herself up and slip her foot through the opening, then her other leg and, with difficulty, her torso. At last she squeezed her shoulders in. A cave. A refuge. Above the sea. Above Reggie.

And now he was there, just below her. His face was ugly-scary as he reached toward the opening, crazy enough to think he could pull her out. She bit his hand. He screamed.

"You bitch!" he yelled, but he drew back. He stared at her, then out to sea. "All right," he said, turning back to her. "You think you're safe? Spring tide. Know what that is? It's coming in fast. Coming right for you." He was smiling.

She looked out at the water, raging and white-tipped, and realized she had no understanding of it, no knowledge of tides or waves, the habits of the sea.

"I'll be waiting right up there," he said, nodding back toward the steps. "I'm staying until you come out, and then I'll grab you and hold you under. I'll drown you like a cat."

Then he was gone. And she was alone.

Panic engulfed her. She should have died when she had the chance, any other way, explosion, gun, anything but this, holding her breath, the ice-cold water on her skin, in her mouth, the salt consuming her, weighing her down, the heaviness of her clothes and shoes, the terror, and then the sea filling her lungs, burning them, bursting them apart, the lack of air, asphyxiation. The kind of death her nightmares were made of.

Declan! she screamed. *Declan!* She was calling his name as if he could hear, as if he could save her, like the deus ex machina of the Greek plays. She began to cry at the idea that she had thought he was the killer. Tears, so difficult for her to produce, spilled out of her now, her mind filled with regret that she could have thought so badly of this man she loved. It was a kind of betrayal to believe him capable of such evil, and that, too, was why she was here, why she had followed Reggie, as if capturing him and stopping the war could make up, in Declan's eyes, for her lack of faith.

Would he find her body? Or would she wash out to sea? Would he forgive her?

* * *

Declan felt Sailor strongly now, the sense of her over-whelming, but there was no joy at all, none of the liveli-ness of her. There was only stark, primal terror. The terror of madness.

Time passed. The water came closer, the waves growing bigger, the spray hitting her face when she looked out. She was stuffed into a space about four feet by four feet, maybe six feet deep, she estimated, with the cave mouth only a bit wider than her own shoulders. She couldn't see or hear anything but the sea. But she knew Reggie was as good as his word, that he'd climbed the steps to higher ground and was waiting for her to come out.

Her body was cramped, weakened and desperately cold, but so far she was still safe. She wrapped her arms around her legs, clutching them, holding on tight to herself. Would the safety last? Even now the ocean had climbed higher, closer. When had that happened? How long had she been here?

She had no idea.

But she was never coming out.

Declan phoned everyone he could think of: Rhiannon and Barrie, Reggie Maxx, Darius, Brodie, Alessande. Tony Brandt. All over town, he left curt voice mail messages. His instinct was to shift into a bird and fly, but he knew his own physical limitations. Unless he had some idea of where Sailor was, and unless she was out in the open, as opposed to in a car or a house, it would be a waste of time and a debilitating waste of energy. Even if he found her, he might be too weakened to save her from whatever was terrifying her.

The last call he made was to Kimberly Krabill. It was a

long shot, but he figured if Sailor was sick or injured and could reach a doctor, Kimberly was the one she'd go to.

Amazingly, Kimberly actually answered the phone. "I have no idea where she is, Declan. But it's funny you should call. Tony Brandt sent me the lab results, not just Sailor's but everything from this case, and I saw something shocking."

"What's that?"

"I happened to look at the killer's DNA just after studying Sailor's, and I found some startling similarities. I'm sure no one else has seen it because there'd be no reason to compare the two, and of course I'll need to do much more work on it before—"

"Just tell me," Declan said. "What does it mean?"

"Declan, I think our killer is an Elven Keeper. Just like Sailor."

Time slowed, then stopped. Reggie Maxx. It had to be him. He'd been with Sailor all afternoon. Not protecting her; planning her death.

Declan more than knew it; he could feel it. They were together, Sailor and Reggie. And she was terrified. But she was still alive.

"Call Brandt, call Brodie McKay at Robbery/Homicide. Tell them it's Reggie Maxx," he said and hung up.

Declan moved onto the deck, closed his eyes and breathed in the salty air. It took all the discipline he had to make himself go still, so great was his need to act. He moved his energy into his astral body. He forced himself to breathe. And wait. After a moment there was a gentle shattering of the boundaries that held him in place as a mortal.

And then he was floating.

He addressed the spirit of Charlotte. "You know where they are. You can see them."

Silence. Darkness. Mist.

"I couldn't save you, Charlotte, but I can save her. Help me."

A tornado of currents circled him. The wind picked up. The mist cleared.

A sound penetrated her fear, a sound other than the storm-ridden sea. It was the caw of some huge bird, like nothing she'd ever heard before, and it was followed by a huge whoosh. Sailor stretched to peer out of the cave opening and gasped.

A terrifying creature, vast and prehistoric, hovered in the sky near her, and the clouds parted, granting it the last light of a setting sun. She glimpsed a wingspan like a small plane, talons the size of her hands. A long flap of the wings, and then it was gone, ascending out of sight.

Above the roar of the surf she heard a man shriek. Reggie. The shriek went on, sending chills up and down her spine, but grew increasingly faint, as if he had been plucked from the cliff wall by this creature from another era and carried off.

Her whole body quivered, unable to understand what she'd just seen, or to reconcile it with the natural world she knew. She was disoriented. She wondered if she was hallucinating.

If Reggie was truly gone, this was her chance to escape.

She pulled herself to the edge of the cave, only to see a wave hurtle toward her and crash against the surrounding rocks. She moved back, terrified. Water pooled on the floor of the cave, some of it sloshing back out to sea, but more of it staying in. The safety she'd felt had been no more than a magic trick. If the water kept rising, this would be her grave.

But it was better than being swept out to sea.

She thought of the cliff she'd climbed down, the steps that were the only way up. How far away were they? Fifty feet? It didn't matter. The water was too deep for her to walk through anymore.

"Sailor."

Was that the wind? Or a hallucination, or…

"Sailor!"

She moved her cramped limbs through shallow water to the mouth of her tiny cave.

In the sea, being tossed about, was a figure. A man. Declan.

"Declan!" she cried. "Declan, I'm here!" She was shouting his name, screaming into the wind.

He saw her. He swam toward her, strong arms arcing through the much stronger surf. When he got close enough, he called, "Hello, love. Ready to go?"

"I don't—I—" She was so cold, she realized, that she could barely speak.

"I can't come in, so you'll have to come out. That's a very tight squeeze. Can you stretch your hand toward me?"

Fear gripped her. She tried to make her arm cooperate, but her reach was pitiful. It was as though she was paralyzed, with no idea how to pull herself out of the cave. Every animal instinct told her to stay. She saw herself as a sailing ship inside a bottle, unable to come through the neck.

"I—I can't," she said.

"You what?"

"I can't. I can't come out. I can't swim."

Declan was moving in and out with the surge, and she realized how hard this had to be for him, how dangerous it was, even for a strong swimmer, to be among these rocks at high tide. If he didn't shift soon, he could well die.

As she realized that, the water swept him against the cliff and he found something to hang on to, maybe the same root that had helped her earlier. She had to lean further out now to see him, but there he was, bobbing like a cork, his chest rising out of the water and sinking back in as he held himself close to the cliff.

A huge wave came rushing toward them, and she moved back into the dark, terrified. Water sloshed around her. She was sitting in it now, inches of it, no matter where she positioned herself.

"Sailor!"

She moved back to the mouth of the cave and peered out to see Declan eight feet from her. She looked down. The water was so high that she could reach out and touch it.

"Look at me," Declan commanded.

The moon had risen. By its light, nearly full, she could see the lightness of his eyes. She kept her focus on them, not the sea. "You don't need to swim," he continued. "Just get yourself out of that hole and into the water. I'll do the rest."

"No." She shook her head. "I c-can't."

"You're Sailor Ann Gryffald!" Declan yelled. "You can do anything you put your stubborn mind to."

"Declan, I'm so sorry. I was wrong about so many things. I—"

"Tell me later. Come on. Time to go."

She began to hyperventilate. Another wave would come and she would lose sight of him again. She couldn't bear it. "Declan," she called, "can you really turn yourself into a bird?"

"You didn't see the show I put on? That was for you."

"Can you be a sparrow?" she called. "Something little? And fly to me. Just come in here with me, be with me."

A wave came, drowning out her words, and when she looked at him he was yelling, angry. "No, I bloody well can't! I'm not watching you die. In sixty or seventy years, maybe. Tonight you're coming with me." He looked at the sea. "This next wave's the one—it'll break, then go back out. When you hear it crash, you push yourself out of there, head first, feet last, just like a baby. Take a deep breath and let go. Fall into the water. I'll be there to catch you."

She was shaking her head, and crying and shivering, not because she didn't believe he would catch her, impossible as that seemed, but because she knew her body wouldn't cooperate, would refuse to let go, would cling to the cave, paralyzed with cold and fear. But the wave was rolling toward them. *I'll stay in the opening,* she thought. *I'll do just that much, not go back into the darkness. I'll just do that.*

She held her ground with her eyes shut, letting the spray hit her and knock the breath out of her. And she heard the last words Declan said, before the ocean stole them away.

"Trust yourself."

The crash of the wave against the cliff was like the world coming to an end.

Sailor willed strength into her arms, pulled herself out of the cave mouth, scraping her belly, her thighs, her knees. She got one foot under her, braced it against the rock, and then, quite certain she would die, took one last breath and fell into the sea.

Chapter 17

"Drink this." Rhiannon offered Sailor a mug of steaming amber-colored liquid.

The beach house was warm and dry and filled with people. Sailor was on the long sectional, swathed in blankets, sitting against Declan, whose arms encircled her. "What is it?" she asked, her hand emerging from a cashmere throw to take the mug. She gave it an exploratory sniff.

"This from the girl who'll try anything?" Declan asked, giving her a squeeze.

That got a laugh out of Barrie, who was on her way in from the kitchen. "Anything as long as it's vegetarian."

"If that's a controlled substance," Brodie McKay said, "I don't want to know."

Rhiannon swatted him on the arm. "It's tea. Chamomile."

Declan smiled. He liked seeing a family in his house, Sailor's cousins, her dog, her cousin's dog and Brodie. The curtains were drawn, closing out the night ocean, muffling its sounds, and a fire burned in the fireplace. The mood was relief to the point of giddiness. Sailor was still shivering involuntarily every minute or so. Until her cousins showed, she'd been sitting on his lap, which he considered a much better arrangement, but he could see the avid curiosity on the faces of Rhiannon and Barrie, and figured Sailor would have enough explaining to do later without the more graphic displays of affection now.

"What I want to know," Barrie said to Declan, "is how you found Sailor."

"Once I figured out that Reggie Maxx was the killer, I knew she and he were fighting it out. But I didn't know where." Sailor squirmed in his arms, but he pulled her in closer. "Charlotte knew, though. A window opened between the worlds, and she showed me the cliff face. It's close by. I knew the exact inlet. I knew Sailor was trapped, like Charlotte's cat had been the night of the full moon, with the tide coming in. It took me no time at all to reach her. And right there for the taking was Reggie Maxx, waiting to see her drown."

"The Elven propensity for revenge," Brodie said.

"It worked in our favor," Declan said. "Charlotte had a need for revenge, too—but not for herself, mind you. For her cat. Reggie abandoned Tamarind on the beach when he dumped Charlotte's body. And nobody messed with Charlotte's cat."

"So Charlotte saved your life, Sailor," Rhiannon pointed out, "which was generous, given that she herself is dead."

"And that you've stolen her boyfriend," Barrie said.

"Ex-boyfriend," Sailor protested.

"And that you said you didn't like her acting," Declan reminded her.

"Charlotte, I take it back," Sailor said, looking skyward. "You were brilliant, you deserved fourteen Oscars."

Barrie sighed. "I have to say, I'm shocked by Darius's role in all this."

"But he was right, it wasn't his attack on me that put me in danger," Sailor said. "It was my own ace detective work."

"Well, that's generous of you," Rhiannon said. "I plan to tell him exactly what I think of him and his vampire version of tough love. Scaring us all like that."

"There should be a censure of some kind," Barrie said.

"How does one censure a vampire?" Sailor asked.

"Good point. So what exactly happened to Reggie?" Barrie asked.

"Brodie knows," Sailor said, nodding at her Elven cousin-to-be.

"When Alessande arrived at the shack," Brodie said, "and saw the situation, she summoned two members of the Elven Circle. A woman named Saoirse and a man called Dalazar. They teleported to where she was, guided by her description. Then they waited. At some point after dark an extremely large bird of prey dropped Reggie Maxx at their feet."

Barrie threw Declan a look. "I can only imagine what the residents of Malibu thought they were seeing."

"Terrible breach of Otherworld security," Declan agreed, shaking his head. "Who would do such a thing?"

"At which point," Brodie went on, "the three Elven dealt with Reggie according to the Old Way. While he was still alive, they cut his heart out. When the moon sets, around 4:00 a.m., they'll burn it in a ritual bonfire somewhere in Las Virgenes Canyon. Peace restored. Case closed."

There was a long silence.

"What about the police?" Barrie finally asked.

Brodie answered, "Reggie will eventually be declared missing and, at some point after that, presumed dead."

Sailor sat up straighter. "In the shack Reggie was talking to Charles Highsmith on the phone. Discussing how to kill me. How on earth did he get caught up in the murders?"

"Reggie found the flasks of Scarlet Pathogen on a property he was selling," Declan said. "He knew he had something special even before he knew what it was. He told Highsmith, who bought the lot in a preemptive bid, but Reggie kept back two flasks. Catrienne Dumarais emptied out one. The other was enough to infect a dozen women. Highsmith guessed what had happened the minute he heard about Charlotte's death. The price of his silence was Reggie becoming his pawn on the Council. And elsewhere. Highsmith loves to own people. It probably didn't hurt that three victims were Darius's clients or employees. Those two loathe each other."

"Will Highsmith go to prison?" Barrie asked. "For conspiracy, or accessory or…"

Brodie shook his head. "Impossible to prosecute without exposing our world. But Highsmith has been advised to leave town before the Elven Circle can separate his heart from his chest. He has now relocated to a small island he owns."

"So Highsmith's getting away with murder," Sailor said.

Declan murmured, "Don't bet on it, love."

"Well, he'll never sleep well," Barrie said. "Would you, if you had three tribes of Elven mad at you?"

"*I'll* sleep tonight," Sailor said, "regardless of who's mad at me."

"Tonight," Declan said, "no one is mad at you."

At that point the front door opened and he turned to see Harriet in the entrance. "I was just going home, Mr. Wainwright," she said, "and look what I found on the doorstep."

In her arms was a gray cat, with no collar or tags, wet from the rain. The cat regarded them calmly, then set about grooming herself.

Magic hour.

The only thing better than being out for a run, mile seven on a perfect stretch of downhill trail, Sailor thought, was spending that last hour of sunlight in bed.

In the right company.

Declan reached for a glass of water on the bedside table and took a long drink. "Performance-wise, you're doing well," he said, "for a woman who half drowned not twenty-four hours ago."

"And you're doing well for a man of advancing years."

He looked over at her. "Am I going to be listening to this forever? When I'm ninety, will you be flirting with the eighty-year-olds and making fun of me?"

"Think we'll still be dating?" She toyed with the white bedsheet, pulling it up over her breasts, suddenly shy.

He pulled the sheet back down. "Well, it will take me at least a century to tire of this." He traced his finger from her throat downward, between her breasts, over her sternum, stopping at her belly, covering it with his hand. The warmth on her skin started a fire inside her. *Don't stop,* she thought. *Keep going.*

Instead he rolled her toward him, caressing her hip, her birthmark. His eyes met hers, so blue she thought she would cry just looking at them. "Anyway," he said, "I'm not letting you out of my sight, not until you've paid me back."

"For what?"

He raised an eyebrow. "The Aventador. You pumped four bullets into it."

She laughed. "Wow, I'm a better shot than I thought."

"At your present salary, giving me twenty-five percent of your take-home, we'll be square in forty-eight years."

"Except I've been fired," she said. "While trying to stop a war last night I missed my shift and I didn't call in. Instant pink slip."

"In that case," he said, pulling her close, "I guess you'll have to marry me."

Her heart skipped a beat.

He pulled back and looked down at her. "Nothing to say? That's not like you."

She gazed up into his eyes and smiled.

"Ah," he said. "The telepathy thing. I'll have to work hard to have any secrets from you at all. Any other abilities I should know about?"

"Yes, many," she said. "But I believe it's your turn."

"Meaning what?"

"Well, you keep saying you can do birds, but except for a fleeting glimpse—in the dark, I might add—of some sad little extinct thing, I haven't seen any. I'm starting to think you're all talk, no feathers."

He laughed. "I was saving it for the honeymoon."

"Uh-uh," she said. "I want to know what I'm getting into."

His hand snaked around her waist once more, moving her effortlessly until she was underneath him, her thighs wrapped around his, her eyes staring up into his shadowed face. "What kind of bird would you like?" he asked.

"Surprise me," she said.

"Really? Anything?"

"Well, because it's my first time…I wouldn't like to find myself in bed with a turkey. Or an ostrich—that would be disturbing. So maybe a bird with your face. And your hands, of course. Your chest." She ran her hands down to his waist. "And this…" She moved her hands lower. "And, of course…this."

"That is not your average bird," he pointed out.

"More like an angel, then," she said. "A dark sort of angel."

His eyes half closed, sleepy. A lock of black hair fell forward onto his forehead. She studied his unshaven face, hardly able to believe her luck that it would be hers to look at for the rest of her life. He inhaled and opened his eyes, meeting her look with the intensity of a hawk, and something inside her awakened. His shoulders shimmered, and the next thing she knew the air itself wavered and then arranged itself into…wings.

He stretched them out and asked her if she would like to fly.

She watched a feather float through the air, in the last moments of sunlight. "Yes," she said, "I would."

* * * * *

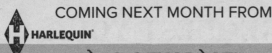

COMING NEXT MONTH FROM

HARLEQUIN®

NOCTURNE™

Available April 2, 2013

#157 THE WOLF PRINCE • *The Pack*
by Karen Whiddon

Time is running out and Prince Ruben needs to claim a mate to ensure his place at the throne. Yet his choice, Willow, is unlike any princess—or woman—he's ever met before. She is a combination of fairy and shifter: beautiful, but dangerous. And when a killer murders one of Ruben's servants and flees to Willow's homeland, he must join forces with her to travel through her terrain, where nothing is as it seems. With treachery around every corner, can Ruben secure the safety of his people...as well as a place in Willow's heart?

#158 BEAUTY'S BEAST • *The Trackers*
by Jenna Kernan

When the family of Samantha Proud, a gifted Seer of Souls, is threatened by a powerful nemesis, she has no choice but to flee...right into the arms of Alon Garza. The Halfling dazzles Samantha with his strength and his charm, and Samantha knows she is protected. But once in battle, when he calls upon his powers, she sees him for who he really is: the son of her sworn enemy. Can she now overcome everything she's always believed to survive and have a new life with this Halfling?

REQUEST YOUR
FREE BOOKS!

2 FREE NOVELS FROM THE
PARANORMAL ROMANCE COLLECTION
PLUS 2 FREE GIFTS!

YES! Please send me 2 FREE novels from the Paranormal Romance Collection and my 2 FREE gifts (gifts are worth about $10). After receiving them, if I don't wish to receive any more books, I can return the shipping statement marked "cancel." If I don't cancel, I will receive 4 brand-new novels every month and be billed just $21.42 in the U.S. or $23.46 in Canada. That's a savings of at least 21% off the cover price of all 4 books. It's quite a bargain! Shipping and handling is just 50¢ per book in the U.S. and 75¢ per book in Canada.* I understand that accepting the 2 free books and gifts places me under no obligation to buy anything. I can always return a shipment and cancel at any time. Even if I never buy another book, the two free books and gifts are mine to keep forever.

237/337 HDN FVVV

Name   (PLEASE PRINT)

Address   Apt. #

City   State/Prov.   Zip/Postal Code

Signature (if under 18, a parent or guardian must sign)

Mail to the Harlequin® Reader Service:
IN U.S.A.: P.O. Box 1867, Buffalo, NY 14240-1867
IN CANADA: P.O. Box 609, Fort Erie, Ontario L2A 5X3

Want to try two free books from another line?
Call 1-800-873-8635 or visit www.ReaderService.com.

* Terms and prices subject to change without notice. Prices do not include applicable taxes. Sales tax applicable in N.Y. Canadian residents will be charged applicable taxes. Offer not valid in Quebec. This offer is limited to one order per household. Not valid for current subscribers to Paranormal Romance Collection or Harlequin® Nocturne™ books. All orders subject to credit approval. Credit or debit balances in a customer's account(s) may be offset by any other outstanding balance owed by or to the customer. Please allow 4 to 6 weeks for delivery. Offer available while quantities last.

Your Privacy—The Harlequin® Reader Service is committed to protecting your privacy. Our Privacy Policy is available online at www.ReaderService.com or upon request from the Harlequin Reader Service.

We make a portion of our mailing list available to reputable third parties that offer products we believe may interest you. If you prefer that we not exchange your name with third parties, or if you wish to clarify or modify your communication preferences, please visit us at www.ReaderService.com/consumerschoice or write to us at Harlequin Reader Service Preference Service, P.O. Box 9062, Buffalo, NY 14269. Include your complete name and address.

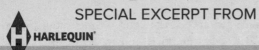
Barrie Gryffald was heading for the local crime editor's desk
when she saw the one person she didn't want to see coming
toward her.

Mick Townsend.

A newbie on the paper, and a thorn in her side from the
instant he'd show up. For one thing, jobs were scarce enough
without extra competition. But that wasn't even the start of it.

Townsend was *w-a-a-a-y* too good-looking to be a journalist.
In a city of surreally gorgeous people, he was truly heartstop-
ping.

Only movie stars were supposed to look like that; there was
something almost preternaturally beautiful about him. Dark
gold hair and green eyes under perfectly arched eyebrows,
cheekbones you could cut glass with. The way he held himself,
that casually aristocratic elegance that was the territory of actors
and, well, aristocrats. He moved like a cat, strong as a panther
and just as lithe. He was tall, too, which made Barrie glad she

was wearing some serious heels tonight, Chanel pumps to go with the little Balenciaga number she'd found in her favorite thrift store.

Mick Townsend stopped right in her path, towering over her in an alarmingly commanding way. "Gryffald."

Barrie put up all her defenses as she coolly replied, "Townsend," and was proud that she didn't blush.

"You're looking very Audrey Hepburn tonight," he said lazily, and looked her over, a direct look that managed to be slow and sexy and aloof all at the same time, which didn't help her state of mind at all.

She sidestepped him and kept walking toward the crime editor's desk. Unfortunately, he turned and walked with her.

"A lady on the scent of a story, if I ever saw one."

"Looks like there's only one story tonight."

"Ah, yes. The Prince of Darkness. *Requiescat in pace.*" *Rest in peace.*

But there was a bitter quality to his voice that belied his words; it seemed more than mere journalistic cynicism, but some deeper feeling.

Interesting, she thought. *I wonder what that's about?*

Find out in KEEPER OF THE SHADOWS by Alexandra Sokoloff, available May 7, 2013, wherever books are sold.

HARLEQUIN®
NOCTURNE™

Gifted Soul Seer Samantha Proud has spent her life
hiding from her enemy, the Ruler of Ghosts. But to save
the living world she must convince his Halfling son,
Alon, to help her.

Although he considers himself a beast,
Alon agrees to protect Samantha, vowing not to fall in
love—no matter the temptation—because she deserves
to find her soul mate…and he has no soul.

BEAUTY'S BEAST

a sexy new tale in The Trackers miniseries from

JENNA KERNAN

Available April 2, 2013,
from Harlequin® Nocturne™.

HARLEQUIN®

A *Romance* FOR EVERY MOOD™

**Stay up-to-date on all your
romance-reading news with the
Harlequin Shopping Guide,
featuring bestselling authors, exciting new
miniseries, books to watch and more!**

The newest issue will be delivered right to you
with our compliments! There are 4 each year.

Signing up is easy.

EMAIL

ShoppingGuide@Harlequin.ca

WRITE TO US

HARLEQUIN BOOKS
Attention: Customer Service Department
P.O. Box 9057, Buffalo, NY 14269-9057

OR PHONE

1-800-873-8635 in the United States
1-888-343-9777 in Canada

Please allow 4-6 weeks for delivery of the first issue by mail.

HSGSIGNUP